Joy's Willful Wager

Seven Unsuitable Sisters
Book 4

BY MAEVE GREYSON

DRAGONBLADE PUBLISHING, INC.

ARE YOU SIGNED UP FOR DRAGONBLADE'S BLOG?

You'll get the latest news and information on exclusive giveaways, exclusive excerpts, coming releases, sales, free books, cover reveals and more.

Check out our complete list of authors, too!

No spam, no junk. That's a promise!

Sign Up Here

www.dragonbladepublishing.com

✺

Dearest Reader;

Thank you for your support of a small press. At Dragonblade Publishing, we strive to bring you the highest quality Historical Romance from some of the best authors in the business. Without your support, there is no 'us', so we sincerely hope you adore these stories and find some new favorite authors along the way.

Happy Reading!

CEO, Dragonblade Publishing

Additional Dragonblade books by Author Maeve Greyson

The Dreamer (Book 4)
The Bard (Book 5)
The Ghost (Book 6)
A Yuletide Yearning (Novella)
Love's Charity (Novella)

Also from Maeve Greyson
Guardian of Midnight Manor (Novella)
Once Upon a Haunted Highland Mist (Novella)

Chapter One

Lady Atterley's May Day Ball
London, England
May 1823

L ADY JOY ABAROUGH, one of the Duke of Broadmere's many
sisters, the fifth of seven to be exact, glumly stared at the
ballroom that positively frothed with fresh-cut flowers and pastel
shades of yellow, pink, and green ribbons woven through an astonishing tangle of light-blue tulle that was draped, bunched, and wrapped
around every possible surface.

She was bored to tears, and a dismal sigh escaped her. She normally enjoyed Lady Atterley's gatherings because the *grande dame* always
provided areas for gaming—exciting games of whist, commerce,
piquet, hazard, faro, and so much more laid out in several rooms. One
had but to choose the game one wished to employ as a means of
emptying the purses of the arrogant lordlings who thought themselves
so much smarter than a mere woman.

"I cannot believe your mother chose not to provide any gaming
rooms," she whispered to Lady Frederica Atterley—Freddie to her
closest confidantes.

Freddie sighed. "I fear that is my fault. She thinks it easier for me
to choose a husband if she keeps them all in the same room and
doesn't allow them or me the distractions of the games."

"At least your brother isn't constantly lobbing marriageable bache-
lors your way," Joy said. At the sight of Lord Pellington, better known

as the malodorous Lord *Smellington*, she sank them both deeper into the safety of the shadows.

"Yes, but your situation is far easier," Freddie replied, "because your brother knows he doesn't get his next share of the Broadmere inheritance unless you marry for love. Your blissful union with an as-yet-unknown man will put him over the fifty percent mark, will it not? Since only Felicity, Merry, and Serendipity remain the unmarried Abaroughs in search of their happily ever afters? I'm sure he's champing at the bit to get you to the altar."

"Oh, he is," Joy assured her, "and he can champ on it till the cows come home, as far as I'm concerned. I am not interested in matrimony—at least, not yet. Not when said attachment will surely end my gambling days and force me to resign as acting founder and organizer of our Reader's Dare Club."

"Oh no. You wouldn't close the club, would you?"

"I would have no choice if no one else stepped up to run it after I wed and took on the responsibilities of wifehood and eventually motherhood." Joy shuddered at the daunting prospect of behaving like a proper lady. She much preferred taking care of their illicit club. Referred to as a book club, the Reader's Dare Club was actually a gaming hell for ladies of Polite Society who could afford to lose a bob or two, all in the name of charity. The morally gray undertaking was one of Joy's best schemes, of which she was very proud. Not only did the club provide generous donations to London's Children's Home and the British Charitable Fund, but the weekly gambling events disguised as meetings to discuss books satisfied her hunger for a dangerous dare. Her like-minded friends had welcomed the distraction with open arms. After all, one could only host so many teas, stitch so much embroidery, and tolerate so many hours of torturous lessons on the pianoforte while muddling one's way through the London Season in search of a passable husband.

"And what are you two conspiring about this time?" asked Lady

Prudence Kettering, better known as Prudie, as she joined them.

"Are we planning the events for the next meeting of the club?" whispered Miss Aurelia Winterstone, her dark eyes flashing with excitement as she bounced over to them. The young woman always reminded Joy of an exuberant puppy. "I still say we should allow a few select men into our elite group. Think how the donation pot could grow."

"They would try to take everything over," Joy said while stretching to scan the ballroom for her brother, Chance, and three of her sisters, Felicity, Merry, and Serendipity. Blessing and Fortuity had sent word that they wouldn't be attending this particular soiree because Fortuity had a writing deadline, and Blessing wanted to use the night to study the stars. Gracie was still in confinement, anxiously awaiting the day of her churching after giving birth to the twins. "I'm surprised you'd want to admit males, Aurelia. Don't you tire of being outnumbered by them in your own home? Especially as stubborn and arrogant as you've always said your eldest brother tends to be."

"Jansen can be a horse's—" Aurelia cut herself off, smiling and nodding at old Lady Billersford as the woman swept past them. The haughty peeress didn't return Aurelia's polite greeting. Instead, the matron turned her face aside, stuck her sharp nose higher in the air, and sniffed.

"Old bat," Joy said, while forcing a pleasant expression at the condescending woman. "How dare she give you the cut direct just because your family is landed gentry rather than nobility." A disgusted huff hissed free of her. "I cannot abide such narrow-mindedness. Does she not realize that when the two of you cut yourselves, you both bleed red? And your horse's arse of a brother is not only a celebrated war hero but a knight. Has the woman no intelligence about her at all?"

"My question," said Lady Constance Burrastone, Connie to a select few, as she joined them, "is, what are we ever to do for entertainment *this* evening? The Marriage Mart is most disappointing, since the majority of the eligible males had prior commitments before this last-minute event." She cringed and reached out to squeeze Freddie's gloved hand. "Please take no offense, my darling. I know our mothers are competitors when it comes to Society's latest event to splash across the tattle sheets, but you and I are friends, and we both know one must plan these things well in advance for optimum effectiveness."

"No offense taken," Freddie said with a genuine smile. "I have no idea what possessed Mother to throw this ball on a whim. Even the decorations appear to have been vomited all over the room rather than tastefully arranged. I honestly think she did it out of boredom."

Joy almost snorted lemonade out of her nose. "Well then...what shall we do this evening to keep ourselves entertained, other than admire the floral vomitus filling the room?"

"Count the number of women Lord Smellington nauseates with his odor?" Freddie suggested.

"Too easy." Joy shooed away that suggestion. "That would be any woman he approaches, and every woman he leaves in his wake."

"We could count the gowns already worn one time too many and not returned to the modiste for freshening with different hems and trimmings." Connie gave a particular lady on the other side of the room a pointed look.

Joy eyed her friend, wondering how she had never noticed Connie's leanings toward mean pettiness before. "Connie, truly? I know you're more creative than that." She took on the tone her mother had always used whenever trying to make them feel guilty—and it had always worked.

Connie's cheeks flushed to an embarrassed rosiness, and she had the good manners to bow her head. "Quite right. Do forgive me. I don't know why I am so out of sorts this evening."

With a teasing wiggle of her pert little nose, Prudie waved the girls in closer. "What about a game of dare? If you complete the dare and win, the rest of us have to make an extra donation to the Reader's Dare Club charity pot going to the children's home this month. If you fail the dare, then *you* have to make the same sizeable contribution that the rest of us would have raised together. What say you?"

The idea had merit, but Joy waited to see how the other ladies reacted. After all, as the founder of their gambling club, she didn't want to behave as though her opinion was the only one that mattered.

"I like that idea, Prudie." Aurelia turned to Freddie, Connie, and Joy. "What say you, ladies? Are we all in for some excitement this evening?"

"I am *so* ready for a bit of excitement," Joy said, "that I am willing to be the first *dare* victim. What shall you dare me to do, dear friends? And pray, make it scandalous enough to hit the tittle-tattle sheets if I fail. After all, every dare must have a result more dire than losing a bit of coin. Don't you think?"

"In that case, I have the perfect thing." Connie moved in closer, her green eyes as dancing and bright as the coppery highlights in her auburn hair.

Joy braced herself. Something in her friend's tone gave her goose-flesh and caused the hairs on her nape to stand on end. She thought the world of Connie, truly she did. But the girl's earlier suggestion of mean-spirited mischief had her concerned. Was that revenge she smelled wafting through the air like stale perfume?

"Enlighten us, Connie. If Prudie, Aurelia, and Freddie second your motion, then I am at your mercy." Literally. Joy never backed down from a dare. Never.

"You, my elite gambler who never loses, shall be locked in the library with a man of our choosing. No chaperone, of course. To play a game of whist for two and bet not only money, but kisses as well."

A thrill rushed through Joy. It set her on fire like a gulp of strong brandy, unleashing a feeling so heady it almost made her dizzy. What a dare this was! So exciting and so full of risk. But if anyone found her in such a compromising position, she'd be ruined if she didn't leg-shackle the poor man into a marriage of convenience. Even she knew better than to push a dare too far. If she were ruined, her sisters would be ruined too.

She lifted a finger and adopted the tone of her most recent piano-forte tutor—the one she had told that she would rather kiss all the frogs in the pond than waste another afternoon beating on the ivory keys of that despicable instrument. "I will take this dare—however, I will only do so if you ladies guard the entrances to the library to ensure I remain undiscovered by a wandering guest. I realize that is part of the dare, but I do not yet wish to marry, nor do I wish to ruin my sisters. A dare is a dare, but I cannot risk my sisters' futures. It wouldn't be fair to them. I will abide by all the other rules, even the kiss, but I have no intention of being forced into wedded bliss that might not be so blissful. Nor am I willing to be unfair to my poor, unsuspecting sisters. I am sure you understand."

Before Connie turned to see the consensus of the group, her eyes narrowed the slightest bit, making Joy wonder what mischief she'd thought to unleash with this dare.

"I don't know if it's worth it if we guard the doors," Connie said. "I mean, what is the dare really, if there is no risk of getting caught? What do you ladies think?"

"Connie, really?" Freddie pulled a moue of distaste. "These dares are supposed to be entertaining and exciting, not lethal to one's freedom and family's reputation." She turned to the other two young women. "Aurelia? Prudie? Between the four of us, we can cover all the doors while Joy empties the pockets of our yet-to-be-named lordling. What say you?"

"What about the kiss?" Prudie asked. "She has to kiss him, or there's really no danger at all if we take the possibility of discovery away."

Apparently, Connie wasn't the only friend feeling a bit out of sorts this evening. Prudie sounded downright cross.

"If it were any of you, you would demand the same precautions I have requested, and you know it," Joy said. "You said yourselves there is no real marriageable material here this evening. Did you not?" She refused to be painted as a coward or a player who called foul whenever they feared they might lose.

"I agree with Joy," Freddie said, ever the faithful friend whom Joy trusted as much as one of her sisters. "What do you think, Aurelia?"

"I agree, and I even have our victim...er...I mean...Joy's opponent in mind."

Joy hardened her stare at Aurelia. Surely, she wouldn't dare choose Lord *Smellington*.

"I think my brother would be perfect," Aurelia said with a mischievous grin. "Jansen, of course. Not Ambrose. Ambrose is much too silly."

"Sir Jansen Winterstone," Connie said, her pleased expression faint at first, then bursting at the seams with wickedness. "Perfect! The arrogant war hero who doesn't give a whit about what anyone says, thinks, or does." Her smile took on a particularly evil glint. "And he is *old* and experienced. The perfect man to give you your first kiss." She twitched her nose and gave a coy tip of her head. "Or, at least, I assume this will be your first kiss."

"My, aren't we sour this evening," Joy said to Connie. "Overdone the lemonade again, have ye?" Joy knew very well that Connie hated lemonade, ever since nearly choking on it one evening to the point of embarrassing herself by casting up her accounts all over the Earl of Cedarswik's shoes. Connie and Prudie had surprised her this evening. Usually, they all got along quite well with very little hissing and spats. But tonight, something was different. It was almost as if Connie and Prudie felt she had wronged them somehow and were subtly on the attack for retribution.

Connie's fair complexion flared as red as her hair, and Prudie hooked an arm around her as if plainly declaring an alliance. "Bad form, Joy. You know how terribly that evening embarrassed our Connie."

"I remember thinking the Earl of Cedarswik deserved it for making such an inappropriate suggestion that caused our poor Connie to choke." That wasn't an apology, but it was close enough. Joy refused to say sorry unless she meant it. "It was merely a shame it happened before supper rather than after, elsewise she could've showered him more fully."

Connie laughed, a genuine, giggling snort that showed all was forgiven. "He was such a cad. Papa had strong words with him that evening."

"As well he should have," Joy said, choosing generosity to win the evening. She casually turned and glanced across the room to where Sir Jansen had last been spotted. And he was still there, staring back at her.

She swallowed hard and sent a nonchalant smile his way. He accepted it with a nod that somehow came off as seductive and most inappropriate. Without thinking, she pressed a hand to her throat in a vain attempt at staving off a sudden rush of heat.

Sir Jansen threw back his head and laughed.

How dare he! The man might be as handsome and tempting as the first cup of chocolate in the morning, but his arrogance immensely diminished her opinion of his masculine beauty. Broad shouldered and a head taller than most in the room. Hair as black as the devil's waistcoat, with enough silver glistening throughout to prove he was well past the age of a young buck. The man commanded everyone's attention—and reveled in it without shame.

Yes, she would greatly enjoy emptying that brazen-faced cove's pockets, then kissing him and sending him on his way. Perhaps the realization that this little Abarough goose was allergic to arrogance might teach him a thing or two. In the end, he would probably thank her for softening his personality enough to snag himself a suitable wife. Rumor had it he was on the hunt for one to provide him a manor house full of children to enjoy the land that, some whispered, he worshipped more dutifully than the Almighty Himself.

She turned and faced him fully, tipping her chin higher with an arrogance that matched his.

The insufferable man dared to bow as if she were royalty.

"Get your brother to the library," she said to Aurelia with an indignant huff. "I hope he brought a great deal of coin. The children's home needs it."

❧

SIR JANSEN WINTERSTONE had watched Lady Joy all night, subtly stalking his lovely prey, who had no idea he intended to make her his wife before the end of the Season. He sipped the overly sweet ratafia and tried not to cringe at the awful taste of the stuff. He should have accepted Lord Atterley's invitation to join him in the smoking room for a decent glass of port and some of the finest tobacco the lord's personal smuggler could acquire. But if he had, he would've lost sight of Lady Joy and been forced to depend on his sister to tell him what the beauty had done while he wasn't there to oversee her and plan his next move. With whom had she danced? With whom had she talked or laughed? Aurelia knew his intentions and had promised to help wherever she could, but had also sworn to do nothing to damage her friendship with Lady Joy, whom she loved and admired as a good, decent friend who didn't act like the sister of a duke.

Just as he was about to approach this golden-haired beauty and ask for a dance, damned if she didn't rush out of the room. He grinned. Perhaps he *had* been a bit brazen with his dramatic bow and the looks he'd given her. She'd obviously read the intentions in his eyes. The flush of color creeping up her graceful throat had made him ache to pull her into his arms and kiss her until she blazed with desire and agreed to marry him.

He didn't give a whit that he was merely landed gentry, and she was a peer, the daughter and sister of a duke. Society and the peerage could all go straight to the devil. He had more land, more money, and more thriving business schemes than any member of England's nobility. Even the king sought his opinion on matters that confused the Crown's inefficient council.

As Aurelia headed his way, bouncing around the perimeter of the ballroom, his old wartime instincts tingled. There was something afoot, and his mischievous sister was a part of it. He braced himself.

"What are you up to, Aurie?" he asked as soon as she reached him.

"Up to?" She dared to attempt innocence, then tried and failed to appear shocked. She twitched a shrug and tucked a dark curl behind her ear—a sure sign she was neck deep in some feminine tomfoolery. "Shame on you, Jansen. You make me sound like a naughty child who can't be trusted."

"You are."

"Jansen!"

"Again, my darling sister," he said, lowering his voice even more, "what are you about?"

She fidgeted from side to side, doing her best not to grin but failing. Aurelia exuded a sense of giddiness, always had, even as a baby. After a few more moments of restless shifting, she pinned him with a daring look. "Come to the library, and you shall see."

"The library?"

She nodded, then unleashed a blazing smile. "Unless you are afraid."

"That ruse has never worked on me, and you know it. Save it for Ambrose. By the way, where is he? I don't want him drinking too much and embarrassing himself all because of that conniving Beatrice." Jansen scanned the room, hoping to find his brother as well as Lady Joy. "And where did your friend go off to? Surely she's not ending her evening this early."

"My friend?"

He glared at his sister and waited.

"If you come to the library, you will see. I'll watch for Ambrose. Last I saw him, he was doing quite well and even danced with Lady Serafina."

"Lady Serafina?" Jansen barely stifled a groan. "That woman is a reborn pine marten. Ambrose would do well to remember that while she might be attractive, her teeth are sharp, and she has been known to bite."

"At least he's not pouting in the corner with a drink." Aurelia swept a quick look to the right, then the left, then turned and looked behind her. "Come along, brother. Are you not up for some entertainment?"

"Entertainment or execution? For whom are you looking?"

"Jansen! Just never you mind. Do you wish to join in or not?"

"I am not moving from this spot until you confess all. The Atterleys are valuable friends, and I'll do nothing to endanger that. It never hurts to have allies in Parliament."

Aurelia exploded with a frustrated huff and stepped closer. "If you must know, my friends and I are bored beyond belief, because there are no gaming tables this evening, and the males in attendance are less than satisfactory possibilities for husbands. So, we devised a game of our own. Would you care to play, or are you scared?"

Immediately intrigued and slightly insulted about not being considered a satisfactory possibility for a husband, Jansen took another look around and noted that the rest of Aurelia's close friends had disappeared from the ballroom as well. "Continue. I am interested but require more information."

"Lady Joy is the first to accept the dare: a card game in the library with no chaperone."

"A card game. With whom?"

"You, dear brother."

Entranced by the plethora of possibilities, he set his ratafia aside and resettled his stance, bracing for Societal warfare. "And why would the lady risk her reputation in such a manner? Risk Society and her brother forcing her into a marriage of convenience after being discovered in such a compromising situation?" While he liked the sound of that, he didn't want Lady Joy to marry him because she wished to save her family's reputation. When they went to the altar, it would be because she wanted to be his wife as much as he wanted to be her husband.

"Ladies Constance, Frederica, Prudence, and I shall watch the doors and immediately slip inside and join the two of you should anyone look to be coming your way. And in answer to your question, that was one of the conditions of the dare that Lady Joy demanded. She refused to be the ruin of her sisters and is not yet ready to marry."

His heart sank. "Why is she not yet ready to marry?"

Aurelia wrinkled her nose. "I cannot answer that. It was told to me in confidence. A confidence I shall not betray. But rest assured, it has nothing to do with you or any other man I know of."

That helped him breathe easier, but not much. While he admired Aurelia for keeping her word to her friend, he wished he could wheedle the truth out of her. His future depended on it. "Nothing to do with a man, you say. Is Lady Joy not of age? Is she not the same age as you?" He had done his research, but perhaps his information was incorrect.

"I believe she is actually a year younger than me, but that is not the point. Neither of us is considered a spinster. Now, stop it. I'm not telling you why she's not yet ready to marry, and her being one and twenty has nothing to do with it. Would you like people judging you because you are nine and thirty? No? I thought not. Why is it a woman is categorized by her age, and yet a man is not?"

Several instances of exactly when he'd been judged because of his age came to mind, but now was neither the time nor the place to get into it with Aurelia. "A game of cards, you say?"

"Yes."

"Does the lady know I never lose?"

"The lady didn't choose you. I did." With a daring upward tip of her chin, she glared at him. "I thought it might serve the *purpose* you shared with me and provide you with a rare opportunity to advance your objective."

"Spoken like a true war general."

She grinned. "You are not the only one who learned a great deal on Papa's knee."

"Lead on, dear sister." Jansen tugged on his jacket to straighten it and smoothed a hand over his hair. Aurelia had done well, and if all went as he hoped, he would forever be indebted to her.

They meandered out of the ballroom and ambled down the hallway to the library, doing their best to be as inconspicuous as possible. When they reached the room's main entrance, Lady Frederica smiled and nodded before taking hold of the latches, sweeping the double doors open, then closing them behind Jansen as soon as he'd entered. The locks clicked, making him smile. Never in his wildest imaginings had he thought to be fortunate enough to be locked in a room with the woman he intended to marry.

The ladies had released the dark-blue draperies from their cords, and pulled them shut across the windows to prevent prying eyes from glancing into the room located at the front of the house and on the first level, easily looked into from the drive where the guests' carriages awaited.

His dear lady in question sat at a small table placed in front of the hearth, well away from the windows in case the slightest breeze caused the draperies to shift and reveal the candlelit area. She shuffled a deck of cards over and over, her long, slender fingers maneuvering the stiff bits of heavy paper with the expertise of a gambling hell dealer.

Without taking his gaze from her, he moved to the cabinet he knew held any number of beverages one might desire while perusing the vast shelves of every book imaginable. "Would you care for a drink, Lady Joy?"

"No, thank you, Sir Jansen. I never drink during games." She lifted her focus from the cards and trained her captivating blue eyes on him. "Are you familiar with German whist, since we are just two rather than four? Or do you prefer piquet?"

"So serious, my lady. Would you not prefer a bit of conversation first, before we choose our game and settle on our rules?"

She smiled, and her eyes twinkled with barely contained mirth. She nearly made him forget to stop pouring when his glass of port was quite nearly overfull. *Get a hold of yourself, man. This is no way to win this lady.* He arched a brow. "Did I say something to amuse you, my lady?"

"What did your sister tell you about our little *arrangement* here this evening?"

He feigned bewilderment. "Something about a lady about to die from boredom. Of course, knight that I am, I immediately sought to render aid and rescue that lady from such a dire fate."

"I see." She returned her attention to the cards, shuffling them some more with a faintly knowing smile tickling across her sumptuous mouth. "Which game do you prefer, Sir Jansen?"

"Games come in many forms, my lady."

She looked up sharply, which was exactly the reaction for which he'd hoped. "Card games only, sir. Those are the only games of which I speak and that shall be indulged in this evening."

Unable to help himself, he laughed. "Did Aurelia inform you that I never lose?"

"She should have informed you of the same about me."

He gave her a sultry look that had the desired effect, causing that delightful blush to once again creep up her temptingly kissable throat. "Winning is a perception, my lady, defined by the person gaining that which they wish, whether it be money or something else, perhaps."

"Methinks your sister told you more than you alluded to earlier, dear sir."

Ha! An opening. "Enlighten me, my lady. Let there be no misunderstandings between us."

She shuffled the cards again, cut them, then shuffled them once more. Just as he was about to accuse her of attempting to wear the faces off them, she set the deck on the table, folded her hands, and locked eyes with him. "If—no, *when*—I win, your pockets will be empty, but mourn not for the loss of your coin, since it will all be donated to London's Children's Home—a most worthy charity, if I do say so myself."

"And *if*, perchance, I win?"

Her eyes narrowed, and the lovely curve of her jaw flexed to a hardened line. "Then you shall have the honor of not only emptying my reticule but also giving me my first kiss."

Her first kiss. *Gads alive.* A fine goal indeed. He seated himself across from her and wet his lips. "Let the games begin, my lady, and piquet is my choice."

Chapter Two

SIR JANSEN *WOULD* choose piquet. After all, it was quite popular in all the gentlemen's clubs—or so she'd been told by her brother Chance. Joy culled the unnecessary cards from the fifty-two-card deck, creating a proper piquet deck of thirty-two. Once finished, she thumped the stack onto the center of the table and offered her opponent a graceful nod. "Be my guest, Sir Jansen. First cut of the cards."

"Oh no, my lady. That right belongs to you." He sipped his port and had the audacity to lick his lips again. Full, tempting lips that made her wonder what his kisses would be like.

Pulling in a quick, deep breath and straightening her spine, she refused to reveal how he affected her. "As you wish, sir." She cut the deck, then sat back and waited for him to do the same, hoping her card would be the higher so she would be required to deal. Dealing put a player at a disadvantage, but since six deals completed the *partie*, it was preferable to deal first so as not to have to deal the last hand. The disadvantage of the first hand could be remedied, but the last hand could not.

He revealed that her card was the highest. "Luck is with you, my lady. First deal is to you, making you the *younger hand* this set and me the *elder hand*. But, of course, you know that. Forgive me for attempting to educate such an experienced lady."

"*Experienced* lady?" She fisted her hands in her lap so he couldn't see how the words affected her. "Do not waste your time on insults, Sir Jansen. I assure you, it will not diminish my ability to win."

"Forgive me, my lady." He rested a hand over his heart and locked his disturbingly golden eyes on her. They were as tawny as the shimmering eyes of the black panther she'd seen at the Royal Menagerie. "I truly meant no insult or innuendo," he said. "Never would I purposely speak to you in such a crude manner. If you wish me to leave your presence, I shall—but I do beg your forgiveness."

His deep voice rang with sincerity and remorse, making her swallow hard again and commit his soothing, rich baritone to a memory she was sure to replay at her earliest convenience.

"I forgive you," she said, allowing enough kindness into her tone to assure him she meant it. "This time."

With his hand still over his heart, he gave her a contrite nod. "Thank you."

"You are welcome." She dealt them twelve cards each, then placed the remaining eight face down between them in two piles of three and five, respectively. "I hope you don't mind my splitting the *talon*. It's how my brother and I always play."

"Not at all." He gave her another of those grins that made her heart flutter. "Do you ever allow your brother to win?"

"Never."

"Now, how could I possibly know you would say that?"

She couldn't resist a smile, but quickly resumed her usual stoic expression that always won the game. She placed a paper and a short stub of pencil that she'd pulled from her reticule onto the table. "Shall I keep score? Or would you rather do so?"

"I trust you implicitly, my lady." Then he winked. "And I also have an excellent memory when it comes to numbers, but I am sure it would be better if you wrote down the score, so there will be no question when it comes time for me to claim my kiss."

She almost choked on thin air and was ever so glad that she'd not asked for a drink, or she surely would have spewed it all over him. "I admire your confidence, sir," she said a little more sharply than she should have.

"Confidence always wins the day, my lady. One's mind is the first step in achieving anything. If you believe you can—then you will."

For some odd reason, she didn't think he was referring to the cards. She so badly wanted to roll her shoulders to rid herself of that eerie warning tingle he'd set free across her nape, but didn't dare do so. It would give her away, revealing how he affected her. "Then I *believe* you exchange first, Sir Jansen. I look forward to winning."

"I shall exchange three," he said as he placed the cards face down on the table, then drew three more from the *talon*. "Naturally, I'm permitted to preview the following pair."

"Of course." He liked to control things. She would remember that and put it to good use. Here was a man who would become most piqued if he found himself unable to manage a situation. "I shall exchange five when you are finished," she said.

"And I shall declare *carte blanche*, my lady. I believe that is worth ten points, is it not?" He revealed his cards to prove his claim.

Damn his eyes. Frustrated by her poor hand, she hid it well with a polite nod and noted ten points on his side of the paper. "It is indeed ten points. Congratulations, sir."

He leaned across the table and waggled a dark brow. "You see, my lady," he said quietly, "I have already won by scoring the first points."

She wanted to tell him to shut his gob and play, but refused to give him the satisfaction. "Indeed. But the game has just begun, dear sir. Do not let down your guard and crow too soon."

A dark curl fell across his forehead, making him appear even more devilish. Joy inwardly cursed, then immediately felt guilty because Mama would most definitely not approve and, since Mama was in heaven, most likely had access to thoughts as well as oaths sworn aloud.

"So unfair," she said under her breath while eyeing her cards.

"What is so unfair, my lady?"

"My mother is able to hear my thoughts and inward cursing," she said without thinking, then jerked back to her senses. "Beg pardon, sir. I did not mean to say that."

"But of course you did, or you wouldn't have said it." His expression struck her as one of admiration. "I find that to be one of your best qualities, my lady. Your brutal honesty."

"When have I ever been brutally honest with you, Sir Jansen? We have barely spoken a handful of times."

"Ahh...but I have watched you at every event, my lady." He chuckled, and it washed across her with the lightness and warmth of an affectionate touch. "And I have heard the complaints of those stung by your tongue."

She didn't know whether to be insulted, intrigued, or fearful because he'd just confessed to *watching* her at every gathering the two of them had attended. Surely Aurelia would have warned her if her brother was...dangerous. She fiddled with her cards, re-sorting them in her hand as if that would both change them and this stressful situation. "I only sting when provoked," she said. "Ask Aurelia. She often sides with me."

"Aurelia adores you," he said with a seriousness that not only enraptured her but made her lower her cards to the table. "As do I."

"As do you?" she squeaked, then swallowed hard for the umpteenth time, silently cursing her heart's infuriating habit of lodging in her throat since he had entered the library. "As do you?" she repeated in a more controlled manner. "What is that supposed to mean?"

"As I said, I adore you. Always have. Ever since I first set eyes on you at Lady Burrastone's opening ball the Season before last. You wore the blue silk that matched your eyes." He gazed off as if reliving the night, then shifted with a heavy sigh. "And then you were the angel that came to me when I was shot on the battlefield in Greece."

He pulled in another deep breath and bowed his head. "I almost died that day, but my angel, that vision of you, saved me by giving me the will to fight and return to you."

Good heavens. Why hadn't Aurelia told her that Sir Jansen was stark raving mad? But the sincerity in his eyes made her heart hurt for him and gave her a rush of emotions that threatened to make her cry. Everything he had said was so…so…*nice*, and he sounded as if he truly meant it. This man was not some dowry-hunting lordling spouting endless nonsense to impress her. He was…real.

"I am glad you didn't die that day," she said ever so softly, then cleared her throat and tapped on the table. "I believe it is your play, Sir Jansen."

He gave another heavy sigh, made even more rumbly with a low, throaty growl. His jaw tightened as he studied his cards. "Indeed. It is my play and time to choose an action." He threw the cards down onto the table, grabbed her by the shoulders, and kissed her more soundly than she had ever imagined a kiss could be. He tasted of port, desperation, and determination, and oh my goodness, she couldn't help but kiss him back. The way his lips pressed against hers. His tongue. His touch. The searing heat of the intimate bond.

Heart pounding, she reached across the table and slid her hands up his broad chest, his muscular neck, and tenderly cradled his face. She breathed him in as she opened to his claiming, to the urgency and yearning he offered, to the temptation of giving herself over without the least bit of fuss. And then a yearning moan escaped her, sharpening the awareness that she needed to break this dangerous connection before she did something she shouldn't and would most definitely regret. She jerked away.

"Oh my goodness, you must stop. We must stop." She pressed her fingers across her throbbing lips as she rose from her seat and backed across the room, putting as much distance as possible between them. The game was over. Both the card game and the dare. She had satisfied the rules. She needed to escape as soon as possible. But there he was with those golden eyes filled with so many things she wished she could ignore. He was a wounded man. Probably a little crazed. She couldn't let sympathy cloud her good sense or tip her over into something even more dangerous—like caring, or affection, or, heaven forbid, a desire for an attachment. "Take the money, Sir Jansen. You most definitely won the game."

"I do not want the money." His demeanor said he wanted to close the distance between them, but thankfully, he remained rooted to the spot. "I wanted the kiss, and I want you, my lady. If not for this silliness devised by bored women, I had intended to ask you to dance this evening and for permission to court you. But when Aurelia presented this option, I couldn't resist."

"Court me?" The very idea made her breathless with excitement, as well as terrified at all the freedoms she would lose if she courted, then married. She simply wasn't ready to be...to be...a *responsible* adult, for lack of a better definition. "You cannot court me."

"Why?" He stepped forward then, making her back up until she bumped against the bookshelves.

"Why?" she asked.

"Yes. Why?" He moved closer. "I know you have no regard for Polite Society's segregation of nobility, landed gentry, and common-ers. Not only have you openly defended Aurelia when she's been treated poorly by a select few, but you've defended me. I've overheard you, and Aurelia has sung your praises."

"I do not wish to marry." If she married, all the good the Reader's Dare Club did would be lost, as would all the excitement, camaraderie, and fun it provided. How would she raise an equal amount of money for her causes without her precious gambling hell? How would she spend her Tuesday afternoons? But the way he looked at her...the way he kissed. He must surely be the devil himself, because he made her want to throw herself into his arms and do all the scandalous things she'd read about in her sister Fortuity's books. Lust. That's what this was. Lust!

"I do not wish to marry," she repeated in a steadier tone that made her proud.

"Why?"

"My reasons are my own."

"You don't wish to marry *me*, or you don't wish to marry *anyone*?"

"I don't wish to marry anyone and lose my freedom, and that is all I am going to say on the matter." She pointed at the door. "Out with you. Now."

"It is locked. Remember?"

"Knock on it," she said, forcing the words through clenched teeth. She had to get out of here, go somewhere she could clear her head and cool down before she exploded into a ball of flames—or worse, did or agreed to something she would soon regret.

He stared at her—glowered, actually, eyeing her as if deciding on the most effective means of attack. "What freedoms are you in fear of losing if you marry? If you were my wife, we could still attend any function you wished. We could still spend part of the Season in London and the rest of the time at my manor in the country. Winterswick is quite a pleasant village in the Lake District. Not that far from Binnocksbourne, so you could visit family any time you wished. Aurelia loves it and doesn't miss Town a bit whenever we're there."

"I do not wish to marry." She couldn't explain it to him. He would never understand. No man would.

"You will not be rid of me," he said, jutting his chin to a stubborn angle that made him even more irresistible. "I mean to marry you, my lady."

Joy rubbed her forehead. How had she ever gotten into such a pickle? She needed to get out of here. She needed her sisters. Heaven help her, she needed to speak with her sisters. They would help her decide if this wanting was merely lust or something deeper. Because, truth be told, she had always admired Sir Jansen from afar. Had she been just as guilty about watching him as he'd been about watching her? She shuddered.

"You need to go," she told him.

He swelled with a deep breath, narrowed his eyes, and shot her a frown so dark it made her weak in the knees. "I will go on one condition."

She could only imagine what that condition was—his demeanor shouted it. "What condition would that be, sir?"

"Two conditions."

"Do not be greedy."

"They are easy conditions," he added with a thoughtful nod.

Unable to resist, she rolled her eyes. "What?"

"Call me Jansen—not sir or mister. Jansen. My Christian name that my wife will use when not speaking to me with endearments such as 'my darling' or 'my love.'"

"If you remain this bossy and rulemaking, the only endearment your wife will likely use is *my horse's arse of a husband*."

She should not have said that. What was it about this man that made whatever came into her head dash out of her mouth?

He grinned, then shrugged. "If need be, I will answer to *my horse's arse of a husband*."

"Your second condition?"

"You will allow me to court you."

"No."

"Then we are going to be in here for a very long while." He eased closer. "Is that what you truly want?"

She couldn't handle that. The closer he came, the more muddled she got in the battle with her emotions, a battle she'd never really had to fight before. She knew how to gamble. She did not know how to do *this*.

Hands thrown up in surrender, she said, "Fine. I will consider it."

He shook his head. "No, my lady. There is nothing to consider. You either agree to court me so I can convince you that you should be my wife, or we will stay in this library alone until Lady Atterley's servants come to douse the candles and discover us. Not even my sister or your friends will be able to remove me or vouch that we were never left alone. Because I will make certain the truth is told. Then you would be faced with yet another option—a marriage of convenience to save your family's name."

"You are a stubborn, infuriating horse's arse."

"Thank you, my darling. You are an irresistible, intelligent beauty. A rare combination, I assure you." He resettled his stance, smiling like the devil that he was. "What will it be, my lady?"

"Fine," she said with an explosive huff. "You may court me."

He gave her a formal bow, then went to the door and knocked. "The dare is complete, ladies. Open the door."

A smiling Aurelia bounced into the room, then came up short. Her smile disappeared. "Oh dear. What did you do, Jansen? Joy has a face like thunder."

"Never mind that," Joy said, pointing at the woman she'd considered to be one of her very best friends. "I would like a word with you." She glared at Jansen. "Alone. You may go."

He threw back his head and laughed as he sauntered out the door. "Until tomorrow, my lady."

She did her best to ignore that, choosing instead to sweep across the room, catch Aurelia by the arm, and tug her far enough from the doorway that they didn't risk being overheard. "I thought you were my friend!"

Aurelia's jaw dropped, and her eyes filled with tears. "But I am, Joy. Why in heaven's name would you say that? What in the world did Jansen do?" She clapped a hand over her mouth and gasped. "Was he rude? Did he molest you?"

"Well, of course he didn't molest me." Joy backed up a step, shocked at Aurelia's choice of words. "Has he ever done such a horrid thing to a woman?"

Aurelia stamped her foot like a petulant child. "Absolutely not. My brother is an honorable man. While I agree that he is stubborn, bullheaded, and annoying to no end, he respects women and would never force himself upon one."

"He kissed me without asking."

"Uhm."

"Uhm, what?" Joy said. "That is all you have to say about that?"

Aurelia avoided looking her in the eye. "He knew about the dare. Knew that if you lost, his winnings would be enhanced with a kiss." She cleared her throat and gave a cringing shrug. "Did you happen to lose the game?"

Joy didn't doubt that he knew about the kiss, because, fool that she was, she had told him herself. "I was in the process of losing the hand, but we had yet to finish. I could've come around and won with the proper cards and strategy." She hated the shrewish tone she'd taken and coughed to hide it. "My issue with you is that you never told me of his habit of tracking me like prey, about his hallucinating about me on the battlefield." She shook a finger. "And you were the one to suggest him for the dare. You *knew* what would happen."

"I didn't know for sure." Aurelia shook her head so fast that her ebony curls bounced in disarray. "With Jansen, you never know for sure." She chewed on her bottom lip, then wet it as if preparing to give a speech. "He is quite smitten with you, Joy. Even more so since he came back from Greece. Where is the harm in his thinking you are his angel?" She held up a hand. "I know that sounds as though his attic's emptied itself, but I swear, he is quite sane." She chewed on her lip some more. "Before Papa died, he warned me that war could change Jansen. It did. It made him determined to make you his wife. Is that not romantic?"

"Romantic? He said he'd been watching me since the beginning of the Season before last. That's over two years. You don't find that strange?"

"Well, he couldn't watch you the entire time," Aurelia said. "He was on the Continent six of those months. Helping the Greeks fight the Ottomans." Her frustration clear, she hugged herself. "Jansen can be such a dear. Can you not at least give him a chance? I know you're the daughter of a duke, but he's quite wealthy and well respected amongst the other gentry and peerage alike."

Hurt that Aurelia would even think her capable of such prejudice, Joy turned away. "You know me better than that. When has someone's class ever colored my regard for them?"

"Then is it simply because you don't want to lose the Reader's Dare Club? Is that why you wish to spurn him?"

"I am not yet ready to marry."

Aurelia shook her head. "Then don't. Simply take the time to get to know him better. Allow him to show you the man that he is. All you know about him is what I've told you, and what you've seen at all these silly parties we're paraded through in search of husbands." She shrugged. "At least, if it's known that the two of you are courting, that will protect you from other men sniffing around for a fine, plump dowry."

Upon hearing that suggestion, Joy remembered why she and Aurelia were such good friends. The girl was brilliant when it came to examining a situation from every angle. "You make a fine point there."

"Then we are still friends?" Aurelia reminded Joy of one of Gracie's puppies after it had been scolded for piddling on the floor. "Please?"

Joy shook a finger, but this time, she wasn't nearly as stern. "No more secrets about your brother. Agreed? I need you on my side, not his. In this matter alone, of course. Can you do that?"

"I can do that."

"Good." Joy released a heavy sigh. "Now, I get to tell my sisters and my irritating brother that I've agreed to court Sir Jansen Winterstone."

BACK HOME IN his personal study, Jansen sat staring at the dwindling fire while partaking in a last, relaxing glass of brandy for the evening. He deemed the battle in Lady Atterley's library a success, but he had yet to win the war and enjoy the spoils. Damn, Lady Joy was a passionate woman—she just didn't know it. The way she had returned that kiss. Opened to him. Her faint moan before she pushed away had nearly undone him. He had to proceed with care to ensure he didn't lose her.

Another sip from the snifter burned its way down his gullet, promising to numb the constant, dull ache in his shoulder. The field doctor had assured him that the bullet had passed straight through, but Jansen wasn't so sure. At times, he swore he felt the grind of metal against bone. Perhaps the bullet had left a few shards as a cruel memento.

A knock on the door finally interrupted the silence of the room. He knew who it was, and it was about damn time. "Come in, Aurie."

"You almost cost me a friend!" She headed straight for the cabinet and poured herself a brandy. "If I lose Lady Joy's good humor because of you, I will torment you the rest of your days. She accused me of conspiring *with* you and *against* her."

"Which you did."

"That is not the point. I had no idea you'd leave her in such a stir. She said you kissed her without permission!"

"I wouldn't exactly put it that way."

"How would you put it?" Aurelia flopped into the chair beside him and nearly spilled her drink.

"Easy there. Our smuggler only comes through once every other month. Mustn't waste a good brandy with petulance." Jansen took another sip of his own drink, drew in a deep breath, then allowed it to ease out. "If she hadn't wanted me to kiss her, she would have never told me about it. She informed me it was part of the stakes."

"She was simply laying out the rules."

"And I simply followed them the way I wished to." He grinned at his sister. He couldn't help it. "I am indebted to you, Aurie. She agreed to court me."

"I know. I finally got her to admit it to me, too, so you, at least, have a witness." She slowly shook her head while staring at the fire. "I worry that you and I both told her your angel story. She probably thinks you're a little rattled in the brainbox."

"Did you make that opinion worse or better?" He eyed his sister, wondering just how loyal she was and to whom. She adored Lady Joy.

"Better, I hope. I told her what Papa said about wars changing men."

"Thank you, Aurie."

"You better convince her to marry you. I don't like it when my friends are angry with me."

"I shall do my very best."

Chapter Three

"I KNOW SIR Jansen is a decorated war hero," said Serendipity, the eldest of the Broadmere flock of sisters, "but that does not mean he is suitable to be your husband." She sat taller as her maid worked to remove the evening's jewelry from around her neck. "And do not accuse me of prejudice just because he is landed gentry and not nobility. I simply feel you could do better."

"I did not ask your opinion of Sir Jansen; I merely told you I had agreed to court him and needed a way out of that agreement. Did you miss that part, or are you simply not listening?" Joy paced the perimeter of the sisters' large, shared dressing room, ready to pinch Serendipity if she didn't get down off her high horse and offer some useful advice. She paused in her pacing long enough to pin her sister with a narrow-eyed glare. "And anyone who says, *Do not accuse me of prejudice* usually reeks of it."

"Here." Felicity, next to the youngest and ever the peacemaker, who believed that either tea or food fixed any situation, held out a cup and a small platter of biscuits. "My newest recipe. They're perfect for nighttime relaxation and calming sleep."

"Laced them with laudanum, did you?" asked Merry, the youngest Abarough sister.

Felicity rolled her eyes and ignored her sibling's teasing. She shoved the tea and biscuits into Joy's hands. "There is no laudanum. I promise. Only lemon and lavender in the biscuits and chamomile tea."

"Have we no brandy?" Joy asked. "This is truly an evening for brandy—or possibly whisky."

"How did this arrangement come to pass?" Serendipity rose from the dressing table chair and bore down on Joy. "What sort of bet did you finally lose? I missed that part, you were talking so fast. How many times have I warned you that your gambling would someday be your demise?"

"I am far from dead."

"Maybe so," Serendipity said, "but from where I stand, your freedom appears to be toddling on its last legs." She frowned while tipping her head to one side. "Or do you love him? I have seen you eyeing Sir Jansen whenever he's on the dance floor with another."

"I do not love him." At least, Joy didn't think she did. Maybe she was talking with the wrong sisters. Blessing, Fortuity, and Grace had more experience in these catastrophic matters than Serendipity, Felicity, and Merry. Joy bit into a cookie, cringed at the cloyingly sweet—yet acidic—flavor, then spat the bite into her teacup. "Oh, Felicity. I am sorry, but this is not one of your better efforts."

Her sister gave a sympathetic nod. "I know. But I didn't want to waste them by throwing them out, so I thought to try them on you rather than the servants. It seemed unkind to force them on the help."

"Thank you ever so much." Joy glared at her sister, whom she knew could usually bake better than any cook alive. "I shall remember your kindness when next we find ourselves in the country close to a pond filled with frogs."

"You wouldn't."

"Blessing taught me well." Joy envisioned Felicity stripping back the covers of her bed and discovering it filled with slimy green visitors. "Now, could one of you please tell me how I can extricate myself from this situation?"

"Tell him *no*," Merry said. "He is a knight. He won't force his attentions on you."

"I cannot do that, remember? He said he would tell everyone about our compromising card game in the library and force me into a marriage of convenience."

"I warned you about gambling," Serendipity said in an annoyingly singsong way. "You cannot win at every hand of cards or roll of the dice and shouldn't be foolish enough to expect to. You usually play for money. What on earth possessed you to play for the right to be courted?"

"I didn't play for the right to be courted. I played for the right to be kissed."

All three sisters stared at her with their mouths agape. Serendipity was the first to recover. "You didn't."

"I always pay my debts."

"How was it?" Felicity whispered, inching closer with excited anticipation.

"Oh my, did he embrace you against that broad chest of his? Crush your bosoms against his rock-hard muscles?" Merry folded her hands and closed her eyes, lost in her fantasy.

"Merry!" Serendipity scolded. "No more of Fortuity's books for you!"

Merry opened her eyes and wrinkled her nose at her sister. "Do not be a hypocrite. I know where you hide your scandalous books, remember?"

"Do any of you possess any useful suggestions at all? Or have I wasted this confessional?" Joy shook her head. "I should have saved it for Blessing or Fortuity, since Gracie's in the country." Thoroughly frustrated and on the verge of panic, she threw up her hands. "I have to think of something before Chance gets wind of this and has the banns read! He'll have me married off before the month is out."

Serendipity puckered a thoughtful frown. "Maybe not. He wants you married, but I am sure he'd prefer nobility. You know he was never too keen on Thorne until he got to know him."

"Thorne is a baron. That *is* nobility, and Blessing loves him. Chance didn't like him because Thorne was an unrepentant rake before he fell in love." Joy rubbed her forehead, wishing the pounding ache would cease. The entire evening had been a terrible disaster. She'd lost at a hand of cards, lost a kiss, and very possibly lost her heart, and could lose so much more because of it. She wasn't one of those swooning debutantes with an empty head, a marriage-minded mama, and aspirations of gaining Society's envy. She didn't want anyone's envy. She wanted her freedom, her personal gambling hell, and eventually marriage and all the responsibilities that went with it. At a later date—much later.

Someone tapped on the bedchamber door, then called out loud enough to be heard in the dressing room. "My ladies." It was Mrs. Flackney, the housekeeper. "His Grace wishes to see you before you retire for the evening."

"We are already retired," Joy lied. She was not in the mood to deal with Chance.

"His Grace gave his word that the meeting would be brief."

"His Grace is a liar," Joy said. "Tell him the flock declines his invitation."

"We are coming," Serendipity called out as she grabbed Joy by the wrist and dragged her along. "Ignore Joy. She is in a mood. Tell His Grace the flock will be with him shortly."

"Tell His Grace to kiss a frog," Joy muttered.

"What is it with you and frogs this evening?" Serendipity tugged harder, picking up the pace. "Come along, Merry and Felicity. You are to come too. You heard Mrs. Flackney. Dear brother requested the entire flock."

A pair of groans echoed behind them. Merry and Felicity disliked Chance's meetings after every soiree as much as Joy did.

By the time they reached the smaller of their townhouse's two parlors, Joy felt in rare form and was ready. Depending on what

Chance had seen, heard, and surmised, this meeting was destined to be rocky from the outset, and she would make him regret not waiting until another time.

He stood in his usual place in front of the hearth and had already lined up four chairs as if preparing to deliver a sermon.

Joy fixed him with her most ferocious glare. *He can deliver his sermon straight to the devil.*

He glared right back at her, his usually dark-blue eyes already flashing to a deep amethyst—a sure sign that he'd gotten wind of her escapades this evening and was not at all pleased. Well, good on him. She wasn't pleased either.

"Do you have something you wish to share, Joy?" he asked.

"No."

"No?"

She huffed. "You do know what the word means, do you not, brother?"

He resettled his stance, shifting his large frame in place as if hunkering down for battle. He'd always done that as a child as well, but it had never worked. The sisters still managed to band together, and either pushed him out of trees or into ponds to pay him back for whatever mischief he'd wreaked upon them. But there were only four sisters to wage war against him now. As each sister was married off, the odds turned in Chance's favor.

"I forbid you to court Sir Jansen Winterstone."

Joy laughed. She couldn't help it. "I am of age, darling brother. You cannot forbid me anything." Why had she said that? Chance forbidding her was the escape clause she needed. After all, as a dutiful, loving sister, she could never in good conscience marry without his blessing. Of course, Sir Jansen could still counter with the scandalous library *tête-à-tête* and force the need for a marriage of convenience.

Merry nudged her in the ribs and whispered, "I thought you wanted out of this?"

"Do you have something to share with the rest of us, Merry?" Chance asked.

"Stop trying to guilt us like our French tutor. It makes you even more ridiculous." Merry jutted her chin higher, a silent challenge for a solo battle with her brother. Joy had never loved her youngest sister more.

Chance rolled his eyes, then turned his attention back to Joy. "Legal age of consent or not, I shall not give my blessing to a union with a member of the gentry. You deserve better."

She deserved to be left alone so she could figure a way out of this herself, and Chance's forbidding her to do something simply made her wish to do it even more. Anything daring and forbidden always tempted her and always would.

"And I have heard rumblings about your book club," he said, but his expression betrayed that he didn't know anything at all. Chance was bluffing, fishing for information.

"Have you now?" She shrugged. "We meet every Tuesday afternoon at Bankerton's Books and Bibelots to discuss the week's most scandalous selection we chose to read."

"Perhaps I should drop in sometime."

"Sorry, brother dear. Ladies only. It is *our* club. Much like White's only admits gentlemen." She pretended to hide a yawn behind her hand. "Is there anything else? The hour grows late."

"Yes—forbidding your courtship was primary, but I also wish to address Felicity and Merry's behavior this evening." He homed in on the unsuspecting two like a hawk switching prey, pointing at Merry. "No more seeking refuge in Lady Atterley's empty nursery. It is decidedly odd, and I am not the only one who noticed. It is bad enough when you sneak off to help the nannies with their charges, but that is explainable. Everyone knows your love for children. But an empty nursery? I mean, really? What were you thinking, Merry?"

"I was thinking I needed some fresh air after Lord Smellington walked by me. If I'd gone to the garden or the terrace, Old Smelly would surely have followed. He gets worse with every Season. You cannot deny it."

Chance closed his eyes and shook his head as if sorely put upon. Rather than defend the malodorous marquess, he turned to Felicity. "The kitchens. Again?"

"I wanted to speak with the cook. I wasn't in there all that long." Felicity squirmed in her seat, then went still at the soft sound of material ripping. "Oh dear. May I be excused, please? I fear I've burst another seam."

Chance waved her away and turned to Serendipity as Felicity hurried from the room. "You must speak with her. Again. Before she eats her way to plump spinsterhood."

"Leave her alone." Joy had heard enough. "She is a dear and perfect just the way she is. If no man can see that, then they can all go to the devil." She rose and charged toward her brother, backing him up with several hard pokes to his chest. "You are not exactly perfect, brother, and neither are any of the other males of the peerage. Everyone has flaws. It is what makes us interesting."

"But—"

"Stop being an arse!" She poked him again. "We love you, but you are not Papa and never will be. Be a good brother rather than a mercenary guardian trying to sell your sisters to gain the rest of your inheritance. Grow up, Chance. Why do you think Mama and Papa drew up the will the way they did?"

He opened and closed his mouth like a fish out of water, making incoherent sounds as if suddenly struck mute.

"Joy," Serendipity said, "do you not think that's a little harsh?"

"Oh, shut your gob, Seri. You are just as bad as he is. I am going to bed." Joy flounced from the room, charged upstairs, and slammed the door of the sisters' joint sitting room behind her. She did the same with the door to her bedchamber. Since there was naught but the four of them now in the house, they'd remodeled the rooms so each of them had their own private bedchamber. Thank goodness, because in her dark mood, she wasn't fit for company.

❧

"NIMBUS. WHAT HAVE you been told?" Jansen asked the black cat that sat at his feet, proudly holding what looked to be a brand-new hair ribbon in his mouth. Jansen took it away and tucked it into his jacket pocket. "You must stay out of Aurelia's ribbons or she is sure to stop allowing you into her rooms."

The golden-eyed feline flicked an ear, appearing more than a little uninterested in yet another lecture about his thieving. Nimbus stole anything he could carry or drag. More often than not, he deposited whatever he nicked into Jansen's bedchamber, which made things rather awkward whenever he helped himself to the belongings of visitors. But Jansen loved the cat. He had rescued him as a kitten from the wreckage of a cannon in Greece, and Nimbus had been with him ever since.

The cat hopped up onto the bed and meowed while kneading his favorite pillow. Nimbus wanted to go to bed, and the feline was right. It was only a few hours till dawn, and Jansen had yet to sleep at all. He hated the nights. The darkness of closed eyes and unguarded slumber allowed the demons to creep back in and attack, making him relive the nightmares of war, nightmares real enough to make his old wounds rage as they had done when brand new. An hour or two of rest was all he usually salvaged from any night. Thankfully, he'd conditioned himself to survive quite well on what little sleep he stole from the terrors of his past.

Grudgingly, he shrugged off his jacket and rid himself of the rest of his clothes, then climbed into bed. The cool sheets caressed his nakedness and helped convince him that once again, together, they would reign victorious over the horrifying darkness and steal some much-needed rest.

The only thing that strengthened his sanity was the memory of Joy's visiting him on the battlefield. That vision had been so real. Her smile, the caring in her touch, and her lilting voice had saved him from madness and death there on that muddy field. Praise the Almighty, he had spotted her at that ball, and every other ball thereafter, for the few months before he'd gone off to war. Of all the women he'd bedded, flirted with, and barely spoken to, only Lady Joy had come to him on the battlefield as he lay there waiting to die. As he'd told her, she was and always would be his saving angel.

Nimbus walked onto his chest, leaned forward, and licked the tip of his nose with his dry, rough tongue.

Jansen gently moved the cat back to the pillow on the lower part of the bed. "Mind your manners, old man. With any luck, we shall soon have our angel sharing our bed. I have it on good authority that she likes cats. What say you about that?"

Nimbus yawned, obviously bored and sleepy.

"I know. Time to fight the demons." Jansen pulled in a deep breath as he lay back and folded his hands behind his head. Tomorrow, he would call on his precious Lady Joy. That thought made him smile and relaxed him even more. He closed his eyes. Then all hell broke loose.

Deafening cannon fire exploded all around. Men shouted, and some even screamed as they fell to the ground in what had once been a grassy meadow, now turned into a sea of churning sludge by horses' hooves, wagon wheels, and blood. His shoulder burned as if a red-hot brand had been shoved through it, skewering him to the wooden cannon wheel he lay against for cover. Shouts in a language he recognized as the Ottomans made him check his supplies. He was out of both ball and powder, helpless except for his saber and bayonet. He dragged himself even tighter against the wagon and fell back, gasping. Blast it all. He was too weak to pull himself under it. Besides, that would be the first place the enemy would look for survivors.

The voices drew closer, gleeful and laughing as they made his fellow sol-

diers cry out with agonizing screams as they murdered them with a final thrust of their bayonets. Lightning flashed, splintering the sky. The clouds opened up, releasing a deluge. Thunder shook the ground as they reached him. The ominous black shadows closed in, reaching for him. He gritted his teeth, refusing to give them the satisfaction of crying out when they ended him. Then something nipped his nose, lightly at first, then harder, making it sting. It rumbled on his chest with a low, throated growl, making the wound in his shoulder ache even worse. He couldn't see. Blinded by more lightning. Something bit his nose again.

Jansen fought through the darkness and opened his eyes to find himself nose to nose with Nimbus. Drenched in sweat, gasping to catch his breath, he cradled the cat's enormous head between both hands and rubbed its ears. "God bless you, old man. Thank you for saving me once more."

Nimbus rumbled with loud purring, butted his head against Jansen's chin, then curled up on the pillow next to Jansen's shoulder and flipped his tail down across his chest. Jansen allowed him to remain there, finding comfort in his old friend's deep, vibrating purrs and soft, silky tail contentedly brushing across him.

"I have to think of a way to rid myself of these demons," he told the cat as he watched the shadows from the sputtering night candle dance across the ceiling and walls. The deep blue of the darkness filtering in with the breeze through the window was softening with the faint blush of the approaching sunrise. He had survived another war with the terrors of his past, with Nimbus's help. "I'd hoped for Lady Joy to share my bed rather than take a room of her own once we married. But if I'm unable to overcome the darkness that overtakes my mind, how can I ask her to share that?"

Nimbus flipped his tail harder as if to say, *Be quiet and try to sleep some more.*

Perhaps the cat was right. He needed to be as rested as possible when he called on Lady Joy. He pulled in a deep, relaxing breath, held it for a moment, then released it. Closing his eyes, he held her vision foremost in his mind, praying she would keep the devils of his past away long enough for him to feel refreshed when he rose from the bed that had been a battlefield ever since his return from the war. He prayed his angel would save him from all that and change the battlefield into a place of peace and love.

Chapter Four

"**Y**OU DO REALIZE her sisters would happily serve as chaperones?" Aurelia asked as their open carriage clattered down the streets of Mayfair. "My presence is unnecessary."

"I am well aware of that." Jansen tipped a nod at an acquaintance strolling along the pristine street of the elites' townhouses. "But I prefer to better my odds. With you at my side, even if one of her sisters comes along too, the odds are even. Two against two. Were I to come alone, I would be outnumbered from the outset. I prefer to start this battle with the best possible advantages."

"Do you always think in either gaming or war terms?"

"Life is a war game, dear sister. One must always weigh the odds to not only survive but thrive."

She shook her head and adjusted her parasol, keeping herself shaded from the warm, sunny day. "All I know is I best not lose my dear friend in all this."

"It is my hope that you'll not only keep Lady Joy as a friend but also enjoy her company as your sister-in-law."

Aurelia smiled, supporting him as she always did. "I hope so too, brother. For your sake as well as mine."

The carriage slowed as it turned onto St. James's Street and came to a halt in front of Broadmere House. Jansen admitted that the place was the most impressive of the homes along the thoroughfare. But then, it would be. It housed a duke. He had never been inside, but

Aurelia had. Yet another reason for bringing her along.

"You know you may have to leave your card in case she is not receiving?" Aurelia said as he helped her step down from the carriage.

"She is receiving."

His sister arched a dark brow, eyeing him much as their mother had whenever he'd been up to mischief. "And how can you be so certain Lady Joy is receiving?"

"Because I told her I would call on her today." He couldn't help but feel a little smug. "And she knows if she doesn't keep her word about courting me, a marriage of convenience or the lack thereof will soon be bandied about by every gossip in the *ton*."

"And it does not bother you that you are *forcing* her to court you? Blackmailing her, even?"

"Not at all. It provides me the opportunity to win her heart." He gallantly offered his arm, then escorted Aurelia up the steps to the front door. But before he could make use of the highly polished brass knocker, she stopped him.

With a subtle nod, she stepped closer and lowered her voice. "Walters is their butler. He is slightly odd, older than Methusaleh, and more loyal than the best hunting hound. He has been with the family since before they were all born and refuses to accept his pension and live the remainder of his days in ease. Bear that in mind, because they are all very fond of him. Mind your tongue."

A bit insulted, Jansen frowned at her. "I am never rude to servants. You know that."

She grinned. "Ahh, yes. But you have never met a butler like Walters, nor have you ever withheld what you consider helpful suggestions that others might consider poking one's nose in where it does not belong."

"Hmpf." With that, he sharply rapped on the door, clacking the brass knocker three times.

The portal opened slightly, but the tall, white-haired man,

hunched over with age, just stood there, silent as a stone. After a long moment of nothingness, he slowly listed to the right, bumped against the door facing, and drew in a deep breath that sounded remarkably like the beginning of a nasally snore. Then he jerked, opened his eyes wider, and cleared his throat. "May I help you, sir?"

"Sir Jansen Winterstone calling for Lady Joy."

"One moment, sir." Walters closed the door in their faces and left them standing on the doorstep.

Jansen turned to Aurelia, amazed that a duke would keep such a man as the majordomo of the household. "Are we to stand here on the stoop like beggars waiting for scraps?"

"No." She pushed the door open and waved for him to follow. "He meant to ask us inside to wait in the entryway. He simply forgot. It happens more often of late."

"How do you know this?"

"Lady Joy is my friend. Remember?"

Amazed, Jansen obediently followed, praying the odd butler wouldn't forget that they'd knocked and set the hounds or footmen on them.

The young duke, whom he had spoken to briefly once or twice, stepped into the hallway and noticed them. "Miss Aurelia? Has Walters wandered off, or were you able to make him understand you wished to see Joy?" As he neared, he swept Jansen with a hard look, then turned back to Aurelia, obviously giving a subtle cut direct. "I assume you wish to see Joy today. Yes?"

"Actually, it is I who seeks the pleasure of Lady Joy's company today, Your Grace." Jansen stepped forward with a formal bow, determined that the man acknowledge him. "We have met, Your Grace. I am—"

"I am well aware of who you are," Broadmere said, "and I am not at all pleased with my sister or yourself, sir. My other sister, Lady Serendipity, informed me about the way in which this courtship began. Bad form, sir. Especially for a knight. Entrapping a young woman and giving her the ultimatum to either court you or marry you."

Jansen paused for a slow, deep breath to cool his temper. Steadiness ruled the day, and it would indeed be even worse form for him to knock this young pup on his arse in his own home. "I am most fond of Lady Joy, Your Grace. It is my greatest hope that while courting me, she will develop like feelings for me."

"I see."

Jansen doubted very much if the duke saw anything other than the dollar signs attached to the will that said his bank account depended on his sisters marrying for love. That stipulation, as well as the size of their dowries, had been the talk of the *ton* for the past four years. But far be it from him to remind the Duke of Broadmere of such things. Jansen had known the young man's father, the fourth Duke of Broadmere, well. Sadly, Chance Abarough, the fifth to take the title, was not half the man his father had been.

"Do you know if Lady Joy is receiving today, Your Grace?" Aurelia asked in a voice so innocent no one could refuse her.

Chance turned and glared up the graceful grand staircase that curved down into the wide, marble-floored entry hall. "I am sure she is. Walters probably fell asleep on the way to fetch her. God bless him. Let me ring for one of the maids." He disappeared into a side room that Jansen could only assume was a parlor or a library.

The housekeeper, Mrs. Flackney, came around the corner at a fast toddle, then pulled up short. "Miss Aurelia, good afternoon to you. Are you here to see Lady Joy?"

Aurelia shifted with a barely perceptible sigh. "Good afternoon, Mrs. Flackney. Allow me to introduce my brother, Sir Jansen Winterstone. He is the one calling on Lady Joy today. Walters went to fetch her, but we haven't seen him since. His Grace went to the parlor to ring for a maid. And now here you are, overseer of all the maids, so I really couldn't tell you if Lady Joy knows she has company or not. Did you come in answer to His Grace's bell?"

"Oh dear." The housekeeper clapped her hands to her chest. "I do apologize. Our Walters appears to be having a very bad day today."

"Think nothing of it," Jansen said. It always paid to get in good with the housekeeper. Mrs. Flackney would know everything that went on in Broadmere House. "I commend the man for holding so tightly to his position and am sure he's doing his best. Would you mind sending word to Lady Joy for us?"

"Lady Joy is right here," Joy said from midway down the stairs. "Walters fetched me. He merely had to rest a moment and catch his breath before he could relay the message that I had a caller." She smiled at Aurelia. "And I am happy to see you too, Aurelia."

"Too?" Jansen seized on the word. "Might I hope that means you are pleased to see me as well?"

"Of course, Sir Jansen." But she sounded as though she forced the words. "Forgive me—I mean—of course, Jansen. And now that we are courting, you must call me *Joy*."

"It would be my *joy* to do so."

"Oh, Jansen." Aurelia groaned and rolled her eyes. "If you court like that, I shall soon cast up my accounts."

Joy laughed, the same lilting sound he remembered from his vision on the battlefield. It very nearly took him to his knees.

"Mrs. Flackney, would you please take care of their things?" Joy asked. "Walters can store them when he makes it back downstairs. Oh, and might we have tea in the garden? It is such a lovely day. Much too nice to spend inside the parlor."

"Right away, my lady." The housekeeper held out her hands for Jansen's hat and gloves and Aurelia's parasol.

After divesting himself of his things, Jansen found himself at a rare loss for words and feeling a bit awkward. He had never courted anyone before, and not only that, the class difference of nobility versus gentry was never more stark than here in this opulent townhouse. He was by no means a pauper, but neither was he this flush in the pockets.

To his dismay, Joy appeared to have picked up on his discomfort. As an avid and successful gamer, she apparently possessed one of his traits—she read people. He hurried to shake free of this rare uneasiness and take control of the situation. "As you noted the loveliness of the day, my lady, after our tea, would you care to enjoy a carriage ride or a promenade?"

"What better way to establish our situation among Society, sir? Is that your intention? I assume Rotten Row would be our destination?"

The minx had him dead to rights, but he didn't care. Her quickness and lack of skirting the issue made him laugh. "I am a proud and yet humbled man, my lady. I would shout our arrangement from the rooftops, if I could."

"I feel quite sure that won't be necessary. The *ton* will shout it for you." Joy led the way through a large parlor and out the doors thrown open to the gorgeous day, showing them to the opulent garden overflowing with every shade of rosebush imaginable. "Mama loved her roses and tended them as carefully as she tended all of us. This time of year was always her favorite."

Aurelia tipped her nose higher and sniffed. "I love their fragrance. So very sweet. What a lovely way to have your mother still with you."

Joy's sad smile made Jansen ache to find a way to wash away her sorrow. But losing a beloved parent was a pain that only the Almighty Himself could heal. "Our mother loved daisies. I remember her weaving them into flowery chains for her and Aurelia to wear like crowns."

Aurelia gasped. "I remember that now, too. Just barely, though. I was so young when Mama passed."

"And your father never remarried," Joy said. "I remember your telling me of their great love. That too was the way of it with my parents. A true love match. A rare thing."

"Rare and precious," Jansen said. "Something worth seeking out and trying to capture by any means necessary."

She stared at him, her cornflower-blue eyes flaring wider and her supple lips, those lips that had tasted so very sweet, barely parted. Then she seemed to shake herself free of the moment, squared her shoulders, and offered a polite smile. "Rare and precious, indeed." A clatter from the doorway caused her to turn. "Our tea has arrived. Come, let us sit over here beside the arbor and watch the pond. Merry released her goldfish in there, and wonder of wonders, they are thriving. She couldn't bear their being imprisoned in those small bowls, so I am so relieved that they haven't died. She would be distraught. If you watch closely, they'll come to the surface to see if we have any treats for them. You will be amazed at their size."

Jansen spotted one of the shockingly large, shimmering fish and laughed. "Nimbus would be enthralled."

"Nimbus?"

"My cat." He'd heard she liked cats and prayed that rumor was true. "While over in Greece, I found him hiding in an old, abandoned cannon. A starving kitten small enough to fit in my pocket. Of course, I couldn't leave him there to die."

"Of course not," Joy said with such sincerity that his heart soared. "I look forward to meeting Nimbus."

"Guard your things when you do," Aurelia warned. "He is an unrepentant thief."

"I imagine that's from when he was a tiny kitten and had to steal to eat." Joy went to the tea cart and shooed the housekeeper away. "I shall pour, Mrs. Flackney, since you appear to be the only servant at our service today. Where is everyone?"

The matron glanced back at the doorway, then lowered her voice. "George and Peter are trying to convince Walters to have a nap. His confusion is much less after he has slept a few extra hours. And, of course, the maids are busy cleaning. I don't mind doing my part to help our Walters."

"Perhaps we should try to hire a helper again. A butler in training?"

Mrs. Flackney gave a sad shake of her head. "Whatever you wish, my lady, but I fear nothing we try will go easily with our Walters. You know he considers it his oath to your parents to maintain this household as he did when they were alive."

"I shall speak to Chance." Joy reached out and squeezed the housekeeper's hand. "I promise."

The matron toddled away, her shoulders slumped with weariness.

"Is there anything I can do to help?" Jansen asked, touched by Joy's caring for her servants. A noble rarely, if ever, touched a commoner. Most behaved as if those of the lower status bore the pox.

She handed him his tea with an unhappy sigh. "Nothing I know of. Poor Walters allows his position to define him. If he no longer takes care of the household, then in his mind, he ceases to exist. I wish we could make him understand he has earned his retirement, but he refuses. Hopefully, this time, Chance and I—and the rest of the girls— can convince him to take on a butler in training without him being offended. He is a dear old curmudgeon. We are all very fond of him."

Aurelia set her teacup and saucer on the table. "I feel the need to wander among the flowers. You two behave." She shook a finger at them. "No patty fingers. No kisses. Only longing glances. Understood?"

Joy laughed and placed her hand over her heart. "Understood."

Jansen glared at his sister, willing her to feel his exact opinion about those particular instructions.

"Aurelia is a dear," Joy said as she watched his sister follow the path and disappear into the roses.

"She is indeed." Deciding to take the bull by the horns after Aurelia's accusation of blackmail—which was founded, but that was neither here nor there—and Broadmere's obvious displeasure with him, Jansen leaned back in the fancy wicker garden chair that groaned and crackled beneath his weight. "How much do you hate me, Joy? For ensnaring you?"

She looked up from stirring her tea as though startled. "Hate you?"

"Yes. For blackmailing you into our courting."

With a look one would expect from a displeased mother scolding her child, she set her tea on the table. "I do not hate you, Jansen, and cannot understand why you would assume such a thing."

"My sister accused me of blackmailing you, and your brother—"

"Do not get me started on my infuriating brother." She rolled her eyes while shaking her head. "Why he has suddenly taken on this high-and-mighty attitude, when I know good and well he would marry me off to a toad if it got him his next percentage of the inheritance, is beyond me. Ignore him. I intend to."

"My only concern, my greatest fear, is that you will come to hate me because you love someone else, and with our courting, are not free to pursue that love." He held his breath, praying he had read her right all these years, and that she had no attachments to anyone.

"There is no one else." She picked up her tea once more and hazarded a small sip. "I do not wish to marry—yet—for reasons of my own. But those reasons have nothing to do with another." She tipped a thoughtful shrug. "Although, I guess you could say, my reasons are because of things close to my heart. But they are *things*, not people."

Intrigued, he had to ask, "What things, my lady? What things might I provide for you that satisfy your heart?" All she had to do was name them, and he would move heaven and earth to lay them at her feet.

With a shy smile and a shake of her head, she looked away, unable to meet his gaze. "You are very kind, sir, but these things my heart protects, these things I will lose once I marry, cannot be bought."

"Tell me, my lady. Let me help you think of a way to keep from losing them. I swear I am not an unreasonable man who would strip away your identity once you became my wife. I understand you wish to keep your *freedoms*, as you said last night, but of what freedoms do you speak? What do you fear losing?" He reached across the table for her hand, but she pulled it away with a teasing grin.

"No, no. No patty fingers. Remember our promise to Aurelia?"

He found her levity annoying. "I am quite serious, my lady. Allow me to help you so we might marry one day before we both grow as old as your Walters."

She narrowed her eyes. "This is our first day of courting, Sir Jansen. I hardly think you've suffered an overly long engagement just yet."

"*Engagement.*" His heart swelled. "A much better term than courting."

"That was a slip of the tongue, I assure you!"

"Oh no, my lady. You called this an engagement." Blackmail or not, slip of the tongue or not, he wasn't about to allow her to reverse course now.

"You are as infuriating as my brother." She rose from her seat and shook a finger at him. "We are not engaged. We are courting."

"We already call each other by our first names. Yet another sign we are engaged."

"We are not engaged," she growled. "Stop saying that."

He so delighted in teasing her, but didn't wish to overplay his hand. "As long as we are officially *courting*, I am happy, my lady."

"Well, heaven knows I would never wish otherwise for you." She flounced over to the pond and crumbled a biscuit across the water's surface. Fish immediately bobbed into view and gobbled up the treats.

"Joy." He stood but didn't approach her. He had made her angry, and that was far from his intent.

She didn't answer, simply crumbled another biscuit for the greedy goldfish that were already larger than his hand.

"Joy?"

"What?"

"Do not be angry with me. I was somewhat teasing in the hopes that you would agree. I apologize, but in my defense, it is because I adore you, my angel. All I want is the right to make you happy all the rest of your days."

"Happiness can sometimes be a complicated thing," she said without taking her gaze from the churning waters of the pond.

"It doesn't have to be."

She turned and eyed him, studying him as if trying to decide what sort of animal he might be. "Happiness is always complicated—or at least, that has been my experience."

"Then allow me to change that for you. Allow me to make you happy by helping you find a way to retain whatever it is you live in fear of losing."

"You have no idea what you are asking."

"I am asking you to trust me."

She shook her head. "I cannot. At least, not yet." She brushed the crumbs from her hands and started toward the door. "Forgive me, but I am suddenly too tired for a ride. Perhaps another time. Yes?"

His heart fell. He had indeed overplayed his hand. "I am sorry to hear that, my lady. Of course I understand." He understood more than she knew. It was written in her eyes. "Please accept my apologies."

"No apology necessary, Jansen. But I must bid you good day. Please tell Aurelia I am truly sorry."

"I will, my lady. I shall call again soon."

"Lovely." She dropped a quick curtsy, obviously in a hurry to be gone from him.

He offered her a nod, then watched her run from the garden. In future, he needed to take better care. Go lightly and not rush her. His lady was delicate prey, flighty as a deer that would bolt at the slightest provocation.

"Come along, Aurelia," he called out, already planning the next visit. He would do better next time. Next time, Joy wouldn't run away. She would run *to* him.

❦

AS SOON AS she reached her room, Joy closed the door tightly shut and leaned back against it, blinking against the frustrating sting of tears begging to be shed. What the devil was wrong with her? She had very nearly confessed everything to Jansen. What power did that man possess to loosen her tongue at both ends and almost make her toss caution to the wind? But she had caught herself just in time. Barely.

At the next meeting of the book club, she would have a word with Aurelia. Something about Jansen's manner made her believe he knew more than he was letting on. Had Aurelia betrayed her trust? All the ladies admitted into the Reader's Dare Club meetings were sworn in, promising never to tell about the ladies' gaming club. The Reader's Dare Club was *their* place, as fine and entertaining as any forbidden men's club like White's or Brooks's or Boodle's.

And he had been so handsome today—so unbearably handsome that she could think of nothing but their kiss.

Good heavens, she needed some cool water. She rushed to the washstand and filled the basin. Thankfully, the water was still quite chilly, since the maid had just freshened it. After wetting a cloth, she pressed it to her temples, dabbed it across her forehead and eyes, then held it to the back of her neck. Much better, she decided with a deep breath.

A dull ache low in her belly provided the answer to part of her problem. Her courses had decided to come. "Well, isn't that just lovely?" That would explain the silliness of wanting to cry. Thank goodness she had begged off the carriage ride. That would have been most awkward and very embarrassing, since she currently wore white muslin with tiny blue flowers. She would have permanently stained her dress.

"Flora!" Her maid had to be somewhere close.

"Yes, my lady?" Flora emerged from the shared dressing room, then slapped a hand to her forehead. "Forgive me, my lady. 'Tis time for your courses, and I completely forgot the date. Your pads and belt are laundered and ready in the stand beside the commode. Shall I fetch some tea or laudanum? How bad are your pains this time? I know 'tis early yet, but you always suffer so."

"Do not remind me." Joy didn't have time for this inconvenience. Tomorrow was the meeting, and invariably, her second full day of courses was always worse than the first. The devil himself wouldn't be able to get along with her by tomorrow. "Tea. Lots of it, please. We shall save the laudanum for tonight."

She took refuge behind the privacy screen, found her supplies, and belted a pad in place. Dear heavens, it was like walking with a chafing pillow bunched between her legs, but if she didn't tie the pad tightly enough, it would slip and not provide protection. Sometimes she hated the maturity of womanhood.

"Shall I draw you a bath, my lady?" Flora called out from the other side of the screen. "Or warm some linens to hold against your belly?"

"Yes to everything, dear Flora. Thank you." Maybe if Joy attacked her womanly time head-on with teas, hot water, and warmed linens, she could convince her body to calm down and behave enough for tomorrow's meeting. She simply had to be there. With the membership as large as it had become, she couldn't possibly shirk her duties for something as annoying as her courses. Some women took to their beds, but not her. Although, to be truthful, it would probably be kinder to those around her if she did.

"Come along now, my lady. Let's get you abed. Your bath will be ready shortly."

"I hate this, Flora. Hate it with a passion."

The maid gave her a sympathetic nod. "I know, my lady. All women do."

Chapter Five

"**G**OOD AFTERNOON, LADY Joy. Miss Aurelia." Widow Bankerton smiled from behind the counter of Bankerton's Books and Bibelots, the book and bauble shop she and her husband had transformed into a thriving London business. "And how are we today?"

Joy had barely pulled herself together after hours of cramping, headaches, and nausea brought on by a particularly vicious round of monthly feminine ills, but she wasn't about to share that personal information with the shop owner. "We are quite well, Mrs. Bankerton. How are you?"

"Happy to report that upstairs is nearly filled," the matron said with a mercenary gleam in her eyes. "The Reader's Dare Club may soon be forced to expand to the third floor as well. Wouldn't that be lovely?"

"Indeed." Joy knew their charities would benefit, but also knew that Bankerton's would profit as well. She didn't begrudge the widow her excitement or her profit. After all, Mrs. Bankerton knew very well what went on every Tuesday afternoon at the Reader's Dare Club, but she was tactful and professional enough to look the other way and deflect any curious male customers in another direction. Sometimes, when business in the shop was slow, she even came upstairs and tried her luck at Faro.

"Good heavens," Aurelia whispered as they climbed the stairs. "It was Connie's turn to arrange refreshments. I do hope she had the foresight to plan for extra."

"If she reviewed last week's receipts with Freddie, that should have given her some idea." Joy plodded along, still nursing a throbbing headache. "If we run short, we shall simply have to shut down early. Everyone will understand—or at least, they should. It is not as if we have a warehouse filled with food and beverages on site."

"Are you all right, Joy?" Aurelia paused on the stairs, offering such an expression of sympathy that the danger of tears threatened to overtake Joy once more.

She hated that she was sometimes weepy during her monthlies, absolutely hated it, though she also realized it wasn't only her monthlies to blame this time. But she couldn't speak with Aurelia about Jansen. Who knew if the girl could be trusted with that particular subject anymore?

Joy massaged her temples and whispered, "A course's headache."

"Ah." Aurelia offered a conciliatory hug. "I understand, and once a month, I curse Eve for tempting Adam."

"If Adam had been a proper man, he would have refused her and asked the Almighty to scold her." Joy had decided long ago that whenever she found herself at the pearly gates of the great beyond, she had a few choice words to share with Eve about listening to that vile serpent.

"But Eve was tempted too, so I suppose we should grant her some grace," Aurelia said. "Temptation can be so hard to resist."

For some odd reason, Joy got the impression they were no longer discussing the first couple who had gotten themselves ousted from the Garden of Eden for flouting the Almighty's rules. "Is there something you wish to tell me?"

Aurelia arched both brows higher. "Something to tell you?"

Joy tugged her friend to a stop just outside the entrance to the second floor. "What is it?"

"Please don't hurt my brother. He truly does care for you. Really, he does."

"Aurelia—"

"I know you agreed to court him, but please don't string him along and give him hopes only to dash them. That would be crueler than cruel."

"You know why I don't wish to marry just yet, and if he finds out the truth about the club, he probably won't wish to marry me either. Think of the scandal. We have all worked so very hard to build it into what it is today, very few understand how much good we do for our charities from its proceeds, and my reputation would certainly be the one to fall, because I founded it."

"We would stand beside you," Aurelia said. "We understand the risks we take."

"I know, but it would still be my fault. Not only because I founded it, but because the *ton* would blame me for leading the rest of you astray. I have somewhat of a reputation when it comes to gambling, you know."

"Just please don't hurt him. Have you any tender feelings toward him at all?"

Joy released a heavy sigh, trying not to snap at her dear friend. Again, she was not about to tell her that she already possessed tender feelings for Sir Jansen Winterstone, mainly because she hadn't quite come to terms with that herself. "I think, with time, I could develop tender feelings for him." A wicked grin came too easily. "His kiss was quite breathtaking."

Aurelia bounced in place and clapped her hands. "I am so very glad. That is all I'll trouble you with today. I promise. Just know he truly does adore you."

"Shall we go in now?" The subject needed to be changed. "If the place has filled to capacity, I am sure Freddie, Connie, and Prudie need us to help ensure things go smoothly."

"Indeed." Aurelia led the way.

"Good heavens," Joy muttered as they stepped through the door. Widow Bankerton had not exaggerated. Every table was full, as was the bar where refreshments could be found. The place was standing room only. They most definitely needed to expand to another floor and recruit more servants from trusted households. After all, a comfortable gamer was a happy gamer willing to stay longer and gamble more, and a portion of every pot went to the house for the benefit of the charities. If they were ever found out, Joy prayed they could use the excuse that this was a novel way to support their favorite organizations, because all the other ways had grown quite stale.

Connie rushed over to greet them. "Good gracious, we have never had such a crowd. What caused the sudden increase in our number of guests? It's not as if we have the luxury of placing an advertisement in the tittle-tattle sheets. I thought poor Freddie would never get all the new ones vetted. Widow Bankerton had to help her." She nudged Joy. "By the way, congratulations on your engagement."

"On my what?" Joy forgot how to breathe. "I agreed to court him, not to be engaged."

Connie made a face and shook her head. "That is not what the tongue waggers say, and they seem quite sure of their sources."

Jansen had to have done this, after all his supposed understanding and sincerity yesterday in the garden. Joy turned on Aurelia. "Tell your brother his antics are not appreciated."

Aurelia shook her head, vehemently jerking it from side to side. "No. No. Jansen would never do something so audacious. I swear to you he wouldn't."

"Then who?"

"If it wasn't me," Aurelia said, "and it wasn't Jansen, which I am certain it wasn't, that leaves Connie, Freddie, and Prudie, since our little group was the only ones who knew about the dare."

Joy locked her glare on Connie, instinctively knowing it was her.

"Why would you do such a thing to me?"

Connie opened her mouth, then closed it and gave a nonchalant shrug. "You watered down the dare when you took away the possibility of discovery and had us guard the doors—and you scolded me that evening. Never scold me. I will not stand for it, and I don't care that you are the daughter of a duke. I will not be treated as a *lesser*." She spun about and flounced away with her head held high, obviously proud of herself for serving Joy a supposed comeuppance.

"Well, I never," Aurelia said in obvious shock.

Joy huffed a bitter laugh. "Well, she did. So much for our friendship. I believe that bridge just turned to ash and crumbled into the abyss." She had been fond of Connie, but not so much as to mourn the loss of their tenuous friendship. What worried her more was Connie's inclusion in the Reader's Dare Club. The girl knew all their secrets and could turn the tables on them in the blink of an eye. "You know Prudie will side with her. She doesn't take a breath without Connie's permission."

"Freddie will side with us," Aurelia said. "But that doesn't change the fact that Prudie and Connie both know entirely too much. They've helped with the club since its inception."

"I do not feel well enough to deal with this appropriately. If I approach them, the *ton* will not be talking about my engagement but about my *enragement*."

"What are you going to do about both?"

"I have no idea." Joy rubbed her throbbing temples, all the while inwardly cursing Connie straight to the devil. *Damn her eyes.* She should have known better than to include the daughter of Lady Burrastone in anything that required secrecy. Mama had never trusted Connie's mother, and apparently, the backbiting acorn had not fallen far from the treacherous oak.

"You need to go home to your bed," Aurelia advised with a consoling hug.

"If I leave, she wins." Joy swallowed hard, trying to tamp down the bitter bile burning the back of her throat. If she lost her tea and toast, she needed to be sure she was close enough to hit Connie with it.

"I am going to go give her a piece of my mind! I simply must."

"Aurelia! Don't!" Joy tried to snag hold of her and missed. It was too late. Aurelia was already nose to nose with Connie and Prudie.

"Oh dear," Widow Bankerton said from behind her. "Is there an additional problem?"

"Additional?" Joy braced herself. What else could be wrong?

The widow drew closer and shielded her mouth with her hand. "Miss Winterstone's brother is in the shop and refuses to leave until he speaks with you. It was all I could do to prevent Sir Jansen from storming the stairs."

"Oh, good heavens." Joy cradled her head between her hands and pulled in a deep, fortifying breath. "Tell him I will be down immediately. I must speak with Miss Aurelia first."

"Yes, Lady Joy. Right away." Widow Bankerton slipped out just as quietly as she'd slipped into the room, and no one seemed to notice. Of course, all eyes were currently locked on Aurelia, Connie, and Prudie. Freddie had also joined the fray, siding with Aurelia, just as predicted.

Joy marched over to the arguing women, who were hissing and growling like a quartet of angry cats. "Stop it. All of you. Unless you've tired of the Reader's Dare Club and wish for it to be done with because of your abysmal behavior. If ladies cannot trust us, they will not only cease to come here, but will more than likely spread the word to their men about what goes on here. Is that what you wish? If so, say as much, and I will announce to one and all that this afternoon is over, and there will not be another. Or you may announce it yourself. I really do not care either way."

"But I was defending you," Freddie said, hurt feelings on her sleeve.

"I know. And I thank you for that, dear Freddie and dearest Aurelia. But if Lady Constance and Lady Prudence wish to behave like selfish, backbiting hussies, I would rather they show their arses by attacking me and no one else. I assure you, their behavior does not bother me in the least. Now, decide what you wish to do and do it, because I have a meeting downstairs"—she glared at Connie—"with my *intended*." Then she turned and stormed from the room, smiling at the round of applause following her.

Upon reaching the ground floor, she found herself so lightheaded that she leaned against the wall and concentrated on deep, calming breaths to cool the rage sweeping through her.

"Joy!" Jansen rushed over, swept her up into his arms as if she were a babe, and carried her to the cushioned window alcove perfect for reading. "You are as white as bleached parchment. Lie here while I send for a coach to see you home so a physician might be called to attend you."

She caught him by the sleeve. "Stop overreacting! I simply need to catch my breath after a rather unpleasant argument upstairs."

"With Aurelia?" He settled down beside her on the cushions, looking shocked. "But she is always so good natured and absolutely adores you. What on earth could have happened?"

Joy bowed her head and massaged her temples. Closing her eyes, she tried to calm her pounding heart. The excitement of being swept up in Jansen's strong arms and held against his rock-hard chest had nearly undone her. "Aurelia and Freddie sided with me against that pair of sorry hussies, Connie and Prudie. They betrayed me."

"I see."

She narrowed her eyes, struggling to hold back angry tears and keep her voice low. "This is not humorous at all. You have no idea of the seriousness of this matter."

"I believe I do." He scrubbed a hand over his eyes, seeming suddenly weary. "A friend of mine visited to congratulate me on our engagement. I came here to ensure you knew it was not I who made this announcement to the *ton*. Is that the serious matter to which you are referring?"

She sighed and nodded. "Yes. What are we going to do?"

The hurt and loneliness in his eyes made her sorry she had asked.

"I had *hoped* we would be engaged," he said quietly. "But apparently, that is not your preference."

It broke her heart to hurt him so. He was such a good man. And Aurelia would make a good sister, even though the last thing Joy needed was another sister. She allowed herself another heavy sigh. "Forgive me. I am not well today, and being stabbed in the back does little for my mood. Since the *ton* believes we are engaged, then we are engaged, as long as you have no problem with a *long* engagement?"

He eyed her with a leeriness she found most insulting. She never broke her word. Why would he think so?

"I mean it," she said. "We are engaged, and I do not say that lightly. All right?"

A slow grin made him even more handsome. "Such a stern beginning to an engagement, but I shall take it and be thankful." He brushed a kiss to her gloved hand, making her catch her breath. "I am the luckiest man in all of creation to have found such an angel."

She couldn't help but snort. "You won't consider yourself so lucky when you have been around me longer. I am anything but an angel. Especially when I am as out of sorts as I am today."

"Oust those two from your book club," he said. "Shall I go upstairs and escort them to the street for you?"

"No." She caught hold of his hand and held it tightly. "Aurelia and I handled it. You must allow ladies to take care of matters involving ladies...or women who claim to be ladies. If you ask me, they are a sorry couple of cows."

He threw back his head and laughed so loudly that Widow Bankerton hushed him. "Beg pardon, Mrs. Bankerton," he said before turning back to Joy. "Shall I escort you home, my lady? I am sure Mrs. Bankerton wouldn't mind fetching Aurelia if you're not yet ready to be seen without a chaperone."

She hated leaving. That was tantamount to surrendering to Connie and Prudie. But she had already said as much to them as she dared. To say more, especially in front of the ladies who had applauded her, could brand her an unreasonable harpy. At least her *guests* had considered her speech a success, and neither Connie nor Prudie had gotten the opportunity to react or reply. There would be the devil to pay later. Of that, she had no doubt. After all, look at the lengths Connie had gone to over a simple reminder that to be mean to others less fortunate than oneself was the epitome of pettiness indeed.

"Please do ask Mrs. Bankerton to fetch Aurelia," she said. "While I believe she could hold her own quite well, I feel terrible for deserting her."

"Consider it done, my lady, and then we shall ride home in style. My carriage awaits outside."

"Then why did you offer to call for a coach?" She eyed him, wondering at that slip of a tongue.

"Because I had no idea how infuriated you might be about the announcement of our engagement. My greatest fear was that you would never wish to set eyes on me ever again, let alone ride in my coach with me."

"You are very considerate."

"Some might argue that point."

"I would not." *Oh dear.* She was very much developing the most tender feelings for this man. "Thank you for everything, Sir Jansen."

"Jansen...remember?"

"Yes. Jansen." Even saying his name felt oh so right. She was indeed in danger of becoming a servant to her heart.

"WHAT A WONDERFUL afternoon with my two favorite ladies," Jansen said to Joy and Aurelia. He couldn't resist saying it, even though the both of them had plainly had a trying few hours. From his perspective, this was an auspicious day. Joy had grudgingly agreed to their engagement, and also agreed to sit beside him in the carriage and let Aurelia have the opposite bench to herself.

"Shall we swing through the park, or are you feeling well enough, my dear?" he asked Joy. She still appeared a bit wan, and that concerned him.

"Perhaps some fresh air would do me good," she said with a hesitant smile.

"You are certain? If you need to go home, I understand completely."

"I am certain I wish to enjoy the park. Carry on." She nodded and appeared to pull in a deep breath, as if determined to put on a brave face. That concerned him too. What on earth had happened back there at the bookshop?

And while Joy appeared pale, Aurelia's colors ran red as fury, a sure sign she was plotting someone's demise.

"Who are you planning to murder, dear sister?" he asked her, only partially in jest. Something dire had to have happened to upset both the ladies, and instinct told him it was something a great deal more than the malicious announcement of his and Joy's engagement. And why had Lady Constance taken it upon herself to do that? What had triggered her to turn on her friend? There was a great deal more going on here than what he had been told. "Aurelia?"

She tore her gaze away from whatever she was glaring at off in the distance and fixed it on him. "What?"

"Such curtness for your favorite brother?"

"Sorry." She rolled her shoulders, resettling herself on the carriage's plush seat. "I fear I was reliving all that was said at the—"

"Aurelia!" Joy kicked at her like a horse, warning that there was worse to come if she continued speaking.

Aurelia snapped her mouth shut, her glower even darker.

"Forgive me, dear friend." Joy leaned forward, reaching for Aurelia. "None of this is of your doing. I have no one to blame but myself. Please, please ignore my rudeness."

"You know I adore you," Aurelia told Joy with a sympathetic smile.

"And for what are you blaming yourself?" Jansen asked, bracing himself for the worst. It had to be something to do with their engagement.

She stared at him for a long moment, repeatedly wetting her sumptuous lips to the point of distraction. "For trusting too many people. When one has a special secret, it should be kept to a select few, rather than sharing it with half the population and expecting it to remain undiscovered by the other half."

"The secret of our courting?"

"No. This secret was well in place before my little game of dare that pulled you into the thick of this madness."

"What in heaven's name are you talking about?"

"She cannot tell you," Aurelia said. "It is a womanly thing you would never understand."

Egads. A womanly thing? But far be it from him to be a coward. "I think you will both find I can be very understanding, and possibly even helpful."

"The Reader's Dare Club is a ladies-only club." Joy spat out the words so fast that they tumbled over one another. "A gambling hell for women. We meet every Tuesday to enjoy gaming, betting, winning, and losing. Some have even been known to smoke and drink a brandy or two on occasion, but we ensure everyone is well set and refreshed before they leave the bookshop, so the males in their lives are none the wiser. The house gets a percentage of every pot no matter who wins, and we donate those proceeds to the London Children's Home most of the time. Sometimes, when there is an increased need elsewhere that we are made aware of, we donate to other charities that we have verified do some actual good for the populace of this area. There." Joy jutted her chin to a defiant tilt. "What say you to that?"

"A gambling hell for women," he repeated, tossing the concept around to examine it from every possible angle. "A ladies' club. Like White's for the gentlemen?"

Joy pulled in another deep breath and jerked a curt nod. "Yes. Like White's."

"What is wrong with that?" He was amazed someone else hadn't thought of it long ago. The idea was a veritable gold mine.

Both Joy and Aurelia stared at him as if he had suddenly sprouted horns.

"Most gentlemen would not agree with you, brother," Aurelia said. "While ladies are permitted a few friendly games here and there at parties or teas, we are by no means allowed the freedom of going to a club and gambling away the afternoon. It simply isn't done—well, it wasn't done until the Reader's Dare Club."

"And what do you fear would happen should word get out?"

"The *ton* would brand us as terrible jades leading polite ladies astray and putting improper ideas about things they shouldn't even think about into their pretty little heads," Joy said. "We—or more accurately, I—would become a social pariah." She gave Aurelia a sympathetic smile. "I am the founder and take full responsibility for leading Aurelia, Freddie, Connie, and Prudie down this path of depravity."

"I believe you are bloody well brilliant and fail to see the problem with your club." Jansen shook his head, suitably impressed by the entire operation. "You are helping charities and giving ladies a way to relieve their boredom in ways much more suitable than taking lovers or embarrassing their husbands in some other foolish manner." He thumped his knee with his fist. "By golly, I believe you should expand to your own building and stop hiding in the bookshop's upper levels. Who knows how much coin you could pull in for the orphans and foundlings, veterans of the wars, and whoever else might be in need? Such an establishment could grow by leaps and bounds."

Joy stared at him, her lovely mouth ajar in disbelief. "You don't wish to break our engagement and forbid Aurelia to be my friend or ever speak to me again?"

"Copper!" he called out to the driver. "Find us a nice, shaded area that is quiet and free of tongue waggers craning their necks and sniffing around." This matter needed to be settled, and settle it he would.

"Right away, sir." Copper tipped his hat and nodded.

Soon, they were sitting in the shade of a sprawling oak, watching the swans gracefully float by on the Serpentine. Jansen handed his sister a spare parasol from the pocket inside the carriage and pointed at the lake. "Please go for a walk, Aurelia. Not too far, but far enough. Understand?"

"I am not a bacon-brained half-wit, you know." She snatched the parasol out of his hand, climbed down from the carriage, and stormed off.

"You should be kinder to your sister," Joy said. "She has had a most trying afternoon being my champion."

"Your afternoon has been trying as well, my lady." He took her hand between both of his and held it. "I meant what I said about your club. It is an absolutely brilliant undertaking." A huff of amusement escaped him. "I am not at all surprised, because you, my angel, are a brilliant woman."

Tears welled in her eyes and quickly overflowed.

"Oh, good heavens. Forgive me. What did I say?" He started to drop to one knee right there in the carriage, but she dove into his arms and sobbed against him, thumping his chest with her fist.

"You are unbelievable. Absolutely unbelievable," she cried, hiccupping out the words.

"In a good way, or bad?" He hated her crying, but rather enjoyed the opportunity of holding her close.

She sniffed and pulled back, wrestling with her reticule for what he could only assume was a handkerchief.

"Here." He held out his, thankful he'd tucked one of his best silks into his pocket before leaving the house.

"Thank you." She sniffed again, tapped it to her nose, then dried her eyes. "Please forgive me. You have no idea how heavy this burden of secrecy has weighed upon me." She shook her head. "And to have you accept me so easily...without accusation...without fault finding..." She crumpled with another onslaught of tears, holding his handkerchief to her mouth as if trying to hide behind it.

"Dear heavens, what has Society done to you women?" He gathered Joy close once more, shushing and consoling her.

"You're just like...just like my papa. So understanding. So open-minded." She shuddered against him, melting ever closer, making him wish they could stay like this forever. "I will most certainly marry you, Sir Jansen Winterstone. I would be proud to be your wife."

"Because of my understanding, or because you are fond of me?" He knew it was petty, but he longed to hear words of tenderness and affection. He prayed she felt both for him.

"Because I have fallen hopelessly in love with you," she said, snuggling herself more comfortably beneath his chin. "And you...understand me."

He closed his eyes and rested his cheek atop her silky head, his heart soaring so high he couldn't breathe. "My angel." A ragged sigh escaped him, and he kissed her rose-scented hair. "I think I loved you from the first moment I saw you—even before you appeared to me on the battlefield and kept me from dying."

"You frighten me when you put me on a pedestal. The more highly you speak of me, the farther I have to plummet." She shifted back and looked up at him. "But I still need us to observe a long engagement."

"Why?"

"Because I need time to not only become accustomed to the idea of marriage but also settle the matter of the Reader's Dare Club. Connie and Prudie are certain to be a problem. I feel it in my bones."

"We already settled it. I shall immediately start looking for a place to lease. Is that building next to the bookshop not empty? If you wish, I shall put my name on it so you will not be incriminated further."

"You will not get involved." Joy scooted back, putting even more space between them. "I have yet to decide what I wish to do. Your acceptance helps immensely, of course, but just because you accepted it so readily, that does not mean the other males of the *ton* will do so. Nor does it mean the ladies who patronize the club will wish to share it with the men in their lives. Not everyone is like you. Openly flaunting what the club truly is could be…messy."

"Why will you not allow me to help you?"

"Because I need to do this myself." She huffed at him. "I started this mess. It is mine to finish. On my own, thank you very much. If you get involved, it will only complicate matters."

"How so?"

"Everyone will think I am a mindless ninny who gets herself into scrapes only to be bailed out by the first man she can trick into doing so by batting her eyelashes and waving around her dowry!"

That was more than mildly insulting. "I have no interest in your dowry, my lady. My only interest is in you, and I wish to be clear on that. As far as I am concerned, you can take your dowry and donate it to one of your precious charities."

"I will not! That dowry is for my children, should something happen to my husband!"

"Then why are we even speaking of it?" Egads, the woman not only drove him to distraction because he loved her, but the minx possessed the ability to irritate him beyond belief.

"You started it."

"I did not, my lady. You brought up your dowry and your eyelashes. I simply offered my assistance in helping you solve your dilemma." How could they tumble so fast from tender words to sparring like a couple of amateur pugilists?

"I do not want your help." She paused, staring at him with those startling blue eyes of hers, chest heaving with emotions he prayed weren't so strong that she would spurn him after all. "I do not want your assistance—I simply need your support and understanding. I must handle this myself. Please try to understand."

It suddenly struck him that one of the reasons he had waited until such a ripe old age to marry was because all the women he'd met had worshipped Polite Society and did whatever the *ton* commanded. He was nine and thirty and had searched forever for a woman of independence and thoughtfulness. One who knew herself and respected herself enough to follow a path for its rightness, not for its acquiescence with Society.

Well, now he'd found her. What did he expect? While it would be nice to have an independent woman who also did whatever he said, that would be a contradiction in terms. He couldn't have it both ways. An independent woman knew her own mind and wouldn't automatically accept his opinion as her own.

"I understand," he said, struggling to fully do just that. Perhaps it wasn't that he didn't understand, but that he just didn't like it. But as he'd already realized, he couldn't have it both ways. "I do not like it, but I realize why you feel this way."

"Really?" She arched a brow.

"Really—or at least, I am trying to, and need you to accept that as enough for now."

"That would only be fair, since you have accepted so much about me."

"Thank the Almighty."

"And what is that supposed to mean?"

"It means I am thankful. What are you angry with me about now?"

With a heavy sigh, she bowed her head and massaged her temples. "I am not angry with you, per se. I am angry at the world. The devil himself couldn't get along with me today, and I should never have emerged from my bedchamber. Please accept my apology for my horrid, snappish harpyness."

"Is that a word?" he asked, unable to resist teasing her.

"What?"

"Harpyness?"

"It is now, because I just used it, and if you are wise, you will accept that and let it lie."

He chuckled. He couldn't help it. "I shall, my lady. I shall."

Chapter Six

"OH, NOT CHARMING Charlie. Please tell me this is another of Chance's poor jests." Joy groaned, earning a sharp elbow in the ribs from her eldest sister.

"Dare I remind you how your voice carries when the music pauses? Do you wish all in the ballroom to hear your cutting wit?" Serendipity gave a disgruntled huff, sounding much like a snorting bull. "From what you told me about your war with Lady Constance, I am surprised we even received an invitation to the Burrastones' spring ball. And when the Duke of Rushden comes over, you will be civil. Is that understood? It is not that poor man's fault that Chance led him to believe you are one of his most ardent admirers."

"As soon as we get home, I am getting an overflowing bucketful of eels from Cook and dumping them in Chance's bed." Joy stamped a foot to seal the oath. How dare her self-serving brother attempt to manipulate her into breaking her engagement to Jansen, expecting her to settle for a vain, effusive duke who was as fake as old Lady Billersford's poorly powdered hair switches, which didn't match what was left of her real hair. "I am engaged to Jansen and intend to remain that way. Chance had best get used to the idea and accept it. Jansen is one of the most successful of the landed gentry. He is a knight and a war hero. Chance's behaving as though I've leg-shackled myself to a chimney sweep is getting very old, and I, for one, am done with it. Has he forgotten, perchance, that if I do not marry for love, he does not get my percentage added to his inheritance?"

"Do you love Jansen?"

"I believe I do."

"You *believe* you do?" Serendipity's fair brows arched higher until they disappeared behind the fringe of blonde curls framing her forehead. "That sounds like a decision of your mind, not your heart."

"I do love him—all right? It simply feels odd to say so to someone other than him. I am not one of those silly girls who shout their love from the rooftops. You should know that, and you should also remember how I feel about losing what little independence I have."

Serendipity blew out a heavy sigh. "Here comes your Sir Jansen now, and Charming Charlie won't be far behind once he works his way around the room after flirting with every female in attendance."

Joy couldn't respond. She was too enraptured by the sight of Jansen, so handsome in his black tailcoat, gorgeous silk burgundy waistcoat, and buff-colored breeches that made even the haughtiest of the nobility greet him with smiles and polite nods, before they respectfully parted so he might pass. His gaze met hers, and he smiled, making her feel safe, warm, and oh so ready to be back in his arms.

"You might as well shout your love from the rooftops, the way you're ogling him," Serendipity hissed in her ear.

"Shut your gob," Joy snapped, holding her smile in place. "Go pester Felicity and Merry for a while. They're still unattached. Remember?" She cut a curt glance her sister's way. "And last I checked, you were unattached as well. Our ranks are thinning, sister. Soon, you will be the one on the chopping block, and then you shall see just how *enjoyable* that situation is."

Serendipity responded by slightly narrowing her eyes. "Be civil to the duke. Promise me, and I shall leave you to it."

"I will be as civil as the circumstances require."

"Joy Elizabeth Marigold Abarough."

"Reciting my full Christian name will not increase my civility," Joy said. "If anything, it just might shorten it. Now, go away. Jansen is nearly through the gentlemen who always stop him for tales about the war."

"Fine." Serendipity spat the word as if it tasted bad. "I leave you to it." She flounced away, craning her neck in search of Merry and Felicity.

"Who won, my lovely?" Jansen gave her a wry grin as he bowed to greet her.

"I did, of course." Joy gave him an adoring curtsy, one she rarely, if ever, used. "She left me alone, didn't she?"

Jansen lifted his head, perking like a hound that had just heard the yip of a fox. "A waltz, my lady. May I have the pleasure of this dance? It will not only be our first, but our first as an engaged couple. Decorum demands we dance at least twice to set the tongue waggers astir, must we not?"

"Is it your wish to stir the tongue waggers even more than Lady Constance already has?"

"Absolutely." He swept her out onto the floor, effortlessly spinning her in time to the music. "If the tongue waggers are obsessed with us, it will give everyone else a brief respite." He smiled down at her. "And might I add that you're even lovelier than the first time I saw you?"

While the compliment set her aflutter, she had much more urgent matters with which to deal. She eyed him, debating whether to warn him about Chance's ridiculous game or simply pray that the Duke of Rushden became more interested in another of the tempting young things in attendance before he reached her.

"What is it, my angel?"

"What do you mean, *what is it*?" She knew what he meant, but had yet to make up her mind about how to handle the situation, and Charming Charlie had very nearly worked his way through most of the room. Unfortunately, he kept glancing her way while speaking to the other ladies.

Jansen arched a dark brow, making himself appear even more devilishly handsome—as if that were possible. "You are either plotting or fretting or both, my lovely. Which is it and why?"

"Explain to me how you have come to read me so accurately in such a short amount of time? I don't believe I like that even one little bit." She was stalling, and he would know it, but she couldn't help herself.

"You are stalling, my lady, and I can read you because, much like yourself, I am a gambler, and my ability to win depends on my ability to read people."

The song was almost over. If she were going to warn him, she had better begin doing it. "Chance informed the Duke of Rushden that I was his most ardent admirer in the hopes of securing a match for me."

Jansen's angular jaw flexed, then hardened with stony anger. "I see."

"For the record, I cannot stand old Charming Charlie."

He narrowed his eyes as he swept his glare across the room, searching for his opponent.

"I love you, Jansen." She squeezed his hand. "And I do not love easily or lightly. Papa always said that the man I finally accepted as a husband would be a most lucky man indeed, because he would be loved to the point of distraction. He said I was just like Mama." She cleared her throat and lowered her voice as the waltz ended. "I took that as the highest of compliments, and you should too."

Even though the song was over, he didn't release her. Instead, he held her close right there in the middle of the dance floor. The other couples meandered away, leaving them standing there alone for all to see. Joy tried to retreat, but he stopped her. Before she could speak, he dropped to one knee and stared up at her in adoration, but didn't say a word. He merely drew her in so she might drown in his golden-eyed gaze. A collective gasp rippled through the crowd.

Words were not necessary. His eyes, his demeanor, spoke to her heart, causing it to overflow. She smiled down at him and squeezed his hand again. With the slightest of nods, she said *yes*, loud enough for everyone to hear.

"I beg your pardon." The Duke of Rushden strode forward. "You overstep yourself, sir," he told Jansen.

Before Jansen could speak or rise from his knee, Joy stepped between the men and squared her shoulders, ready for a fight. "He does not overstep himself, Your Grace. I am engaged to Sir Jansen. I fear you are misinformed and have been led astray."

The passably handsome duke with his auburn hair and hazel eyes stared at her for a long moment, then shifted his focus back to Jansen, who now stood towering over him. He proffered a formal nod. "Let me be the first to congratulate you, then, Sir Jansen. Well done, old man."

Jansen gave the man an amicable yet smug tip of his head. "Thank you, Your Grace. I consider myself the most fortunate of men to have won the heart of my angel."

"Indeed." Then the duke turned and walked away, heading straight for a trio of debutantes from last Season who would surely grant him the adoration he felt he deserved.

Jansen offered Joy his arm. "My lady."

A shiver ran through her as she took it and allowed him to escort her to the long wall of double doors thrown open to Lady Burrastone's elaborate garden.

"That went much better than expected, and I am glad," she said as they stepped out onto the torchlit veranda.

"Yes," Jansen agreed. "I would hate to kill the man in a duel."

Startled at the murderous jealousy in his tone, Joy stepped back. "You would kill a man over a ridiculous misunderstanding?"

"I would kill any man who attempts to take you from me," he said matter-of-factly. "You are mine, my angel. Any man who dares think otherwise will not think that way very long."

"Swear to me you will never hurt my brother." Chance might be an annoying horse's arse, but never would she want him dead. "Swear it, or we will never marry. He is my only brother, and does what he does, even though it is usually misguided and bad form. He does what he does out of love and trying to protect me and my sisters."

"I swear I will never hurt your brother"—Jansen sucked in a great, deep breath, then whooshed it out—"other than flooring him for being an insulting idiot."

That relieved her worries somewhat. At least Jansen wouldn't *kill* Chance. A pop on the nose or a punch in the eye might even knock some sense into her brother, although she truly doubted it.

"Thank you," she whispered. "That is all I ask for him."

"Lady Joy?" a footman called from the doorway. "Lady Joy?" He bore a silver tray with a single white envelope in its center.

"Yes. I am Lady Joy." Joy rested a hand on Jansen's arm, more for support than to hold him back. Who knew what the note held—and it had to be dire for something like that to be delivered at a party rather than her residence. It had to be either from Lady Constance or her mother, Lady Burrastone. They were probably discreetly asking her to leave for causing such a scene. That would not be a problem, since such gatherings were far from her favorite forms of amusement.

She took the note and was mildly surprised when the footman hurried away. Apparently, no response would be required. As she read the words, a nauseating chill washed across her.

Everyone will know. I will see to it—they will hear my *truth:*

The Reader's Dare Club keeps the Broadmere family accounts fat and full, restoring them from where the duke drains them away with drink, gambling, and whoring. A pity one of the sisters has to ensure the family does not fall from grace and become paupers.

I want my money back. Now.

One hundred pounds by teatime tomorrow. In the hollow tree that stands in Mayfair's mews. Behind Lord Denby's residence. I feel sure you know the one I mean.

Pay or everyone will know my truth about your illicit club. Do not test me. You will fail.

"Who could have…" She stumbled to one side, grateful when Jansen caught her.

He helped her to a nearby bench. "What did it say?"

Unable to speak, she handed it to him while staring across the garden and not seeing anything. Who could hate her so much to make up such a lie about her family and threaten her in such a manner? Connie and Prudie wouldn't stoop so low—would they?

"We should get you home," he said. "I am concerned for your safety. We must show this to your brother, as well, and speak to that damn footman. I will have the name of whoever gave this to him, and I will have it tonight."

"We cannot show it to Chance. He doesn't know about the club. Only my sisters know. Please…please don't tell him." She snatched the horrible note back from him and reread it, still unable to believe its words. "What woman would send this? No men other than yourself know about the club, and how in heaven's name would they ever come up with such a lie about my family? I have ruined us all. Utterly ruined us."

He caught hold of her and forced her to look at him. "You have not ruined anyone or anything. This is merely a battle we must and will win. Lady Constance and Lady Prudence. Are they not your archenemies now? One of them must have sent it. Do you not agree?"

She slowly shook her head. "I cannot imagine either of them behaving this way. Truly, I cannot. I know they can be mean-spirited and petty, but never could I see them as…as…a pair of heartless blackmailers and liars."

"Tuck the note away and come. I am escorting you home. Whoever sent that has to be here, and that means you are in danger. I'll not have it, my angel. I will not allow anyone to harm you."

"Harm me? Haven't they harmed me enough by sending such a threat?"

"Threats are painful, my love. But trust me, there are worse things to endure. Let us fetch Aurelia. I'll not leave her here unguarded, either. I cannot depend on Ambrose to protect her. He is nigh on useless whenever there is endless drink that costs him nothing. Once I see you safely home, I shall return and investigate more fully."

Joy folded the note even smaller and stuffed it into her reticule while glancing all around to see if anyone was watching her. That might give her a clue as to the miscreant's identity. "Let us find Aurelia and Serendipity. I'll tell Seri I'm feeling unwell and must leave. I'll share the truth with her once she and the girls get home."

"Agreed. That would probably be best." He helped her stand and steadied her for a moment before they assumed the demeanor of a loving couple with not a care in the world.

As they entered the ballroom, Connie and Prudie rushed over, terror in their eyes and suspiciously identical squares of notepaper clutched in their gloved hands.

"I did not do this," Connie blurted out. "I swear I did not do this—never would I do this." She shoved her note into Joy's hands. The only difference was the threat that they would blame Connie for the blackmail.

"And I had nothing to do with this either," Prudie said, her fears making her face a bright red. "Never would I do something so dastardly—I swear it on my father's grave." Her note was much the same as Connie's, only threatening to blame her for the blackmail rather than Connie.

"I got one too," Aurelia announced matter-of-factly as she joined them. She handed it over to Jansen, as if knowing her big brother would happily take care of it and the sender.

"I wonder if Freddie got one too?" Joy looked all around, then realized she hadn't seen her friend all evening.

"Freddie declined," Connie said. "Something about feeling unwell, but I took it as a snub because of our argument at the bookshop."

"Someone is targeting us because they know us to be the ones running the Reader's Dare Club," Joy said. "And between the four of us, they stand to gain four hundred pounds. Can any of you recall any disgruntled players? Anyone bitter over losing a particular pot, or protesting how a game turned out?" Joy tried to think of anyone who might have fussed a bit more than the usual disappointment at losing, and couldn't recall a single name. "No one I know ever became overwrought—especially when they knew a portion of their losses was going to help the children."

"I cannot think of a single, bitter soul," Connie said with a despondent sniff.

"Nor I," Prudie agreed.

"Come, Aurelia. We are taking Lady Joy home." Jansen nodded at Connie and Prudie. "We will do our best to discover the truth, ladies. If you think of anyone or anything else that might be helpful, do let us know."

Both Connie and Prudie nodded while clutching their notes to their hearts.

"FOUR HUNDRED POUNDS." Jansen almost cringed at the amount once they found themselves safely seated in his carriage and rolling toward Broadmere House. "An astonishing amount. Such blatant greed."

"Freddie keeps the books and would have notified me of anyone losing anywhere close to that amount of money. We do have rules regarding the limits of acceptable wagers for this very reason. We don't wish anyone to overextend themselves." Joy clutched the neck of her pale-blue beaded reticule as if trying to strangle it. "And if Freddie received a note this evening, at her home, that brings the demand to a total of five hundred pounds. I wager she got one, and we shall hear about it tomorrow."

The more Jansen thought about it, the angrier he became. How dare someone threaten his angel. As far as he was concerned, Lady Constance and Lady Prudence had earned a good comeuppance, but not his precious Joy, Aurelia, or the amicable Lady Frederica. All the ladies had done with their daring club was help feed and clothe the poorest children of London while giving the richest females of the *ton* a somewhat innocent diversion every Tuesday afternoon.

"I will deliver the money," he said, "then hang back to capture the blackguard and bring him to justice."

"It cannot be a *him*," Aurelia said. "This despicable person must be a woman. Remember?"

"Unless it is a disgruntled husband, brother, or father who discovered the woman's losses." Joy yanked off her gloves and twisted them along with the beaded strings of her reticule. "You don't think it could possibly be someone's personal maid, do you? One whose lady confided in her about her losses?"

"I still feel we must warn your brother, my angel. He should not be blindsided by this matter." Even if the duke didn't like him, Jansen would want to know it if Aurelia were in danger, and felt it was common courtesy to warn Broadmere. "And we may be forced to call in the Bow Street Runners, depending on what I'm able to discover once I return to the ball to speak to the footman who delivered the notes."

"I am well and truly ruined. I'll be lucky if Chance doesn't dump a bucket of eels in my bed."

"What?" Jansen eyed her, wondering if he'd heard that correctly. "Did you say *eels*?"

"Never mind." With a shudder, Joy closed her eyes and bowed her head. "How could I do this to my family? My reputation does not matter—but poor Felicity, Merry, and Seri. What have I done to them? What have I done to Aurelia and Freddie?"

He gathered her closer, ignoring Aurelia when she started clearing her throat in a most annoying, chaperone-like way. "I shall put you out on the side of this road if you continue that nonsense, Aurelia." He gave her a sharp glare to underscore the threat.

"Sorry." But she didn't sound it. With a heavy sigh, she propped her chin in her hand and stared out the window into the darkness.

Jansen turned back to his beloved, lifting her face to his. "Joy," he said softly.

She opened her eyes and gave him such a despondent look that he cradled her closer still. "What?"

"We will overcome this. I swear it."

Crestfallen, she reached up and hesitantly touched his cheek. "Can you swear no one will be ruined? Not my sisters? Not Aurelia? Not Freddie?"

"For now"—he paused and kissed her forehead, breathing in the delicate rose scent of her fragrance and reveling in her warm softness pressed against him—"all I can promise is that I will get to the bottom of this foulness and end it—and I will protect you."

"There goes Ambrose," Aurelia said as a carriage pulled alongside them. She winked and kicked Jansen in the shin. "Put me out here. I shall ride home with my *favorite* brother."

"Copper!" Jansen thumped the roof, not about to pass up a chance for some private time with his angel. "Transfer Miss Aurelia to Ambrose's carriage. I feel certain he needs assistance. Once again, my brother has overindulged."

"Right away, sir." Both carriages halted in tandem as if driven by the same man.

"Behave yourself, brother," Aurelia told him before patting Joy's hand. "All will be well, my future sister. Jansen won't allow any harm to come to you."

"I know," Joy said with a sigh. "I just wish he didn't have to. I am more worried about my family and Freddie."

"Take the long way to Broadmere House, Copper," Jansen called out to his driver once he'd seen Aurelia safely ensconced in his brother's carriage.

"The long way?" Joy eyed him as if she were about to refuse.

"I thought a longer ride might give us time to think of a plan. I swear my intentions are not nefarious."

"Well, drat you, then."

He laughed and pulled her back into his arms, unable to resist her wit or her enticing softness. Closing his mouth over hers, he reveled in her taste as she opened her sumptuous lips to his and pressed even closer. She hungered for him as much as he hungered for her.

"My darling," he whispered against her mouth. "Would that we were already married."

She pushed out of his arms with a heavy sigh, making him regret saying something so stupid. "If we were already married, then I would also be the ruin of you. At least this way, with us merely engaged, I have only succeeded in somewhat tarnishing your reputation. Do you wish to break it off?"

"Heavens no, and don't ever ask that again! My reputation can go to the devil. All I need is you as my wife."

She eyed him as if she felt sorry for him. "What makes two people fall in love? What makes them click like pieces of a puzzle snapping together?" She slowly shook her head. "I am so thankful you came into my life, but I regret this mess I have unceremoniously dumped into your lap."

He eased her close once more and stroked her cheek with the back of his finger. "Perhaps our love is fated? Destiny, even? Who knows? All I know for certain is that after that first moment I saw you, I couldn't get you out of my mind."

"Did you try?" She sounded somewhat insulted.

"What would you say if I said I did?"

"That you are a poor judge of the tenacity of the Abarough sisters."

"Ahh…but you were not as entranced with me as I am with you." He kissed her again, nibbling his way across the seam of her mouth and groaning as she slid her hand up his chest.

"Perhaps I hid my entrancement better than you hid yours—and perhaps now, I feel sorry for this mess I've given you."

He kissed her soundly once again, then forced himself to pull away and thumped the ceiling of the carriage. "Broadmere House, Copper."

"Yessir."

She stared at him as if he had just struck her. "Did I do something wrong?"

"No, my love, but if we are confined to this carriage for much longer, I will do something—and I am not referring to discovering the identity of the blackmailer."

"What do you mean?"

"I do not wish our first time together—in the biblical sense—to be on a carriage seat while rolling down the road. Our first time should be, will be, special."

While wetting her lips, she shifted with a deep breath, all the while keeping her gaze locked with his. "My sisters, the married ones, have…*advised* me on what to expect."

He pondered that revelation, unsure if it was good or bad. "Indeed."

She offered him a wicked grin. "Do not worry. Blessing, Fortuity, and Grace are all three madly in love with their husbands and described their marriage beds in glowing terms."

"So might I take that to mean you look forward to *our* marriage bed?"

"I didn't look forward to any marriage bed—until you kissed me. Once you showed me how lovely that could be…" She paused and pulled in another deep breath while fanning herself. "I am very much looking forward to it now."

He groaned and shifted in the seat. This conversation was causing him extraordinary discomfort. "We really should get you home." He craned his neck out the window, relieved to see the lights of Broadmere House not too far in the distance. "Ah…almost there."

She laughed and gave him a coy toss of her head. "Are you in such a hurry to be relieved of my presence?"

"I am in a hurry for relief, my lady, but it would not do for me to describe that relief any further."

"With another woman?" Her tone took on a murderous pitch. "If you ever bed—"

"I would never and will never, my lady. You are the only woman I will ever bed. I swear it now and will swear it again when we repeat our wedding vows." Her jealousy inflamed him even further, a most dangerous development indeed. "I love you, my angel, with a passion and a fury I have never felt before. Trust me, my love. I would never be unfaithful to you. No woman exists who could ever hope to lead me astray. You own me, body and soul, through eternity and beyond."

"You are going to make me cry."

"Happy tears, I hope."

"Ecstatic tears, my future husband. Ecstatic because I never thought I would ever find a man like you."

The carriage rolled to a stop before he could reply, and Copper opened the door and set the steps so Joy might disembark with ease. Jansen walked her to the door but was loath to let her go once they reached it.

"I do not wish to say good evening, my lady." He cupped her cheek in his hand, losing himself in the deep blue of her eyes, made even darker with the emotions and shadows of the night. "But I must return to the ball and discover what I can."

"Then I will see you tomorrow? To hear what you find out?"

"I swear it."

She stood on tiptoe, gave him a quick kiss, then dashed inside before he could pull her into his arms for more.

"Ah, well, probably for the best." He loped back to the carriage. "Back to the Burrastones', Copper."

"Yessir."

Changing his mind, Jansen thumped the ceiling before the carriage took off, then hopped back out and climbed up onto the driver's seat with the man. "Sorry, old fellow. I've a few questions that you might be able to help with." He motioned at the road. "Continue to the Burrastones'. We can chat while you drive."

"As you wish, sir." Old Copper, loyal to the bone and a man of few words, barely flicked the reins, and the horses set off at a respectable trot. "How can I be helping you, then?"

"Someone chose to deliver some rather upsetting notes at the ball this evening. These notes were delivered to the addressees by a Burrastone footman. Did you happen to notice anything unusual outside the residence?"

Copper scrubbed a gnarled hand across his mouth. "Can't say that I did, sir. All seemed quiet and normal enough. Didn't notice no one behaving in any way out of the regular."

That wasn't what Jansen had hoped to hear, but granted, someone carrying notes in their pocket or reticule would not easily be spotted. "Well, with any luck, the footman can give me something more to go on."

"Is our Miss Aurelia in danger?" Copper cleared his throat and rolled his shoulders. "I'll be thrashing somebody's arse for them if they've bothered our Miss Aurelia."

Copper and his wife had always doted on Aurelia, treating her as if she were their own child rather than the daughter of their employer, while Jansen's father still lived. When Jansen's father, the senior Mr. Winterstone, passed, Jansen kept them on because he knew he could trust them.

"That miscreant with the notes upset our Aurelia," Jansen said. "But fret not—I intend to make whomever it is pay."

"I'll be helping you with that, sir. Just give the word."

"Thank you, Copper. I shall bear that in mind."

They rolled up to the Burrastones', and Jansen noted the festivities appeared to be winding down. He'd best get a move on. Hopefully, the sender of the notes was still there—or at least the footman who had delivered the missives. Since this was Lady Constance's home, she would be the likeliest to point him in the direction of the servant who had handed out the letters. He searched through the dwindling crowd, hoping she had not already retired to her private chambers.

Just as he was about to give up hope, he spotted her. "Lady Constance! Might I have a word?"

The look she gave him reminded him of a terrified animal trapped in a snare. Could she possibly be the blackmailer and had only sent herself a threatening note to conceal her part in this terrible plot?

"I would like to speak to your footman. The one who delivered the unusual post this evening." He watched her closely, reading her as if they were caught up in a game of cards.

"That's just it, Sir Jansen," she whispered. "I cannot find him, nor do I know him. Mama said she had brought on extra servants for the evening, which is nothing out of the ordinary. He must have been one she hired for tonight only, and if so, who knows if we can ever find him, because she brought on at least a dozen or so from several agencies across London. According to our permanent staff, the temporary hires have already left for the evening."

"Well, isn't that convenient?" *Damn and blast.* He should've chased the man down and questioned him before seeing Joy safely home, but he'd been so concerned for her safety and well-being that he'd not wished to leave her side. Circling Lady Constance as if she were prey, he remained silent. Sometimes, the weight of silence convinced even the worst of the worst to confess.

Tears streamed down her face. "I swear to you, Sir Jansen, I had nothing to do with this. Lady Joy and I might fuss and fight at times, but I would never attempt to ruin the Broadmere name—or hers. I spread the word about your engagement because I noticed her attraction to you. Never has she ever been that attracted to any man before, and I have known her for years and years. But I swear—I would never do something as horrid as blackmail and threaten to ruin the Duke of Broadmere's sterling reputation."

Much to his dismay, he decided she was telling the truth. Any lady of Polite Society who would stand there and sob, giving no care about tears dribbling down her cheeks and staining the silk of her yellow gown, was more than likely telling the truth. "There, there, Lady Constance," he said, in a half-hearted attempt at easing her distress. "I shall ensure Lady Joy hears of your loyalty when next I speak with her." He backed up a step, putting more distance between the two of them. "I will catch this blackguard. Have no fear."

"I do hope so." She sniffed, swiping at her cheeks with her gloved hands. "Do excuse me. I am such a mess that I must retire."

He bowed. "Good evening, my lady."

"Good evening, Sir Jansen."

No matter how many tears she shed, he still didn't fully trust her, even though he had her to thank for his engagement to his angel. She bore watching, and watch her he would.

Chapter Seven

JOY PACED BACK and forth across the parlor, occasionally pausing to part the curtains and glance out the window, up and down St. James's Street. Where on earth was Jansen? He needed to arrive while Chance and Serendipity were out.

Merry and Felicity sat together on the settee, offering her no comfort whatsoever.

"Pacing will not make him arrive any quicker." Felicity rose and headed for the bellpull. "Shall I ring for tea and biscuits? My newest recipe is quite tasty, if I do say so myself."

Joy remembered the last new recipe Felicity had tricked her into trying and shook her head. "No, thank you. As soon as Jansen arrives, he and I will proceed to the hollow tree in the mews. The payment has to be in place by teatime, remember?"

Felicity yanked on the pull. "Well, it won't hurt for you to have a little something to nibble on until he gets here. It might settle you." Remorse crept into her tone. "And I promise this recipe won't make you spit the biscuit into your teacup like last time."

"Which of us is going with you?" Merry asked.

"Going with me? Why?" Momentary panic fed the frustration already churning Joy into a knot of misery. Why would either of them wish to come with her?

Merry laughed. "To keep Serendipity from having nine kinds of fits, for one thing, when she returns and discovers you gone with your intended…" She pointed at herself and Felicity. "One of us had better be gone with you. Even though you are engaged, you're still expected to have a proper chaperone. You know that. What happened at the ball last night—and I am referring to your going out into the garden *without* a chaperone—was not wise. Especially with you worried about the release of rumors so vicious they could ruin us all."

Joy glared at her usually fun-loving and adventurous sister. "You sound just like Seri."

Merry jumped to her feet. "You take that back, or I am off to find crickets for your stocking drawer."

"Well, at least that would keep one of you busy while I attempt to snare a blackmailer this afternoon."

"One of us must come with you," Felicity said. "What would Mama say?"

Joy halted halfway across the room, ending her fourth or fifth circuit. She had walked back and forth so many times, she'd lost count. "Do not bring Mama into this. You know as well as I that she would be thrilled with Jansen. A lot more thrilled than our bacon-brained brother seems to be."

"She would still insist upon a chaperone," Merry said. "Look at it this way, at least it's one of us and not Seri."

"Seri and Chance won't be back until well after teatime, and it's my turn to plan next week's meals with Cook and Mrs. Flackney. So…" Felicity nodded at Merry. "Merry wins the title of chaperone for today."

"Fine. Do what you must, since you are too cowardly to cross Seri." Joy threw up her hands. "I won't need a chaperone if he never arrives!"

Walters appeared at the door and cleared his throat. "Sir…" He paused and frowned before turning to whoever stood behind him in the hallway. "Your name again, sir?"

"Sir Jansen."

"Let him in, Walters. Thank you ever so much for announcing him." Joy rushed to the door and smiled at the elderly butler, who frequently forgot what he was attempting to do mid-task of late. "That will be all, Walters. Thank you again."

He gave her a solemn bow and shuffled off.

Even though she wanted to rush into Jansen's arms, she restrained herself because of her loose-tongued sisters. Felicity and Merry were the worst of the bunch when it came to tattling. Probably because they were the youngest and had always been coddled and indulged. "Do come in, Sir Jansen. I realize we don't have much time. I have the money ready. We can leave right away."

"*We?*"

He gave her a look she didn't like one bit. A look that said he intended to see to this task alone. To the devil with that. She jutted her chin higher. "Yes. *We*, as in I intend to accompany you."

"No, you will not."

She let her jaw drop, shocked that he would even suggest she should remain at home, while he planted the payment the blackmailer had demanded and then lay in wait to snare them. "I most certainly will go if I wish to, and I do wish to. The money came out of my personal account."

"She means her personal stocking drawer," Merry said. "And I agree. She needs to stay here. This is not a task for a woman."

"I also agree." Felicity linked arms with Merry. The two always banded together.

"Shut your gobs," Joy told her sisters, then whirled about as Jansen snorted with laughter.

He threw up his hands as if to fend her off. "Forgive me, my angel. I should not have laughed." He cleared his throat. "But you are still not coming with me. I will not have it."

"You have no right to refuse me."

"I have every right. You are my intended. My future wife. You know as well as I that my decisions carry the final word in my household."

"As I said, I am going. This is not your household, and I am not your wife."

"Joy—"

"Do not utter my name in that tone. I am neither a child nor a dog."

"You are not going. I forbid it."

"*You forbid it?*" Enraged amazement swept across her. He dared to *forbid* her? Was this what it would be like if she became his wife? She pointed at the door. "Get out."

"What?"

"I said, *get out.* Go home. I will handle this myself."

"The devil you will." He charged toward her, thrilling her immensely, much to her dismay. When he caught hold of her by the shoulders, she readied herself for the opportune moment to surprise him with a punch in the nose. But it didn't come. He somehow mesmerized her, glaring at her as if trying to make her burst into flames. "You will remain here, where it is safe. End of discussion."

"I will go or we will not marry." She glared back at him, daring him to refuse her further.

"What?"

"You heard me." She fisted her hands so tightly that her knuckles popped. "I am going. You may come along and protect me, but I am going, or we will not marry. This is my *situation* to handle, and I will not be treated like a child sent to the nursery with Nanny while the adults go off and do exciting adult things."

"Exciting adult things?"

"Stop repeating my words. It is most irritating." She would not have the sort of marriage where her husband was a gamekeeper, and she was the contented little guinea fowl who always obeyed. "I am of age, and I like to think I am an intelligent individual capable of tending to myself and making my own decisions. I realize *usual* husbands treat their wives little better than their horses or hounds, but I will not be married to a *usual* man. I am an equal and intend to remain that way. Exactly as my mama was with my papa."

Unsmiling, Jansen widened his stance and folded his arms across his broad chest. "You will not leave here to deliver that money. Either I take it there and wait to capture the devil, or you miss the deadline and deal with the repercussions."

It was then that she realized he was between her and the only door. *Drat it all.* She had not planned this battle well, and that was quite unusual for her. But she could still call his bluff. "Fine. Our engagement has ended, then. I release you. Get out."

"I do not release *you*, my lady." He eased back and placed himself directly in the doorway. There was absolutely no way she could skitter around him now. "And since everyone saw you accept my proposal at the ball last night, I am certain the *ton* would be most interested to discover why you broke our engagement when we appeared to be so smitten with one another." And then he smiled. A smug, victorious smirk that made her itch to throw something at his head.

So angry she was about to cry—and that made her even angrier—she stamped her foot. "I am going!"

"You are not going."

She shrieked and shook her fists. "Then I will never marry you, and if you refuse to release me from our engagement, then we will be engaged *forever*, and neither of us will *ever* marry. I will never choose a date." She stamped her foot again. "There. What say you to that?"

He shrugged. "Fine. At least you will be safe." He held out his hand. "Give me the money so I may place the bait in the tree. The hour grows late, and I need time to hide myself and lie in wait for our scoundrel."

"I will not give you the money."

"Fine. I will use my own money." He turned to go.

"Stop!" How could one person be so bloody infuriating? She charged toward him, shaking a finger. "You will stop this very minute!" She had used her last bargaining chip by refusing to marry him, and yet the fool persisted. Did his stubbornness know no boundaries? "I want to go."

"I realize that." His calm tone made her ready to scream. "But you are not going because it is not safe. I love you, Joy, and will not allow you to put yourself in danger just because you're too hardheaded to know I am doing this for your own good."

"I am not a child!"

"Then stop behaving like one and see sense for both our sakes."

He had the way blocked, and there was nothing she could do. It also didn't help that her two infernal sisters weren't siding with her. Whatever happened to family loyalty?

She marched over to the desk, yanked open the center drawer, retrieved the velvet pouch containing one hundred pounds sterling, and threw it at him. "Take it straight to the devil for all I care!"

"Thank you." He caught it and tucked it into his coat pocket, then nodded at Merry and Felicity. "I trust you two can keep her here, or must we tie her to a chair?"

"You wouldn't dare," Joy said, ready to scream.

He grinned. "I *would* dare, my lady. I would dare anything to keep you safe." He returned his attention to her sisters. "Well?"

"We will keep her here," Merry said.

"Definitely," Felicity agreed. "Even if we have to recruit helpers to come sit on her until you return."

"Do not bother returning," Joy snapped. "Even if you have the culprit in hand. I do not want to see you ever again!" She didn't mean that. Even she knew she didn't mean that before she said it. But by heavens, *he* didn't have to know that. "We will never marry! Not ever!"

The clock on the mantel chimed, drawing everyone's eyes to the time.

"The hour grows late," Jansen said, then fixed her with a look that both thrilled and frightened her. "We will discuss this further upon my return, because return I shall, my lady, and you will see me."

"I will not," she lied. "I will never receive you again. Even if I have to live in my bedchamber." That sounded childish and petulant even to her, but there was no helping it now. After all, one could not exactly un-ring a bell. "Get out!"

With a nod and a touch of his forehead, he headed out the door, then paused in the hallway. "Keep her here, Lady Merry, Lady Felicity. You know how stubborn she is." Then he charged away.

Joy shook a fist at her sisters. "If you try to stop me—"

"If you leave, we'll send a runner to fetch Chance and Seri, and tell them where you've gone," Felicity said with a sternness that reminded Joy of their mother. "Then Chance will learn about your club and everything else. How do you think that will go over? Much less your running after a man without a chaperone?"

"I hate you, Felicity."

"Then you might as well hate me, too, because I intend to help her," Merry said, but her tone was sympathetic. "We do this because we love you, Joy. And you know it."

Joy threw herself into the chair behind the desk. She was well and truly beaten. What in the devil had the world come to?

❧

JANSEN CHARGED INTO the mews, almost running to get to the hollow tree in plenty of time to stow the money inside it and hide. Gads alive, he prayed he hadn't overplayed his hand with his precious angel. Surely she hadn't meant what she'd said about breaking the engagement or never setting a date. She had told him she loved him—more than once. He'd tasted the passion and yearning in her kisses. Most of all, he had tasted her acceptance and their ever-strengthening connection. Surely, once he presented her with her blackmailer, and her anger cooled…surely then she would toss aside the silliness of the words she had shouted in anger. They *would* marry. She would set a date, and they would marry.

Spotting the old hollow tree, he dashed to reach it and deposited the velvet bag inside the hole that was at about the height of his waist. As he did so, he noted four other bundles already inside the small well of the trunk. So, Lady Frederica *had* received a note as well. Apparently, their blackmailer was thorough.

He quickly scanned the area, searching for a place to lie in wait until the scoundrel showed to gather his or her ill-gotten gains. The cobblestone mews was lined with stables and lodging for the elites' coachmen and servants, who not only took care of the horses but also maintained the carriages and tack. Thankfully, the stable closest to the blackmailer's tree belonged to an old wartime friend, the Earl of Denby. Jansen slipped inside and took his post behind a narrow door where he could see the tree through a missing knothole in the wooden planks.

"Come along, you greedy bastard. My future wife wants to meet you," he said under his breath as he peered through the knothole.

"Can I be helping you, sir?" asked a young man from behind him.

"I am a friend of Denby's," he said without taking his gaze off the tree. "The earl knows I am here, and as soon as my business is finished, I assure you I shall be on my way."

"And what business might that be?" asked a deeper voice, obviously an older man.

Jansen risked turning around, determined to keep matters brief. "I am in the process of snaring a blackmailer. Once I finish, you shall see."

"Oy, a blackmailer? Cowardly lot, that is." The older man, round as a barrel and clad in a stained leather apron, resettled his iron hoof nippers and farrier's hammer in his meaty fists. "We can be helping you, then, sir. Crowdy and Pip, at your service."

"Thank you, gentlemen." Jansen pressed his eye back to the hole, praying the blackmailer hadn't come and made off with the payment while he explained his presence on someone else's property. "The scoundrel's parcels are in that tree. He—or she—should be along any time now."

"Well...we was headed outside to do a bit of work." Crowdy waved the hoof nippers in the air with every word, as if conducting an orchestra. "But we can wait a bit. Don't want to be scaring your scabby cove away."

"Thank you, gentlemen. I appreciate that." Jansen stared at the tree through the hole in the plank, willing the miscreant to show up and trip the snare. But the *scabby cove*, as Crowdy had named them, took their sweet time, making him wait. And wait. And wait some more.

A stray dog meandered past, sniffed the tree, then hiked its leg and relieved itself, making Jansen wish he could do the same.

"Anything yet, sir?" Pip whispered.

"No. Nothing." Jansen straightened, rubbing his lower back, which had started to ache from his stooping to peer through the hole. "I would have thought they'd have been along by now."

"Want me to stroll by and peep in there to make sure they didn't come whilst we was talking to you early on?"

"Hold fast. Let me check the time." Jansen popped open his pocket watch and huffed. It was well past teatime. In fact, it was nearly six o'clock. "Check the tree, Pip. But don't look as if you're looking into it. Understand?"

The boy nodded. "I can be right sneaky when I need to be, sir."

"He can at that," Crowdy said, "'specially when he's trying to get out of his duties."

Pip had the presence of mind to hang his head and assume an abashed look. "You said I been better here of late."

"You have at that." Crowdy nudged him. "On wi' you, now. See what you can see."

Jansen took one last look through the peephole and nodded. "Remember to meander along."

"To what?" Pip stared at him as if he had spoken in a foreign tongue.

"Walk along and don't look like you're looking into the tree," Jansen explained.

Pip brightened, then gave a jaunty salute and headed out onto the cobblestone road. He sauntered along, lifting his face to the sun as if prouder than proud that he had gained a brief reprieve from his duties. Jansen had to admit, the lad *wandered* in a most convincing manner. As Pip passed the old tree, he casually glanced over, then halted, went to the tree, and looked into it closely. With a grimace that made Jansen's heart fall, the lad looked back at him and shook his head. "'Tis gone, sir. Nothing in there at all."

"Damn and blast it all!" Jansen rushed to the tree and looked for himself. Pip was right. Nothing in the hole but filth. All five bundles were gone. "Damn, damn, damn!" he muttered. The thief had come and made off with the money whilst he was explaining himself to Crowdy and Pip. Deep in his heart, he knew Joy would crow like the proudest rooster and tell him that if he had allowed her to come along, they wouldn't have failed to catch the blackmailer. And maybe she was right. He hated that. It was a dangerous precedent to set.

"Did either of you notice anyone walking past?" he asked Crowdy and Pip, praying they saw someone or something.

Both shook their heads.

"Damn and blast!"

CHIVALRY DEMANDED HE immediately confess to the failure. To wait until tomorrow would not only be cowardly but also look as if he had delayed sharing his news until he came up with a *believable* story. His angel was no fool, and with her, honesty was imperative—especially since he was currently on her wrong side and about to sink himself even deeper.

He sat in the parlor, nursing a cup of tea that Lady Felicity had insisted upon placing in his hands. Port, whisky, or brandy would have been so much better, but the young lady hadn't offered him anything other than tea.

Now she and Merry sat there staring at him as if he were about to march to the gallows—and he was, in a manner of speaking.

"A biscuit?" Felicity held out a plate of pale, crumbly-edged disks speckled with dark dots of who-knew-what throughout the baked dough.

"No, thank you, my lady." He was not hungry and wouldn't be until he had cleared the air between himself and Joy.

"Explain how you managed to fail," Joy said from the doorway.

"You come right out with it, do you not?"

She sashayed into the room, her muslin skirts of pale pink swirling around her tempting curves. "I see no reason to tiptoe around the facts. Again, how did you fail? We must know so we don't do the same thing next time."

"Next time? How do you know there will be a next time?"

"If you had the opportunity to earn five hundred pounds in the blink of an eye, with little to no effort, would you not do it again?" She took his teacup away and placed it on the cart. Turning to her sisters, she gave them a curt nod. "I am quite certain Sir Jansen prefers brandy to tea right about now. Maybe even whisky." She narrowed her eyes at him. "Am I correct, Sir Jansen?"

"Quite correct, my lady, and a whisky would be delightful." At least if he had to sit here with his neck in the noose, he would have a proper drink to go along with it. He risked a smile. "Thank you."

His lady love did not return his smile. Instead, she fetched him the drink, then perched on the edge of her seat, eyeing him with the stern ferocity of an archangel about to take her mighty sword and cleave his body from his soul.

After a deep draft of his whisky, he squared his shoulders and sat taller, ready to confess. "I believe our blackmailer slipped in and took the money whilst I was explaining my presence to the Earl of Denby's servants. It was his property upon which I hid."

"You do realize that had I gone with you, one of us could have explained our presence while the other kept an eye on the tree?"

"Yes, my lady. Of that, I am painfully aware, I assure you."

"*Painfully* aware. Good." She idly chewed on her bottom lip while studying him. For the first time since they'd met, he had no earthly idea as to what she might be thinking. "I suppose now we wait to be contacted again."

"Five hundred pounds is a great deal of money," Merry said. "Would it not take them a while to go through it?"

"It depends." Felicity rose and fluttered about the tea cart like a nervous butterfly unsure as to where to alight. "Five hundred pounds can be a great deal of money for some and a mere pittance for others. It depends on their habits."

"And their luck and propensity to gamble," Jansen said. "They will be sorely tempted after winning this particular hand."

"Indeed." Joy rose and went to the window. "Next time I go along. Agreed?"

"It depends on their demands and where they wish the money dropped."

She turned and glared at him. "You persist in this stubbornness? Even after today's failure?"

He slowly shook his head. "I will not have you endangered, my lady. Even if it makes you hate me, I will see you safe before all else."

She snorted in a very unladylike manner and returned to staring out the window. "You may go now, Sir Jansen. That will be all."

"You will not dismiss me like a servant. We have much to discuss."

"We do not, and you will not tell me what to do," she said, obviously struggling to keep her tone even. "This day has wearied me beyond compare, and I intend to retire early, whether you leave or not." She flicked a hand at him. "Sit there till the very hot place that spewed you forth freezes over. I no longer care."

"Joy!" Mercy and Felicity said in shocked unison.

"And you may sit with him," she told her sisters before marching out of the room.

Jansen watched her go, his heart plummeting lower than he ever thought possible. She no longer cared. Perhaps the worst emotion, or lack thereof, that ever existed. At least if she hated him, that passion might eventually revert to love. But to no longer care...

He pushed himself up out of the chair, bowed to the Abarough sisters, and left Broadmere House, uncertain if he would ever be allowed to return.

Chapter Eight

JANSEN STOOD WITH his back against the wall, staring at the arched entrance to his main parlor. They had expanded the area by removing the temporary walls between it and the formal dining room that joined the garden at the back of their townhouse. This gave their guests plenty of space to mill about and enjoy the evening. From his vantage point, there was but one guest who interested him. Joy had yet to arrive, even though Aurelia had sworn to him she would come.

He rarely entertained, but Aurelia had said this would be the perfect way to coax Joy out of her self-imposed exile to her bedchamber. She said it would be his best chance of talking to her. Jansen wasn't so sure about that but was willing to try anything. He had to win back his angel. Had to make her understand that he wasn't trying to clip her wings, merely protect her.

Nimbus perched on the ledge behind him, taking in everything with avid interest.

"No stealing tonight, old man," Jansen said to the cat. "Understood?"

The feline flicked an ear, obviously shrugging off the order.

A tap on Jansen's shoulder made him instinctively go for his sword. Luckily, it was locked away in the cabinet in his dressing room. He turned and faced Aurelia. "You know better than to startle me."

"Sorry." With a motherly scowl, she tipped her head toward the guests milling about the room and settling down at tables to play whatever games the particular spot offered. "As the host, you are supposed to mingle. We talked about this. Remember?"

"I remember I told you that there was only one guest with whom I wished to *mingle*." For the umpteenth time, he scanned the room. His heart sank even lower. His angel had not yet arrived, and he very much doubted that she would. "She is not coming."

"It is early yet. I promise—she is coming. She wouldn't disappoint me by staying at home unless something dire had happened."

He jerked to stare at his sister. "What happened? Has another threat surfaced? Is she in danger?"

"Calm down," Aurelia said in a low voice. "To the best of my knowledge, nothing dire has happened. I just used that as an example. Pull yourself together. You are behaving worse than Ambrose."

"Where is Ambrose, by the way?"

"With Lady Serafina again. It does not look good." She wrinkled her nose, making a sour face. "I fear he is quite smitten with her."

"Heaven help us all if he marries that woman."

"Look!" Aurelia whispered excitedly. "Your angel is here. I told you she would come." She rushed across the room, gracefully weaving around the tables to greet Joy.

Jansen remained rooted to the spot. For the first time in his life, he wasn't sure what to do. Broadmere and his sisters—Serendipity, Felicity, Merry, and his precious angel—eased into the room, taking in the party's offerings with interest, or something akin to interest. Joy didn't look at all pleased to be present. Jansen willed her to look his way, but she didn't. Unsmiling and aloof, she ambled along with a glass of lemonade a servant had pressed upon her.

Gads alive. She was loveliness itself in a sapphire-blue silk that reminded him of the gown she had worn the very first time he ever saw her. But this one was enhanced with a gossamer layer of sparkling silver lace, making her even more ethereal. She looked up and met his gaze. Thankfully, she didn't look away when their eyes met. Instead, she held him prisoner, pulling him in and daring him to challenge her.

And challenge her he would. He needed his angel. Couldn't live without her, in fact. Plowing through everyone in his path, he went to her and offered a formal bow. "My lady. Thank you for coming this evening. I appreciate it more than you will ever know."

She returned a curtsy so slight it was barely noticeable. "I didn't wish to disappoint Aurelia. She is a dear friend."

"We left much unfinished between us. I beg you hear me out."

She shifted with a deep breath, her delicate nostrils flaring, but didn't release it with a sigh as he expected. Instead, she held it for a long moment, then allowed it to ease out. "Not here. Not yet. All right?"

"What must I do to win your forgiveness?"

"You can start by listening to me when I speak. Did I not just say, not here? Not yet?" She fiddled with her silver reticule that matched her gown, looking ready to swat him with it.

"Might I interest you in a game of whist, then? German whist. Just the two of us rather than four?"

She stared at him as if judging the purity of his heart and soul and finding both lacking. "There will simply be either winning or losing, understand? If anything is wagered, it will be coin only." She narrowed her eyes. "Are the stakes understood as I explained them?"

He bowed again. "You have made yourself quite clear, my lady."

He offered his arm and held his breath, praying she would take it. Take it she did, and allowed him to lead her to a table. With any luck, he could coerce her into forgiving him and erase the dark cloud of unhappiness that floated between them. He helped her into her chair, then seated himself opposite her.

"Do you wish to deal or shall I?" he asked.

"This is your house. You deal." She looked around as if uninterested in the entire affair, but then she somehow softened. "Is that your Nimbus? What a sleek fellow he is."

"Yes." Jansen shuffled the cards and started dealing. "I have always gotten the impression that he believes this to be his home, and he simply allows me to live here with him."

She almost smiled but stopped herself, making his heart ache to erase the misery between them. "Blessing's cats are much the same. As are Fortuity's, but hers seem to get more pleasure out of tormenting Ignatius than Fortuity or Matthew."

"Ignatius?"

"The lone dog of the household. A rambunctious little pug who considers himself one of the cats."

He studied his hand and sadly realized he had dealt himself a fortuitous start to the game. If anything, he wished to lose to her. Not win. Yet if he purposely threw the wrong cards, Joy would know. She understood the game too well for any sneakiness to slip past her. He threw the appropriate card and braced himself, hoping she had an even better hand than his. "You love animals?"

She narrowed her eyes, staring down at the card he'd discarded and comparing it to her hand. "Yes. I love animals," she said slowly. She tossed a card, then lifted her gaze to his. "Not as much as my sister Grace, though. She is a bit of a fanatic about her animals. Never expect to be served meat at her table unless Wolfe decides to share his platter with you."

"I look forward to meeting them."

Joy frowned, but it was more than a simple frown. Her expression was one of dismay and disappointment. "Yes. I am sure you do," she said, her voice cold and detached.

"Joy, my angel—"

"Stop. Right now. Just stop it." She glared at him. "We are in the middle of a room full of people. Now is not the time."

"I assure you they cannot hear us over Aurelia's pianoforte."

"Are you insinuating that your sister bangs on the keys?"

"I am not insinuating anything. Listen to her." Jansen flinched as

Aurelia found the wrong note yet again, then he played his next card. "That is the thirteenth trick, my lady. I win the first stage. We are now starting the second."

Visibly perturbed, Joy scowled at her cards. "So we are."

They played on in silence, discarding and picking up cards faster and faster.

"And that is the end of the hand, my lady. It appears I have won."

"Drat," she said under her breath. "So you did."

"As for the stakes, I ask nothing more than your forgiveness for behaving like a hulver-headed fool." He set the cards aside and folded his hands on the table. "But in my defense, I need you to understand it was only because I needed you safe. Always, your safety is my greatest concern."

She didn't speak, simply glared at him until he wanted to squirm like an errant schoolboy. "I would rather pay you in coin, for once I am angry with someone, I tend to hold tightly to that anger—and coin is the stakes we agreed upon."

He ignored the part about the stakes. "Grudges are beneath you, my lady. Remember Alexander Pope's *An Essay on Criticism?* 'To err is human. To forgive, divine.' You, my angel, are divinity incarnate."

"You border on blasphemy, sir."

"Jansen—or your *horse's arse of a husband.* Remember?" He risked a smile, then wished he hadn't because her glare hardened.

"You, dear sir, are not my husband."

"Yet." In for a penny, in for a pound. "I would also like a wedding date along with the forgiveness I won, my lady."

"We agreed upon coin only for the stakes. Or have you forgotten?"

"When you spoke about the wager, I said you had made yourself quite clear. I did not say I agreed to the stakes as you stated them."

"I will pay you your coin, sir," she said loudly enough to make heads turn, since Aurelia's pianoforte recital had ended. Silence fell across the room, and everyone stared at them. "This is ridiculous. As soon as I pay you, I am leaving." She reached down beside herself in her chair, then scooted back and looked under the table. "It is gone. My reticule has gone missing."

"How can that be, my lady?" Jansen matched the loudness of his voice to hers. He knew exactly how that could be, but wasn't about to pass up this opportunity that his old friend Nimbus had provided him. He joined her in searching the floor all around and under the table. "I see nothing, my lady. Did you perhaps leave it in your carriage or the cloakroom?"

"Neither, and you very well know it. I had it with me. It has to be here."

"As I said earlier, my dear lady, I do not desire your coin. Your forgiveness and a wedding date are ample payment for me."

A low murmur rippled through the crowded room. Snippets of *all she has to do is forgive him* and *a June wedding would be lovely* danced through the air.

Joy jumped up from her chair and shook a finger at him. "I had my reticule. Give it over to me. Now."

Jansen stepped back from the table and lifted both hands. "My dearest, I do not have it."

Serendipity appeared at Joy's side and hugged her as if trying to keep her from fainting dead away. "You are causing a scene," she whispered without moving her lips.

Jansen was thankful his hearing was impeccable, as he was able to listen in on the sisters' conversation.

"Forgive him and promise him a date, for heaven's sake," Serendipity said.

"Are you in collusion with him?" Joy fixed her sister with a murderous glare. "My reticule was obviously stolen."

"Who came close enough to steal it?" Merry asked as she and Felicity attempted to encircle Joy and block her from everyone's stares.

"I don't know." Joy was close to tears. Jansen could hear it in her voice. Just as he opened his mouth to tell her about his resident feline thief, she marched over and thumped his chest with her fist. "Fine. I forgive you." She thumped him again. "And we will marry once you meet Blessing, Fortuity, and Grace. If you successfully survive all the Abarough sisters, then I am yours."

Applause filled the room.

Jansen offered his arm. "Come. Let us go to the library, where we may talk in private."

"With us," Serendipity said, searing him with a narrow-eyed glare.

"I would consider nothing less." Jansen caught Aurelia's eye and jerked his head for her to follow, then escorted Joy and her sisters to the library. Deeply engrossed in a hand of cards, Broadmere didn't seem to notice as they left the room. Just as well—when Jansen confessed about Nimbus's rather embarrassing habit, he would rather deal with the Abarough females than their haughty brother, whom he still itched to punch in the nose. Something told him that the fifth Duke of Broadmere probably did not like cats.

"Would anyone like a brandy?" Jansen asked as the ladies filed into the room.

"Definitely," Joy said as she seated herself in the chair closest to the fireless hearth.

"That would be lovely," Serendipity said. Merry and Felicity each agreed with a nod.

As he was pouring, Aurelia slipped into the room.

"Ah, Aurie. It appears that Joy's reticule has gone missing. Would you mind?" He set the six glasses of brandy on the tray and took them over to the table in front of the chair and settee where the ladies had seated themselves.

Aurelia rolled her eyes and shook her head. "I shall only be a moment."

Before she exited the room and closed the door behind her, Jansen added, "And bring him with you, if he will cooperate, so Joy might properly be introduced."

"What is that supposed to mean?" Joy asked as Aurelia departed.

"All will be made clear momentarily." Jansen seated himself, praying his forgiveness wouldn't go up in smoke along with the invitation to meet her sisters to secure a wedding date. A familiar, rapid pecking on the door made him frown. Had something else gone awry this evening? "Yes?"

Severns, his butler, entered bearing an eerily familiar pair of small white envelopes. "Do forgive the interruption, sir, but these just arrived for Lady Joy and Miss Aurelia. The veiled woman delivering them stressed that they were quite urgent."

"A veiled woman?" Joy asked.

Severns bowed as he handed over the note addressed to her. "Yes, my lady. Dressed all in black as if in full mourning, and her face hidden behind a black crepe veil."

Setting her drink aside, Joy tore into the note and read it aloud:

I am not greedy, but I need more. Fifty pounds this time or I'll do the same as I promised last time. Same place. Tomorrow by teatime. You know what I will do if you do not pay me.

She looked up, straight into Jansen's eyes. Her fear and sheer desolation made him go and kneel beside her.

"Another hundred pounds?" he asked, aching to pull her into his arms and console her.

She shook her head. "Only fifty this time," she said, her whisper weak. She caught hold of his hand and squeezed. "Why? Is it greed that drives this person?"

"Probably, my love. Either greed or envy. Both do terrible things to people. Once Aurelia returns, we shall see if hers says the same. We failed to invite Lady Frederica, Lady Constance, and Lady Prudence to tonight's gathering, but if Aurelia's note is the same, I see no reason why they didn't receive notes as well."

She held her head, rocking forward and back. "I cannot imagine who this might be."

The library door swung open. Aurelia stepped into the room, followed by a loudly meowing Nimbus, jumping and leaping to snatch hold of Joy's reticule. "He wants it back." She held it out of his reach. "You are not a crow, Nimbus! Just because it is shiny does not mean it is all right for you to steal it." When no one laughed or reacted, she frowned. "What has happened now? I thought to at least get a smile from Nimbus's antics."

Jansen rose and handed her the note. "Yours is on the table there. See if it is the same as Joy's."

Aurelia opened it, compared the two, then blew out a heavy sigh. "The same. Fifty pounds as well." She handed Joy her reticule. "Nimbus is your thief. I am sure the shiny beads caught his eye as soon as you arrived. Please find it in your heart to forgive him."

Joy turned and glared at Jansen. "Tell me you had no idea where my reticule might be."

"I never said that. I asked, *Whatever could have happened to it?*"

"I do not appreciate dishonesty," she said. "While I realize you didn't outright lie, nor did you volunteer the truth."

"Because I love you—and stand before you, a desperate man willing to do anything to get you back."

"I promise he loves you." Aurelia hugged Joy. "Please grant him some grace on this. Please?"

The look in Joy's eyes as she crossed her arms over her chest shot terror through his heart. She was plotting. He would bet his last coin on it.

"I will grant him grace if he agrees that I come with him tomorrow to drop off the money. Same place. Same time. No different dangers to worry about." She jutted her chin higher, glaring at him. "What say you to that offer, my horse's arse of a future husband?"

The somewhat dubious endearment thrilled him, and he bowed

low to her. "I cede to your wishes, my angel. Tomorrow. We go together."

⚬⚬⚬

FIFTY POUNDS STERLING knotted in an old rag sat on the table. Joy scooped it up and shoved it into her reticule then went to the window to watch for Jansen's arrival. She refused to put the money in another little velvet bag. The blackmailer could bloody well purchase their own fancy little purses to hold their stolen coins.

She swallowed hard, trying to slow her wildly thumping heart. A sense of calm was essential. After all, she couldn't very well allow Jansen to see her fraught with aggravation and anxiousness. Even if he did suspect her unease, she doubted he would go back on his word to allow her to accompany him. However, she had no doubts at all that he would scold her about her unease until they caught the annoying little miscreant. At least if she maintained a calm façade, he would be less likely to nettle her about joining him rather than staying safely at home.

"He is here," Merry shouted from the hallway just as Joy spotted his carriage turning down their street.

"Merry! Ladies do not shout about the arrival of visitors." Serendipity shook her head. "That girl."

"Leave her alone," Joy said. "Her childlike liveliness makes the house a brighter place." Not only that, but Merry's exuberance was somewhat magical. One found it most difficult to remain grumpy whenever around her.

"Are you certain you must go?" Serendipity handed Joy the parasol that matched her lavender spencer and the field of dainty purple flowers embroidered across the white muslin of her gown. "And where is your bonnet?"

"Calm down, Seri, it is right here, and yes, I must go." Joy donned the straw confection decorated with white lace and more purple silk flowers and tied the ribbon under her chin. "See? Properly tucked and tied."

"I do not like this," her sister said.

"Nor do I, but it must be done." Joy turned at the thump of boots in the hallway that came ever closer. "Good afternoon, Jansen."

Grim as death, Jansen nodded at Serendipity from the doorway, then shifted his full focus on Joy. "I assume there is no changing your mind."

"You assume correctly."

He offered his arm. "Then come along. We have a thief to catch."

"A thief," she said as she slipped her arm through his.

"Yes, because this blackguard has successfully stolen my peace of mind by endangering you and endangering *us*."

She allowed herself a heavy sigh as they descended the front steps, crossed the walkway, and climbed into the carriage. "They have taken my peace of mind as well. With any luck, today will change all that."

"I sincerely hope so."

Jansen sat opposite her in the closed carriage, not only surprising her, but also adding a layer of uncertainty she currently didn't need. Why hadn't he seated himself beside her? It bothered her. Was he that angry about her forcing his hand to allow her to come along?

"I am glad we were able to convince Seri that this venture did not require a chaperone," she said, fishing for a comment she could pick apart for the truth about his sitting across from her.

Jansen didn't respond, simply glared out the window as they headed toward the mews. She tried to read him but failed miserably. He was so morose. She had never seen him like this before. Surely he wasn't *that* sour because she had insisted on coming. "At least this time, we allowed ourselves more of a window of opportunity by leaving early."

"I suppose so." Eyes narrowing, he rubbed his chin slowly, then dropped his hand to his lap and fixed her with a look she didn't quite comprehend. "I need you to do as I ask while we are there. For your own safety. Do you understand, and will you please swear to do so?"

"I promise I am not going to do anything to endanger myself." And she meant it. She found her frustration with his protectiveness had somehow lessened. His worry for her safety, now that he'd allowed her to accompany him, was actually quite nice. It reminded her of how Papa had always protected Mama. "All I intend to do is help you watch for the fool so you can catch her."

"You are sure our enemy is a woman?"

"A woman delivered the last set of notes."

"That does not mean our blackguard is female. Delivery persons are easily hired and, for extra coin, convinced to wear any dress or persona one wishes."

She pondered that as the carriage rolled to a stop. If that were the case, and well it could be, their blackmailer might be anyone. "What if they hire someone to pick up the payments? Will we be able to make them tell us who hired them?"

Jansen gave her a look that chilled her to the bone. "Yes, my lady. I assure you, they will tell us who hired them—one way or another." He nodded at the hollow oak in the distance. "There is our tree."

Common sense bade her hand him the bundle of coins. She felt certain he would not approve if she darted forward and deposited them in the tree herself.

He rewarded her with a grateful smile as he accepted them. "Thank you, my angel. The fewer our battles with each other, the more I can focus on the real foe."

"I know…and I am sorry about that. It's just that I have an extreme aversion to being coddled. There is no need for it when I am a perfectly capable woman."

"There is a need for it because it enables me to concentrate on the battle rather than have my mind clouded with worries about you. I am now and will forever be your protector."

She understood that now—didn't particularly like it, but understood it, and in time, would surely be grateful for it. As long as he was willing to give her as much leeway as possible when it came to her independence. "Let us hope that today is the last of this particular battle."

"Indeed."

He deposited the money into the tree, then motioned for her to join him in the stable. "Allow me to introduce you to Crowdy and Pip. The gentlemen I met the last time I was here." He gently eased her forward. "Crowdy, Pip, this is Lady Joy Abarough, the target of the blackmailer."

"Good afternoon, gentlemen," she said.

The grimy man wearing the leather apron bowed, then caught hold of the young lad's nape and "helped" him bow as well. "Good afternoon, your ladyship. Sorry for your troubles."

"Thank you, good sir. It is my hope we capture the scoundrel today." All the while, she kept glancing at the hollow tree. If they missed the thief again, she would never hear the end of it from Jansen.

"We best leave you to it, then," Crowdy said. "Me and Pip here will work in the back and keep as quiet as possible."

"Thank you so much, gentlemen." She stayed by the old door with the missing knothole, pressing her eye to the opening to watch the tree. "Were the other parcels in there yet?" she asked Jansen.

"Yes. All we must do is wait." He took a position in the shadows, squinting to see through the crack of another split board. "I am glad the Earl of Denby hasn't replaced these overly weathered portions."

"I'm surprised he hasn't been *coerced* into doing so by his neighbors. These dilapidated boards are an eyesore. I'm sure they think they should be replaced immediately."

"He's a jolly fellow everyone likes. I'm sure he uses that to its fullest advantage." He resettled his footing, leaning with both hands propped against the wood. "This could take a while, my angel."

"I know, and as you well know, patience is not among my virtues." Slightly bent to peer through the knothole was not a comfortable stance, and her neck started stinging with mounting stiffness. Of course, every fiber of her being was tensed tighter than a pianoforte wire as they waited to catch their thief.

"Which of your remaining sisters will I have the pleasure of being tested by first?" he asked with quiet thoughtfulness.

She pondered that while blinking against being mesmerized by the swaying branches of the hollow tree in the distance. "Gracie will be last because to visit her will require a trip to the Lake District. Her churching is soon, but even then, she rarely comes into Town. She hates to leave her beloved country lodge." Joy rolled her shoulders and wished she could remove her gloves and lean against the boards like Jansen. But she daren't do so. She had enough scandalous things being tossed around about her without being seen outside, in public, not wearing her gloves. "I believe Fortuity would ease you into the Abarough gauntlet. One never knows what sort of mood Blessing will be in, since we just learned another little Knightwood will be joining us next year."

"Would it be appropriate for me to congratulate Lady Blessing and her husband?"

Joy wrinkled her nose. "Best wait and see what sort of day she is having. Last time my dear sister was with child, we saw an entirely different side of her." She straightened and stretched. "Good heavens, I didn't realize how trying this would be. I do not wait well."

"I should have had Copper stay close with the carriage rather than in the next street over. You could have waited in it and been a great deal more comfortable."

She turned and pondered him, touched not only by his words but also by his handsome profile in the shadows. "Thank you," she whispered.

He didn't pull his focus from the tree. "For what, my lady?"

"For not pouncing on the opportunity to say *I told you so*, and *that is why you should have stayed home*. That means a great deal to me."

He gave a heavy sigh and barely shook his head. "I love you, Joy, and only want you safe and happy."

"And I love—"

"There!" Jansen sprang around her and shot out of the stable.

She hurried out after him, but remained just outside the door, amazed at the young lad in the distance, little more than a child, dashing away with a cloth sack thrown over his shoulder. Jansen gave chase, but it was easy to see that even in his fine physical form, he was no match for the spry youngling. The boy wiggled through a loose board in the fence farther down the mews, successfully cutting Jansen off.

"Damn and blast it all!" Jansen shouted with an enraged growl. "I cannot believe I lost him again!"

Joy was torn between going to him or giving him time to come to terms with this latest downturn. It wasn't as if he hadn't tried to catch the youth. Good heavens, as fast as that boy had been, it would have taken one of Gracie's fastest hounds to overtake him. "Jansen…"

Shoulders slumped, he hung his head. "Yes, I know. I failed again."

Devil take it all, she hurried over and took both his hands in hers. "*You* did not fail. The vile little wretch was as fast and slippery as an eel."

Eyes closed and head still bowed, Jansen shook his head. "I failed you. Again."

"Sir Jansen Winterstone! You will look me in the eye immediately."

Jaw set, he opened his eyes and glared at her, disgust for himself shimmering in the depths of his golden-eyed gaze. "Yes, my lady?" he asked with strained quietness.

"I cannot bear to see you like this," she said just as quietly. "You did all you could." She squeezed his hands and gave him the most understanding smile she had ever given anyone. "We will outsmart them next time. I promise."

"How can you make such a promise?"

"Because I am wise beyond my years. All knowing, even. We women are like that, you know."

He arched a brow. "Truly?"

"Truly." She tugged on him. "Come along now. Let's find Copper and go for a carriage ride. An unchaperoned carriage ride. And I will not have you hurting my feelings this time by sitting across from me. We two are meant to be side by side. Understand?"

He finally smiled. "I understand, my lady, and I do beg your forgiveness for hurting your feelings. I assure you, that was not my intent."

"I should hope not." She took his arm, then opened her parasol and propped it on her shoulder to shade her face. Serendipity would be so proud. "Now, come along. I might even be in the mood for a kiss or two, since we find ourselves in such a daring state."

"Kissing in a carriage while driving through Mayfair?" he teased, feigning an expression of shock. "Is that wise, my angel?"

"As I already told you, I am wise beyond my years. We'll sort it out. I assure you."

"Lead the way, my darling. Lead the way."

Chapter Nine

J ANSEN PLACED THE long, narrow, blue velvet box in the center of his desk. He was almost afraid to open it, leery that the jeweler, Master Eibertson, had not gotten it right. This gift had to be perfect, because his Joy was perfection incarnate. A silent laugh huffed free of him. Well...at least in his opinion, she was perfection incarnate. Her brother and sisters might disagree.

Aurelia exploded into his office without knocking. "Is it here? Did he really finish it so quickly?"

"Yes and yes, dear sister. Come. Let's have a look at it, shall we?"

She hurried around his desk and hopped with excitement beside his chair, clapping her hands as if what the box held was intended for her. "Well, open it, then. Hurry."

He slowly opened the box and gave a sigh of relief. "It is exactly as I intended. What do you think, Aurelia? Will she adore it as much as I adore her?"

"Oh my, it is lovely." Aurelia clasped her hands to her chest and leaned over it closer. With a teasing glint in her eye, she shook her head. "But there is no possible way she can adore it as much as you adore her, because your adoration of Lady Joy Abarough is beyond compare."

Lifting the box and moving it so the contents caught the light, he ran his thumb along the softness of its velvety exterior. "I cannot wait to give it to her. As soon as Copper brings the carriage 'round, I am off. Would you care to come along as chaperone? It is a lovely day, and I'd thought to take her back to the Serpentine, to our shady oak and the swans."

"I would be honored."

"Perfect." Jansen snapped the box shut and slid it into the inner pocket of his jacket. "Shall we be on our way, then? I'll wait for you at the door while you fetch your parasol and bonnet."

"Lovely." Aurelia skipped down the hallway in the opposite direction as Jansen went to the door and donned the hat and gloves Severns had waiting for him.

"The carriage is here, sir," the butler announced as he turned from the long, narrow window beside the door.

"So it is." Jansen turned and looked up the stairway, his excitement and anticipation building. "Aurelia!"

"Coming!" True to her word, she appeared at the top of the stairs and skimmed down them, her feet flying. "I am so excited. I cannot wait until she sees it."

As Severns opened the front door, Jansen offered his arm and escorted her to the awaiting carriage. "Now, you know I shall wish you to meander off a bit for when I give it to her? I fear you won't see her initial reaction."

"That is all well and good. I shall easily be able to tell how much she loves it when she shows it to me upon my return to the carriage."

"You are the best sister a brother could ask for."

"I believe I have told you that for years. Have you not been listening?"

Laughing and in even higher spirits by the time they reached Broadmere House, they struggled to assume a modicum of decorum before knocking on the door.

"We must be serious now," he said. "I don't wish her to suspect anything."

"Absolutely." Aurelia quieted well enough, but her eyes still danced with glee.

Walters answered the door but didn't say a word, simply swung it open wide and waved them inside, leading them to the main parlor. Jansen found that somewhat disconcerting. What if the man did that with someone who might be a danger to the family? He made a mental note to ask at his first opportunity.

Felicity, Merry, and Serendipity joined them first, not seeming the least bit surprised at their presence, so the old butler must have simply recognized him and Aurelia. That made Jansen feel somewhat better, so much so that he decided not to mention their odd admittance for now.

Then his precious Joy entered the room, brightening it even more. He went to her and bowed before taking her hand. "My lovely angel."

"What have I told you about teetering pedestals, sir? I am simply me—not an angel." But she lit up even more at the compliment. "And what adventures are you and Aurelia up to today?"

"A ride in the park to check on our swans on the Serpentine," he said, "and we thought you might enjoy coming along."

"I would love to," she said without hesitation.

"Parasol and gloves," Serendipity said while Merry and Felicity groaned and rolled their eyes.

"Must you always kill the joy in everything?" Merry asked Serendipity.

"She would've gotten those things without your nagging," Felicity added.

"We mustn't side against Seri, sisters. She'll begin to think we despise her." Joy went to the bellpull.

"Sometimes we do." Merry clapped a hand over her mouth, then scurried from the room with Felicity in hot pursuit.

Serendipity glared at the door, then gave Jansen a forced smile. "Excuse me. I need to have a word with my sisters." With an unmistakable huff, she disappeared after them.

"Oh dear," Jansen said, hoping such a development wasn't a bad omen.

"Don't worry," Joy told him, "Seri will reign supreme. Merry and Felicity are too young to know how to handle her—yet." When Walters appeared at the doorway, she added, "Please have Flora bring down my parasol, gloves, and hat. Thank you, Walters."

He turned without a word and ambled off.

"I don't believe the man has said a word since we arrived," Jansen couldn't help but comment. The butler was a man of few words, but he had always spoken the required niceties.

"He is angry," Joy said. "We banded together and informed him of the butler in training we had hired. The man reports here the end of next week, and Walters considers it the gravest insult to his abilities, even though we assured him it was no such thing."

"Ahh…injured pride?"

"Most definitely." She accepted her things from a maid and donned them. "We have insulted him irreparably and can't think of a way to convince him it is for his own good." With a heavy sigh, she shook her head. "'Tis a sad time for poor Walters—and for us. He has always been our butler."

"It is a hard thing to accept one's limits." Jansen knew that from personal experience, and he was still wrestling with those lessons. He offered his lady love his arm. "But today is too bright and fine for such dark thoughts."

"Indeed."

Once they were all comfortably seated in his barouche, he instructed Copper to head for the park, before nodding at Joy. "Parasol, my lady. If I bring you home with a red face or freckles, your sister will surely have my hide."

"Seri can go to the devil. I love the warmth of the sun on my face." She tugged the brim of her bonnet forward. "I am currently shaded enough. Should the angle of the sun become a problem, then I will deploy my parasol."

"As you wish—besides, Copper will soon have us 'neath our friendly oak from the other day."

"There, you see? Plenty of shade and no parasol needed. I don't wish to frighten away the swans by waving that frilly thing about."

Soon they were once again parked beneath the sprawling oak beside the Serpentine. Jansen nodded at Aurelia and mouthed, *Take Copper with you.*

His sister rolled her eyes. "Copper—could you come along while I go for a short stroll?" she asked as she rose to disembark. "I saw the largest eel last time, and it frightened me terribly. It was so huge, I believe it could rise up out of the water like a sea monster."

"Absolutely, Miss Aurelia," the driver said. "I'll protect you from some old eel. Never you worry."

As they strolled away, Joy turned to Jansen, giving him such a side-eyed glare, he had to hold his breath to keep from laughing.

"A sea monster eel?" she said, "Seriously?"

Jansen shrugged. "You know Aurie. She can overdress it a bit at times."

Joy caught her bottom lip between her teeth and appeared worried. After a long moment of watching Aurelia and Copper walk along the banks of the lake, she hesitantly asked, "Why would she do that? Is something wrong? Are you angry with me about something?"

Alarm shot through him. "No, my angel. Nothing is wrong. She knew I simply wanted some privacy to give you this." He pulled the velvet box from his pocket and placed it in her hands.

Her perfectly kissable lips barely parted, making him hungrily wet his own.

"I hope you like it," he said quietly. "I had it made especially for you."

She carefully opened the box and gasped. "Oh my heavens— how...how...exquisite." Ever so carefully, she drew the silver bracelet out of the box and examined the silver and gold symbols that Master Eibertson had so expertly crafted at Jansen's request. "How in the world…"

"I told Master Eibertson what I wanted." Jansen touched the gold heart locket dangling from the silver chain. "To symbolize the purity of our love." Then he touched the next amulet attached to the delicate bracelet. "A gold anchor for our eternal bond and a silver dove for the peace that shall always be between us. The silver book is for your Reader's Dare Club, and that fine golden tiger with the ruby eyes symbolizes your ladies' gambling hell. Silver angel wings because you are ever my angel, and last but not least, the golden playing card, the queen of hearts with hearts of rubies, because that is who you are to me, my love: the queen of my heart."

Tears streamed down her face. Happy tears, he prayed.

She offered him her wrist. "Put it on me, please. I shall wear it always."

"You like it, then?"

"Oh dear heavens, I absolutely adore it." As soon as he secured it around her wrist, she wrapped her arms around his neck and hugged him tightly. "Jansen, you are too wonderful for words."

Cradling her close, he closed his eyes and breathed easily for the first time since the jeweler had delivered the bracelet. "No, my love. I am not wonderful—I am thankful beyond words."

She kissed his neck, sending a surge of stronger yearning through him. "I love it, and I love you."

"I hope this somewhat atones for my failing you."

She immediately pulled away, making him wish he hadn't said that. "You did not fail me." She patted his chest and straightened the folds of his cravat that she had crushed. "You are a very nice, large, handsome man. No one could expect you to catch a slippery street urchin who possessed the speed and cunning of a rat. Only one of Gracie's hounds could've hoped to catch that little…that little…"

Jansen grinned. "That little what?"

"My manners and my mama watching from heaven forbid me from saying what I wish to say. I believe you understand, though. Do you not?"

"Fully, and I quite agree." He noticed Copper and Aurelia were heading back. That meant that one of Society's loose tongues was probably headed their way also. That, and the fact that Aurelia was anxious to know Joy's reaction to the special gift. "But I am glad you love our engagement bracelet. I wanted something unique."

She smiled down at it, turning it on her wrist and touching each of the charms. "I cherish it more than you will ever know, and as I said, I shall wear it always. Seri and the girls will adore it as much as I." She looked into his eyes and grinned. "I'm sure they'll also be jealous, and that is never a bad thing."

He lifted both hands in surrender. "Far be it from me to start a war among the Abarough sisters."

"A friendly war," she said while shaking her arm and making the bracelet dance and rattle with the softly tinkling sound of the precious metals.

"Do you love it?" Aurelia asked as she climbed into the barouche and joined them.

"Beyond words," Joy said. "Your brother has made me feel so special and so loved."

"You are, my darling," Jansen said. "I swear to you that you are."

⋙✦⋘

"Now, you have to set a wedding date." Envy and excitement filled Merry's voice as she gently turned Joy's wrist to make the bracelet sparkle in the sunlight streaming in the parlor window. "What a lovely gift. And so very thoughtful. It is you, Joy. It is absolutely you."

"Thank you, dearest. I must admit, I feel ever so fortunate." Joy ignored the comment about choosing a date. She wasn't quite ready for that just yet.

"Then why wait to have the banns read?" Felicity asked. "And I can start planning your wedding breakfast. What shall we have? Hmm?"

"Not yet."

"Why not?" Serendipity asked as she smiled down at the bracelet. "Chance gave you his blessing. Grudgingly. But he gave it after speaking to Mr. Sutherland the elder."

"Why was he speaking about me to our solicitor?" Joy asked.

Serendipity rolled her eyes. "Some nonsense about checking the will for terms regarding marriage to commoners." She threw up her hands to stave off any outbursts. "But pay him no mind. Mr. Sutherland set him straight. All that matters is true love—not status."

Indignance rising, Joy was ready to storm out of the room, find her brother, and pummel him. "Chance can go to the devil! He is such an arse."

"Joy." Serendipity gave her the same long-suffering look Mama had always used whenever one of them resorted to language considered inappropriate for young ladies.

"You know I am right."

"I know." Serendipity deflated with another sorely put-upon sigh. "I just wish you were more *appropriately* eloquent about it." She clapped her hands. "Now—about that wedding date."

"Not until he has met Fortuity, Blessing, and Grace."

"You truly expect me to believe that if one or all of them do not approve of him, then you will set him aside and break off the engagement?" Serendipity arched a brow.

"Well…"

"Joy—be honest."

"Do not use that tone with me." Joy pressed her hands to her middle. Every time she heard the word *wedding*, thousands of tiny, winged creatures fluttered so wildly through her innards that she almost cast up her accounts. What was wrong with her? Surely that wasn't normal. "I simply cannot manage it just yet. I am so...so..."

"You are afraid," Serendipity said, her voice filled with amazement. "Why?"

"Why? Are you so thickheaded that you cannot comprehend why? I know nothing about running a household or a husband. All I know is gaming."

"You will learn, and it's not as if you won't have a housekeeper to help you." Serendipity hugged her. Merry and Felicity joined in.

"We will help too," Felicity said. "I can teach you all about meal planning and budgeting the pantry properly with your cook."

"And when the babies come, you know I am happy to help," Merry said. "Why, I would even move in for a while until you found a proper nurse and nanny."

"And my help is always there for you," Serendipity said. "I know we fuss and fight, but we Abarough sisters always lift each other up. No matter the circumstances. You know that, dear sister."

"I know." Joy pulled in a deep, shuddering breath, then blew it out. Confessions were always so hard. "I'm just afraid. I truly am. Afraid of being an adult. A wife. A mother. Instead of a carefree daughter and sister."

"Remember what Mama always said?" Serendipity gave her another gentle hug. "Everything changes. Nothing in this world remains the same except for love, and even that can change...hopefully for the better. It deepens. Becomes richer. Grows even stronger. Is that the sort of love you see between yourself and Jansen? If it is, then you must be brave and embrace that love and the change that comes along with it. Change isn't always a bad thing, you know. Sometimes, it's just...different."

"I still do not want to set a date until Fortuity, Blessing, and Grace have met him. I just don't feel it would be right." Not only that, but it would buy her some time to come to terms with all these *changes* her sisters spoke of so casually, but in her mind were absolutely catastrophic. "And there is the matter of the blackmailer yet to settle. How can I set a date with that misbegotten fool still on the loose? Who knows what mischief they would attempt to stir if they heard about my wedding?"

"I think it's time to tell Chance and call in the Bow Street Runners," Merry said. "You said you've suspended the club meetings ever since the blackmail started, haven't you?"

"Yes, the club is suspended, but we operated for quite a while. And you know Chance will have nine kinds of fits when he hears about it. I truly don't wish to deal with him right now."

"Well...nine kinds of fits or not," Serendipity said, "the Bow Street Runners would make short work of this foolishness."

"What do you prefer on your buffet for your wedding breakfast?" Felicity asked from the desk in the corner. She sat with her quill poised above a fresh sheet of paper.

"I cannot begin to think of food right now." Joy hugged her middle even tighter. "Too many winged demons have me churning."

Merry went to the bellpull. "I'll ask Mrs. Flackney for something to calm you. She makes the best digestives, and you'll feel so much better."

"Less talk about a wedding would make me feel better," Joy retorted.

"Of course, there must be chocolates at one end of the table and an absolutely gorgeous wedding cake for the center," Felicity said. "That goes without saying."

"Did you hear me, Feli? I don't want to talk about it."

"Hot rolls, buttered toast, tongue, ham and eggs. Maybe even kippers," Felicity continued as if Joy hadn't said a word. "And I have the very best recipe for fruit jams. They would go so well with a larger variety of breads other than the usual rolls and toasts. And honey.

There must be honey available, too. How would you feel about including some custard tarts? Those would be loveliness itself."

Joy almost gagged on the rise of bile burning at the back of her throat. She stamped her foot. "If you continue, I shall cast up my tea and biscuits all over you!"

Felicity stared at her, open mouthed in shock. "Forgive me, Joy. I was only trying to help."

Lovely. Now Joy felt even worse for hurting dear Felicity's feelings. "Forgive me, Feli. There is just *so* much to deal with. Can we leave it for another day? Please?"

"Of course." Felicity set aside her quill and slid the paper back inside the center drawer of the desk.

Walters appeared in the doorway. He bore a silver tray that held a single envelope—a disturbingly familiar single envelope. When no one addressed him, he cleared his throat but still refused to speak.

"Walters," Serendipity said, "you are being childish. Now stop it this instant. You know we love and consider you a member of the family. Stop this sullenness at once."

Stoic as ever, the butler jutted his chin higher, held out the tray, then cut a hard look Joy's way.

"You are being ridiculous, Walters." Joy marched over and snatched the note off the tray. "Thank you. That will be all."

"I shall ask Chance to speak with him," Serendipity said as the man turned and left. "Again."

Joy ignored her and tore into the envelope. Her heart fell, and her bile rose, burning the back of her throat even worse.

I am not pleased. How dare you frighten my delivery boy? You will pay. Even more. Just you wait and see.

"Well, isn't that lovely?" She handed off the note to Serendipity. "Jansen will be enraged."

"As well he should be," Serendipity said. "It is time for the Bow

Street Runners."

"Not until I speak with Jansen." Joy refolded the note and tucked it down inside the front of her dress. It would be safe and secure there until she had a chance to show it to her betrothed. "I owe him that much."

"Very well, then." Serendipity nodded at the desk. "You might send him a note to warn him."

"I will." Joy touched her beloved bracelet, running her thumb across the smoothness of the golden heart. Jansen would sort this, and then she could get on with convincing herself that change wasn't such a bad thing after all.

Chapter Ten

"**THEY ACTUALLY NAMED** their son Quill Seshat Ravenglass?" Jansen stared at Joy with an expression she couldn't quite fathom. He was either bewildered, amused, or both.

"It's because of her writing. Tutie takes it very seriously. Have you read any of her books?" Joy very much doubted that he had. He didn't strike her as a man inclined to read romantic stories—even if he was the most romantic man she had ever met.

"I cannot say that I have."

"I rather doubted you were familiar with them." She glanced out the carriage window and almost groaned at the blustery day. It was raining buckets, and the sky was as dark as a blanket of gray flannel. She truly hoped that wasn't an omen as to how this visit would go. One never knew quite what one might find in the Ravenglass household, what with all the cats, Ignatius the pug, and little Quill, whom Fortuity kept at her side when she wasn't writing. The Ravenglass nanny had an extraordinarily easy position, since Fortuity doted on her son. "I wonder if we should have chosen another day?"

"It is England, my angel. It rains. Incessantly."

"I know, but we've been blessed with so many sunny days. Is it greedy of me to wish for another?" Joy shifted in the seat and nearly cringed when her reticule crackled with the latest note from the blackmailer. She hadn't shown it to Jansen yet, but was determined to do so before the day was out. *Visit Tutie first, then show him the note later.* A solid plan. She hoped.

"We're nearly there," she said as they turned onto Chesterfield Street. "Ravenglass Townhouse is just up ahead." She noticed he didn't seem nervous at all. If she were meeting members of his extended family under such inauspicious circumstances, she would be unraveling at her seams. "You are so sure of yourself. Not nervous a bit?"

"Is your sister beastly?"

"Of course not."

"Then why should I be ill at ease? I am meeting future members of my family." He took her hand. "And I am enjoying yet another rare bit of time in your presence without a chaperone. Is your sister unwell? She is normally much more strict."

"Seri has been a bit lax of late. Perhaps she is trying to entrap you in case you change your mind."

"I would never." He pressed a kiss to the back of her gloved hand. "You are my angel. I cannot imagine life without you."

"Teetering pedestals, sir," Joy reminded him. While she thoroughly enjoyed being adored, Jansen needed to understand she was far from perfect. "You hold me up so high, the heights are dizzying at times."

"I will always be here to catch you, my angel."

The carriage rolled to a stop. Copper opened the door and placed the steps while holding an umbrella ready. He held out a hand to help her. "Careful does it, my lady. I tried to choose the spot with the shallowest puddles."

"Thank you, Copper. I am sure you did."

He escorted her up the front steps of the townhouse, ensuring the umbrella shielded her from the rain while Jansen followed behind them. The Ravenglass butler, Thebson, opened the door before they fully reached it.

"Good afternoon, Lady Joy." The servant held the door open wide, waving them inside. "And you, good sir," he said to Copper, "will find a place out of the weather. Round back in the mews. Once you have seen to your horses, come in the servants' entrance for some hot tea. Lady Fortuity always insists on that practice when the weather is foul."

"Thank you kindly, sir," Copper said with a bob of his head. "And please thank the lady of the house as well."

Thebson nodded, then closed the door and set to taking Joy and Jansen's wet things. "Dreadful weather, is it not, Lady Joy?"

"It is at that, Thebson, after all that wonderful sunshine. And do let me introduce you to Sir Jansen Winterstone."

The butler bowed, then accepted Jansen's hat, coat, and gloves. "Welcome to Ravenglass Townhouse, Sir Jansen."

"Thank you, Thebson," Jansen said. "I am very pleased to be here."

"Lady Fortuity and Master Quill, along with several more cats than were here the last time you visited, await you in the parlor, my lady. Do follow me." The butler turned on his heel and led the way.

Joy did her best not to laugh. Thebson hated the cats as much as Blessing's butler did. Joy often wondered if the men ever got together to bemoan their fate of serving households filled with felines.

"Joy!" Fortuity rose from the floor where she had been on the rug with Quill and his toy soldiers. "Look, Quill! Auntie Joy has come to visit."

"Doy! Doy!" Quill crowed, clapping his hands as he toddled over to Joy at something akin to a run.

"There is my little man!" Joy scooped him up and hugged him. "I have a friend for you to meet." She turned and nodded at Jansen. "This is Sir Jansen Winterstone. Can you say *hello* and make him feel welcome?"

Frowning, the child eyed Jansen for a long moment before finally uttering, "'Lo."

Jansen bowed. "It is a pleasure to meet you, Master Quill."

Beaming with pride, Fortuity rushed over and took the cherub from Joy. "He seems to be going through a time where he doesn't trust as readily as he once did," she told Jansen. "Nanny says it is quite normal, though."

"I am sure it is," Jansen said with a polite bow.

"Jansen, this is my *older* sister, Fortuity," Joy said, grinning because she knew Fortuity hated being referred to as such. "Tutie, Sir Jansen Winterstone—uhm—my intended."

Fortuity's eyes went wide. "Intended?" She held up a finger. "A moment, if you please." She hurried to the parlor doorway. "Nanny!" An older woman appeared almost immediately and took charge of young Quill after Fortuity gave him the required kisses on his chubby little cheeks and waved at him. "Bye–bye. Time to play with Nanny."

Quill clapped his pudgy little hands and gurgled at his smiling nursemaid.

Once they departed, Fortuity yanked on the bellpull. "This calls for a toast. I had heard rumors, but Seri refused to confirm anything. She said I had to speak with you." She waved at the pair of settees on either side of the rug covered in toys and cats of various sizes. "Please, have a seat. Just be careful where you step. Cats and toys. The cats will move. Sometimes. But the toys will trip you. At a little over a year of age, I fear my son has yet to conquer the art of tidiness."

Joy pointed at the cats. "That one is Horatio…I think. That one is Jervis. And the very large one is Wellington. Where are Rumbles and Ignatius?" she asked Fortuity.

"Both are in the mews, currently under the watchful eye of Mr. Turnmaster. Rumbles refuses to leave the side of a lady feline that showed up three days ago, and Ignatius rolled in a fresh pile of horse manure. He is not permitted back in the house until the groom has bathed him."

Jansen snorted as he seated himself, making Joy smile.

"Jansen has a cat named Nimbus who steals anything he can carry." Joy sat beside Jansen and shook her wrist to make her bracelet rattle. Fortuity was much like a crow. If she spotted anything shiny or heard metal rattle, she always perked with interest.

"And what have we here?" she asked after instructing a maid to bring tea. She gracefully sidestepped toys and cats, then caught hold of Joy's hand. "Oh my goodness. How lovely." She playfully shook Joy's hand to make it rattle again. "The wedding date? And why have none of the banns been read? Are we to have a special license, then?"

"She refuses to set a date until I receive the approval of every Abarough sister," Jansen said.

"I see. And whom do you lack now?"

He made a face as if struggling to remember. "Lady Blessing and Lady Grace."

Fortuity beamed. "Well, at least I wasn't last." She plopped down on the settee across from them, and two unknown cats jumped over the back of the sofa and joined her. Both purred loudly. "Ahh...yes. Meet Sweetie and Pet."

"Sweetie and Pet?" Joy eyed the pair of black-and-white cats that were almost identical. "Where did they come from?"

Fortuity sadly shook her head. "I have no idea. They just showed up. We fed them, and they took up residence."

"You can hardly blame them," Joy said.

"Now." Fortuity narrowed her eyes, settling her gaze on her sister. "A date?"

"We already told you—he has yet to meet Essie and Gracie. Once he meets them, we'll set a date."

"You honestly expect me to believe that if one of us doesn't like him, you will send him away?"

"You sound like Seri, and do stop talking about him as if he is not sitting right here."

"Thank you," Jansen said with a grin before turning to face Joy. "But I would like to hear that answer as well. Would you send me away, my angel, if one of your sisters does not like me?"

"Of course not," she said quietly. "I would merely"—she cleared her throat—"have a robust conversation with that particular sister."

Fortuity laughed so loudly she startled the cats, making them hiss. "Oh my. Forgive me, pets. I am sorry. It's just I have never seen Joy like this before."

"Like what?" Joy said, bracing herself for what her sister might say next.

Fortuity looked at Joy, then at Jansen. Her smile widened exponentially. "Happy with something other than a deck of playing cards." She nodded at Joy's wrist. "But I see by those amulets that he fully understands you, and I am glad." She rose and gave a dramatic bow, then curtsied. "I hereby bestow upon you my full blessing and hopes for an eternity of happiness."

A door thudded somewhere deeper in the home, and happy barking and the clicking of toenails on the marble floors echoed down the hallway.

"Oh dear," Fortuity said. "Brace yourselves. It appears Ignatius has had his bath."

A pudgy blur sped into the room, yipping happily. He tried to jump onto the settee with Joy, miscalculated the height, hit his chest with a soft thud, then fell back and landed with a grunt.

"Let me help you, old boy," Jansen said, bending to let the wriggling pug sniff his knuckles before he picked him up and deposited him on the settee between himself and Joy.

"Oh my, Ignatius." Joy laughed as she petted the snorting little dog that always looked as though he were smiling. "I am happy to see you, too, but you appear even more wiggly than usual."

"He is always like that after a bath," Fortuity said. "But if Quill were still with us, he would be much calmer. He is a gem around him. It's as if he understands that Quill is a baby and must be coddled and protected."

"And the cats tolerate him?" Jansen asked.

"Oh, yes." Fortuity laughed. "It is as though they understand that sweet Ignatius is totally harmless." Her mirth faded, making her smile sad. "And how goes capturing that rotten blackmailer?" she asked Joy.

"Not well at all. Seri is ready to tell Chance everything and call in the Bow Street Runners." Joy folded her hands in her lap, wishing the subject hadn't been broached.

"I think that a wise idea," Jansen said quietly. "I know you didn't wish to explain your club to your brother, but after two failed attempts at capturing the dirty cove, I don't feel we're left with much of a choice."

Joy slowly shook her head. "Chance will have nine kinds of fits."

"Chance's fits don't usually bother you," Fortuity said. "Why does this one?"

"Because he doesn't like Jansen."

"But Seri said he gave his blessing?"

"Yes, but grudgingly so."

"A bucket of frogs, then?" Fortuity arched a knowing brow.

"I prefer eels while here in Town. Easier to come by."

"What are you ladies talking about?" Jansen asked. "Eels? Frogs? By the bucketful?"

Still rubbing Ignatius's velvety ears, Joy nodded. "When we were children and one of us had a tiff with one of the others, we filled the bedsheets of our enemy with either frogs or eels, then covered them with a blanket for the owner of the bed to find when it was time to retire."

Jansen chuckled. "And your parents allowed this?"

"Our parents allowed us to work through our battles with no interference as long as no one picked up a weapon that might actually do bodily harm. We were allowed to learn diplomacy, reasoning, and the art of getting along firsthand."

"What a novel approach to parenting." Jansen chuckled again. "As the eldest, I was expected to set the example for the young ones and *help* them get along."

"More is always expected of the elder siblings," Fortuity said with a pointed look at Joy. "As the fourth child of eight, I enjoyed the pleasure of being in the middle. Chance, Serendipity, and Blessing were considered the eldest after all the rest of us came along."

"Merry is the baby," Joy said. "She is a *little* spoiled, but not too badly."

"It appears to me that with seven sisters, your brother is a master of diplomacy," Jansen said.

"He is a master of being a horse's arse," Fortuity said at the same time as Joy. They both bubbled with laughter at the disparaging chorus about their brother.

Joy fidgeted with her reticule, making it crackle so much that Ignatius barked at it.

"Why in heaven's name did you not leave that with Thebson?" Fortuity asked. "You know it would be secure with him."

After a deep breath and a hard swallow for courage, Joy worked open the drawstring bag and drew out the note. "Because of this." She handed it to Jansen. "It is the latest from the blackmailer."

"When did you get this?" He stared down at the folded bit of paper with the broken seal.

"Yesterday."

"And nothing since?"

"No."

He opened it and read it aloud:

I am not pleased. How dare you frighten my delivery boy? You will pay. Even more. Just you wait and see.

"That sounds ominous," Fortuity said. "You must call in the Bow Street Runners. The time for secrecy is over."

"I soundly agree," Jansen said. He tucked the note into the inner pocket of his jacket. "Do you still have the previous notes?"

"I do." Joy's heart sank. She dreaded what Chance would say. For the first time in her life, she realized that her brother's opinion of her mattered more than she liked. He would be disappointed in her. Again.

Jansen reached over and took her hand. "It will be all right, my angel. I swear it will."

"I simply hate having to get Chance involved. This is my problem, and he should not have to be a part of it."

"The blackmailer dragged him into it with the first threat. You had no control over that."

"Yet and still…"

"I know, my love. Yet and still."

❦

IT HAD TAKEN some artful negotiation, but with Fortuity's help, Jansen convinced Joy to let him handle the issue of the blackmailer in an effort to delay any confrontations with her brother. He didn't know if the Bow Street Runners could address the matter without speaking to Broadmere, but it was his hope they could—for his angel's sake.

He laid out each of the blackmailer's notes on his desk, studying them. The three were written in the same hand. Decidedly feminine. Maybe. Some men were known for their flowery script. It was a mark of breeding and education. No matter how hard Jansen tried to write with such artistic swoops and whirls, his evil left-handed *scratchings*, as the headmaster had always called them, were often barely legible. But his forced right-handed writings were even worse. Oftentimes, he couldn't read his own letters whenever he attempted to do the socially acceptable thing and write with his right hand.

A light knock on the door interrupted his study of the papers. "Yes?"

Aurelia entered and added her notes to the collection. Again, they were all identical except for the wording between the threats to Joy and the threats to Aurelia. "By the way, Ambrose is heartbroken. You need to speak with him. Again."

"I warned him about Lady Serafina."

"No. A different lady, and I use that term loosely, shattered his soul this time, as he puts it."

Their brother had a flair for the dramatic. "And who is this lady who is guilty of shattering his soul?"

"A lightskirt from the theater. She discovered a lord willing to take her on as a mistress and keep her in the manner to which she wishes to become accustomed. As soon as she received the key to her cozy little nest, she informed Ambrose that his services were no longer required." Aurelia sighed. "You know he falls in love with every woman he beds."

"That is not an appropriate manner of speaking for a lady, Aurie."

"I am not a lady—I am a miss."

Jansen blew out a heavy sigh. They'd had this particular conversation before. "Be that as it may, you should strive to always behave like a lady. Agreed?"

She rolled her eyes but nodded. "So will you speak with him today? Before he either shoots himself or drinks himself into oblivion?"

"I will speak to him after I meet with the Bow Street Runners. I expect them at any time."

"I shall leave you to it, then."

As Aurelia headed to the door, Jansen couldn't help but think something else was wrong. She wasn't her usual exuberant self. "Aurie."

She paused with her hand on the latch. "Yes?"

"Tell me."

"Tell you what?"

"You know very well *what*. What is troubling you?"

"You are a good man, and just because Chance Abarough was born with a ridiculous title attached to his name, he thinks himself better than you. It is not right, and I am bloody well sick of it!"

Jansen rounded the desk and went to give her hand a consoling squeeze. "It is the way of things, dear sister. You know that."

"You are a better man than he could ever hope to be!"

"What is it the vicar always says? We are all equal in the eyes of the Almighty?"

She snorted. "And yet some are more *equal* than others, according to Polite Society."

He affectionately chucked her under the chin. "My Joy's opinion is all that matters. You know she looks at things the way we do. She did not allow her brother to separate us, now, did she?"

"No. Sweet Joy is a reasonable person."

"Then cease giving Broadmere any further room in your pretty head. He is not worth it."

"I shall try, but it will not be easy."

"Nothing worth having is ever easy, and peace of mind is worth having."

Aurelia snorted again. "Don't forget about Ambrose," she said as she stepped out into the hallway.

"I shall speak to him this afternoon. I promise."

After a nod of approval, she swept down the hallway and disappeared around the corner.

Jansen leaned against the doorpost, staring after her long after she was gone. It wasn't like Aurelia to let societal prejudice get her in such a stir. But then again, she had always fought on his side. Even when they were children, and she was a tiny little thing, she valiantly stood against anyone who might tease him. The memories made him smile. He and Aurelia had always been close. Poor Ambrose had often said he was the odd man out, and sadly, he was correct.

"Mr. John Rathbun of the Bow Street Runners, sir," Severns said from behind him.

Jansen turned and greeted the man with a polite nod. "Thank you for coming so quickly, Mr. Rathbun."

"You served with my brother against the Ottomans," the gentleman said. "Saved his life, in fact. When we received your request, I was honor bound to give your case priority."

"I knew your name seemed familiar." Jansen escorted him into his office. "Your brother is a good man. How is he?"

"Sadly, he passed this past December," Mr. Rathbun said. "The war failed to kill him, but consumption did not."

"I am sorry, Mr. Rathbun. As I said, your brother was a fine man."

"Thank you, sir. Now...your case?"

"My intended, Lady Joy Abarough, is being blackmailed." Jansen went to the liquor cabinet and held up a glass. "A drink for you, sir?"

"Just the one, thank you." Mr. Rathbun noticed the letters on the desk. "Are these the evidence you spoke of in your note?"

"They are indeed." Jansen poured two whiskies and handed one to the detective. "My sister is also being blackmailed by the same culprit, as are three of her friends: Lady Frederica Atterley, Lady Constance Burrastone, and Lady Prudence Kettering."

Mr. Rathbun glanced up from the fiend's letters of demand and arched a bushy brow. "What is this Reader's Dare Club of which they speak?"

"My intended enjoys gaming. As do many of her friends. So much so, she devised the Reader's Dare Club for ladies. A female gambling hell, so to speak, and a portion of every pot is donated to charity. Usually, the London Children's Home. As White's is to the gentlemen, the Reader's Dare Club is for the ladies."

Both of Mr. Rathbun's wild auburn brows arched nearly to his hairline. "I see."

"And my intended's brother, the Duke of Broadmere, is unaware of the true intentions of the club. He believes it to be a weekly book club for the ladies."

"And you would like to keep it that way?"

"You understand me perfectly, Mr. Rathbun." Jansen sipped his whisky, relishing the burn as it went down. "The scoundrel obtained the first payment without being detected. The second payment was picked up by a young lad with the speed and agility of a sewer rat."

"Hence the final note where they say they are not pleased and intend to make you pay even more—either money or worse?" Mr. Rathbun sipped his own whisky, then held one of the letters up to the lamp, studying the script in the golden glow of the flame. "This is not the cheap paper of a poorer criminal. I wager this is some of the best stationery that coin can purchase." He took another sip and frowned down at the notes littering the desk. "Does your Lady Joy have any thoughts on the blackmailer? A disgruntled gambler, perhaps?"

"At first, we suspected a pair of the ladies I named off. They'd had a bit of a disagreement with Lady Joy. But since they are being blackmailed as well, it seems unlikely that one of them would be the guilty party."

"Unless they did that to conceal themselves," Mr. Rathbun said.

"True." Jansen refolded all the letters and handed them over to the detective. "Find the man or woman, Mr. Rathbun. My lady love needs peace of mind, or she will never grace me with a wedding date."

Mr. Rathbun smiled. "I shall do my best, sir. I shall do my very best—in honor of my brother."

"Good man."

"I shall tell you of my findings within a few days. Good day to you, sir."

"Good day." Jansen watched the man go, certain he would handle the case with his full attention. His brother had been a good man, a man of honor. Jansen had no doubt that Mr. Rathbun was the same. That was one of those things that could be sensed without saying.

And now it was time to deal with Ambrose.

Jansen allowed himself a heavy sigh. He had never gotten on all that well with his only brother, and had both regretted and wondered at that fact. Perhaps it was because they were polar opposites. Ambrose was dramatic, overly sensitive, and thought worse about himself than any other person ever could. The man had not an ounce of pride or sense of self-importance. No matter what he achieved or how well he did, Ambrose never celebrated himself. Nothing was ever enough.

Mounting the stairs to Ambrose's floor, Jansen picked up on his brother's wails before he even reached his bedchamber door. "Ridiculous." And all for a tart who would more than likely have given him the clap if she hadn't already peppered him with it.

He reached Ambrose's suite of rooms and knocked. "Let me in, brother. Aurie is worried about you."

"But you are not, of course," Ambrose said through the door before resuming his wailing.

"You know better than that."

"Do I?"

"Open the bloody door and stop behaving like a sniveling fool!"

The door swung open, and Ambrose left it that way, choosing instead to throw himself face down on the settee and resume his sobbing. "I loved her. I truly loved her."

Jansen shook his head, eyeing the brother who looked nothing like him or Aurelia. He had often wondered if Mother and Father had found him as a babe somewhere and brought him home because they felt sorry for him. For the life of him, he couldn't remember Mother's confinement or churching after his brother was born, as she had done after having Aurelia. Ambrose was a head shorter than their sister, almost blond, and possessed the slight build of a thin lad still waiting to become a man. But at the ripe old age of three and twenty, Ambrose was well past puberty, even though one could hardly tell it because he rarely needed a shave.

"Ambrose."

His brother remained face down in the cushions, sobbing as if someone had died.

"Ambrose—this must stop. You do this for every woman you have ever sampled."

"That is because, brother, unlike *you*, I only sample the women I love."

"Bloody hell," Jansen muttered. He went to the settee, grabbed Ambrose by the scruff of the neck, and set him upright. "From what Aurelia tells me, this is a blessing. What about Lady Serafina? I thought you loved her?"

"You were right about her," Ambrose said, still sniveling. "She possessed the cruelty of the slyest predator and had the teeth and claws to match."

"Well, at least you had the good sense to rid yourself of her. Now, get a hold of yourself, man. With your style and charm, you always have a lady beside you. And as soon as that lady steps away, another takes her place."

"Until they find someone else with a title or a knighthood."

Jansen deflated with a heavy sigh. That again. The dreaded rankings of Polite Society. What was it with his siblings today? Was it something to do with the phase of the moon, perhaps? "Make yourself into the person you want to be, Ambrose. Is that not what Mother and Father always told you? You can be anything to anyone. Just set your mind to it and do it."

"Can I be a duke? A marquess? Or even a baron?" Ambrose stumbled over to the liquor cabinet littered with several dirty glasses. He filled one of them, drank it in one long draft, then filled it again. "No. I cannot be any of those things. No title for poor old Ambrose. All I am is the younger brother of a war hero. A shadow. A nothing."

"You are not a nothing. Our parents willed you land. A house. A generous allowance. You have everything you need to make yourself into whom you wish to be. Stop wasting your life and *live* it."

"I cannot because I am no one! How can you not see that? With no title, no status, I am a nothing."

"Go to the colonies, then. Make yourself into a hero there. They have no High Society and answer to no king. Make yourself into an important man of business. You've a head for numbers. For design. Help them build the cities I am sure they all long for since leaving England to tame that land."

"And just how long do you really think I would survive in that barbaric land?"

"As long as you bloody well wanted to, damn you! Stop being such a coward. Believe in yourself."

"That is so easy for you to say. You have everything!"

Jansen forced himself to hold his ground rather than storming over to shake his maudlin brother. Father would be so ashamed, and so would Mother. What had happened to Ambrose? Why was he so...so...*different?*

"I do not know how to help you, Ambrose. Honestly, I don't. What can I do to make your life better? How can I help you achieve the happiness you so richly deserve?"

"Put a half ounce of lead between my eyes and bury me beside Mama," Ambrose said so quietly that Jansen had to lean forward to hear him. "Mama understood me like no other."

Jansen had no answer for that. Mother always had understood Ambrose and was the only one of them who possessed the power to calm him whenever he got like this. "I could never harm you, brother. Sometimes, I want to shake you, but I could never harm you."

Shoulders sagging, staring down at the floor, Ambrose sniffed. "I know. I love you too, brother. No matter how much I complain about the darkness of being in your shadow."

Jansen sat on the settee beside his brother, rubbing his eyes, which were gritty with weariness. The demons had been particularly insistent on not allowing him to sleep last night. "I need you to fight for yourself, Ambrose. Aurie and I do our best to fight for you, but you have to fight too. Can you do that? Will you try to do that? If not for me, then for Aurie?"

Ambrose leaned back and rested his head on Jansen's shoulder. "Fighting is hard, Janny, and I am so very tired."

"You haven't called me Janny since you were a tot."

"You will always be Janny the giant killer to me," Ambrose whispered. "I remember how you ran off those boys whenever they threw taunts at me. I remember how you always protected me and Aurie."

"And I always will. As long as I live and breathe."

"You know I am not like you, Janny. I never will be. I am...different."

Jansen's heart ached for his sibling. He was at a complete loss for how to take away Ambrose's pain. "I don't care if you are different. You are my brother and always will be. No matter the circumstances. Nothing could ever change that."

"Swear?"

"I swear on my life, Ambrose. I will always love and protect you."

Chapter Eleven

"**A**ND WHAT SHOULD I expect from this visit, my angel?" Jansen wasn't nervous—more curious, actually.

Joy eyed him as if carefully considering how to word her answer. "Aurora, also known as Rorie or little Starpeeper, is a wild two-year-old who effectively runs the household with her extremely hard-of-hearing grandmother, Thorne's mother, Lady Roslynn, and their army of cats. Blessing thrives on the furor, as does her husband, Thorne."

"Starpeeper?" Jansen repeated slowly, wondering at the odd word as the carriage turned onto Brook Street.

"Before Rorie was born, *Starpeeper* was what we all called her, since we didn't know she was a girl. Essie is an avid astronomer, so Starpeeper was the perfect name, no matter if it was a girl or a boy. Someday, I shall show you Essie's old observatory that Papa built for her at Broadmere House. Thorne is attempting to recreate it at the Knightwood residence. He's been overseeing its construction since they married, and it's nearly finished. To Essie, that gift is more precious than any jewels he could ever buy her."

"Your family is very…"

"Careful what you say, dear sir."

He laughed, but his mirth quickly faded. "I was merely searching for a word to describe such a unique family of independent and intriguing individuals. I wish Ambrose could take a lesson or two from you and your siblings."

"I know I have yet to meet him, but I could try to talk with him. Might that help?"

Jansen slowly shook his head, bleakly staring out the carriage window without seeing anything at all. "I don't know, my angel. Every time I try something I think might help, it seems to drive him deeper into his misery. I am at a loss as to what to do about him. I have never seen him so morose."

"I will talk to him, and if that fails, Aurelia and I shall lecture him until he improves. Never underestimate the power of women intent on a cause."

The carriage rolled to a stop. Copper opened the door, set the steps, then helped Joy step out into the sunshine. Jansen descended after her, then stood on the sidewalk, gazing up at the townhouse that used to belong to the most notorious rake the *ton* had ever known. Perhaps if an Abarough sister could reform such a man, Joy might be able to help Ambrose reclaim himself after all.

They ascended the front steps and made use of the brass door knocker. From within the house could be heard the loud, exuberant squeals of a small child. The door opened the barest crack, and a man—Jansen assumed it was the butler—peered at them with only his one eye showing.

"Welcome, Lady Joy," said the servant, without opening the door any wider. "Please mind your step and rush inside when I swing the door wide, as Lady Roslynn, Miss Rorie, and an untold number of cats are currently marching in the hallway, waging war on France."

"Thank you for the warning, Cadwick. We shall take care so none escape." Joy's sympathetic smile seemed to calm him.

"That would be *most* appreciated," the sorely-put-upon butler said gratefully.

Jansen held his breath to keep from laughing and prepared to bolt into the house as soon as the door opened wide enough.

Cadwick avidly watched something behind him, then swung open the door. "Come in. Quickly, if you please."

"Charge!" shouted a silvery-haired matron from her bath chair at the other end of the hall. The golden-haired tot at her side squealed in agreement, lifted a wooden sword, and thundered down the marble-tiled way with what looked to be nearly a dozen cats galloping alongside her.

"Doy-Doy!" The wooden sword clattered to the floor. The battle quickly forgotten, the child barreled into Joy's embrace.

"There is my sweet Rorie." Joy swept her up and spun her around. "Are you and the kitties terrorizing poor Cadwick again?"

Rorie bobbed her head. "And Fance."

"Oh, and France too? Well done."

"Yep." The child nodded again, then narrowed her sparkling blue eyes and pointed at Jansen. "Who dat?"

"Wait! Wait!" The elderly woman held an ear trumpet to her ear while waving them closer. "I want to hear too."

A young blonde woman, whom Jansen could only assume was Joy's sister, Blessing, swept down the stairs, looking slightly pale. "Joy! Forgive me. I completely lost track of the time. This dreaded sickness… If I am not starving to death and stuffing myself silly, I am casting it all back out again." She locked eyes with Jansen, giving him such a look that he almost backed up a step. "So this is him?"

"Sir Jansen Winterstone, meet my sister, Lady Blessing Knightwood—arguably the fiercest of us all."

Jansen offered a proper bow, then tipped a nod at the disorder in the hallway. "I fear we interrupted a most important campaign against France."

"It would seem so," Blessing said, "and it is a pleasure to meet you." She frowned and glanced all around. "And where is your chaperone, dear sister?"

"Since we are engaged to be married, Seri has relaxed that requirement…somewhat. And she knew we were coming to visit you."

"Engaged?" Blessing repeated slowly, then exploded with a happy squeal. Now Jansen understood where the child had gotten that trait. "And what is the date? Since none of the banns have been read, I am assuming it will be longer than a month from now?"

Joy glanced at him and smiled. "I wanted all my sisters to meet my intended before I set a date."

"I had better not be the last sister," Blessing said.

"We have yet to visit Gracie—calm down."

Blessing turned to Jansen. "Have you ever known anyone to calm down whenever someone told them to do so?"

He failed to stanch a laugh. He couldn't help it. "No, my lady. If anything, it makes them worse."

Blessing nodded. "He will do." She waved them closer to the matron glowering at them from her bath chair. "Forgive me, Mother Roslynn. I did not mean to ignore you."

"Just because I can read lips does not mean I do not wish to be closer." The elder sniffed, then offered Joy and Jansen a regal nod. "Good afternoon."

Jansen bowed and spoke louder. "Good afternoon, my lady. Sir Jansen Winterstone, at your service. I am here for your inspection, for I intend to marry Lady Joy."

Lady Roslynn hiked her nose higher and swept him with a sharp gaze. "We shall see. Wheel me into the parlor, Sir Jansen. Rorie and I shall conquer France at another time."

"Right away, my lady."

"Cadwick," Blessing said, "tea in the parlor, please and thank you."

The butler nodded and hurried away.

Jansen noticed Rorie with her head resting on Joy's shoulder, very nearly asleep. He touched a finger to his lips and nodded at the tot. Joy smiled back at him and gently rubbed the little girl's back while slowly swaying. The sight made him ache for children of their own. Joy's ease with young Quill and now Rorie assured him that she would be the very best of mothers.

"Sir Jansen," Lady Roslynn said in a snappish tone, "hast thou forgotten thine assigned duty?"

Assuming the elder wished to continue the pretending, either for the sake of her granddaughter or perhaps even for herself, Jansen played along and offered a deep bow. "Nay, my lady. This knight is at your service." He went to the bath chair and wheeled her into the parlor. "Where dost thou wish thy throne placed, my lady?"

Lady Roslynn chuckled and pointed at a spot between the pair of settees in front of the hearth. "Over there will be fine, Sir Jansen. Thank you for humoring an old woman attempting to teach her granddaughter the loveliness of chivalry, even though she appears to have gone to sleep."

"It is my pleasure, my lady." An irritated hiss caused him to hop aside. "Forgive me, beastie. I did not mean to get too close to you."

The large cat, colored in patches of orange, brown, black, and white, flattened its ears and hissed again.

"Hera! That is most unbecoming of a lady. He will not trouble you or your babies," Blessing said to the cat.

"Her babies?" Jansen asked.

"She had them under the settee to the left and will not allow us to relocate them. Each time we move them somewhere quieter, she brings them back." Blessing shooed the cat aside. "See to your babies, madam. Now."

"She wishes to be in the parlor because she is curious," Lady Roslynn said. "She simply desires to be a part of every conversation."

Jansen wondered if the elderly woman was speaking more about herself than the cat.

"You know you could set a date without meeting Gracie," Blessing said. "I cannot imagine your breaking anything off just because she might not approve of him."

"So, I take it you approve of him, then?" Joy shot back at her sister.

"Of course. He is tolerant, considerate, and likes cats. What is there not to like?"

"Yes, my angel," Jansen said, unable to resist preening just a bit. "What is there not to like?"

"Your relentless stubbornness, for one thing. However, we cannot set a date without speaking to Gracie first. It would hurt her feelings because he has already met everyone else. It's going to be bad enough that she is last."

"Yes." Blessing grinned. "Indeed, it will be."

Jansen sensed a strong sense of competitiveness between the sisters, and it gave him an entirely new respect for Chance. Poor old bloke. Outnumbered by so many wily women. No wonder he possessed such a vicious disposition. "It is our hope to attend Lady Grace's churching. Perhaps that will ease her frustrations with being last."

"I am sure it will," Blessing said. "And how are you with children?"

"Blessing!" Joy said sharply.

"It is a valid question."

"I look forward to children of my own," he told Blessing.

"And how *many* are you looking forward to?" she asked.

"Blessing! What would Mama say about such impertinence?" Joy shook a finger at her sister. "That is a most private matter to be decided between a husband and wife, and you know it. No one asked you how many babies you wanted."

"I was merely making conversation."

"Rubbish! You are placing your sharp little nose where it does not belong."

Jansen fully expected one of them to throw something at the other, but within moments, they were both laughing and chatting about something else. He stared at them in bewilderment.

"Do not feel bad," Lady Roslynn said to him. "Since my hearing started to fail, I struggle to keep up with the sisters' conversations as well."

"I am simply amazed we're not disturbing little Rorie. How is she sleeping through all this?" he asked.

"That reminds me." Blessing hurried over to the bellpull. "I'll ring for Nanny."

Soon, the sleepy tot was trundled off upstairs by a cheerful, red-cheeked woman nearly as round as she was tall, but it didn't slow her. She moved with professional spryness.

"And what of your blackmailer?" Blessing asked as she returned to the settee.

"Forgive me for asking," Jansen said, "but how is it that all the sisters know about everything?"

"Papa always called it the sister network. We are but a note away, and we always keep each other informed," Joy said. "And as for our blackmailer, Jansen turned the matter over to the Bow Street Runners with the caveat that they do their best to keep Chance entirely uninformed about the matter."

"You should pay them double for that. Chance will never let you hear the end of it if it comes to his attention." Blessing leaned forward and barely touched her mother-in-law's hand. "Mother Roslynn?"

The lady stirred, opening her eyes wider. "Forgive me. I fear it is time for my afternoon's rest." She nodded at them before turning back to Blessing. "Would you be a dear? I hate being a bother."

"You are never a bother, Mother Roslynn. Never." Blessing rose, tucked the lady's lap blanket more firmly around her, then wheeled her away. As they left the room, Lady Roslynn delighted Jansen with a regal wave.

He rose to his feet and gave her such a formal bow that she left the room smiling.

"My, aren't you the charmer," Joy said, but her words dripped with admiration and affection.

"One can but try."

"Did Mr. Rathbun say when we might expect an update?" She

caught her bottom lip between her teeth, nervously chewing it.

"A few days, my darling. I am sorry, but the man has to have time to gather more information and speak to everyone."

"I hate this," she said, rubbing her forehead. "If I had ever known it would come to this, I never would have done it."

He reached over and took her hand in his. "I will let nothing harm you or yours. I swear it."

She bowed her head. "I know. And for that, I am grateful."

"It is not your gratitude I seek—but your love."

She studied him for a long moment, her expression one of awe and bewilderment. "But why? Why me?"

"Because you are the part of my soul that has been missing all this time."

The color on her cheeks heightened, thrilling him immensely.

"I mean it, my darling," he said. "We were meant to be."

⚜

"NOW, YOU TWO understand what you are setting yourselves up for?" Jansen asked.

Joy eyed the closed door to Ambrose's suite, then looked at Aurelia, remembering everything her friend had said about her morose brother. "Yes."

"All right, then. Deep breaths, ladies. It is my understanding that Ambrose has not bathed in several days. By now, he should rival Lord Smellington."

Joy braced herself, but the room's odor still very nearly knocked her back out into the hallway as soon as Jansen opened the door. It wasn't just unwashed male that stank so very badly, but rotted food, and a distinct underlying aroma of something growing somewhere it shouldn't—an earthy moldiness. She pressed her handkerchief to her nose.

"Get up, Ambrose," Jansen ordered his brother. "Lady Joy and Aurelia have come to speak with you."

What Joy had thought was a pile of unwashed clothing on the settee moved, pushing itself upright. Ambrose squinted at them, his greasy hair hanging down into his eyes. "Go away. All of you."

This was Ambrose? Jansen and Aurelia's brother? There was no resemblance whatsoever, and this slight, childlike man was more of a beggarly stable lad than an adult of the gentry.

"I will not go away. You will clean yourself up and listen to me this instant, Mr. Winterstone. Your wasting of a perfectly good life is over." Joy clapped her hands, mimicking her mother and the speech she had given Chance the one time he had made the mistake of bemoaning his extremely blessed circumstances. "You should be ashamed of yourself."

"Ashamed of myself?" Ambrose sputtered and spat, his eyes wide and bloodshot. "I was cursed with this life in his shadow. I never asked for it."

"Would you rather be the resident of the workhouses, then? Or a street beggar, perhaps? It is my understanding that you possess land, a house, and an allowance generous enough to keep them both in order. Many would gladly live in such an abundant shadow."

"What do you know? You were born with a title, you little—"

Jansen stepped forward and lifted Ambrose by the throat. "Insult her and die. Brother or no brother, you will not speak in such a manner to my angel. Is that understood?" He threw him back onto the settee, dusted off his hands, and stepped back. "Keep him respectful, Aurelia, or you will have but one brother."

"Yes, Jansen." Jaw set, Aurelia shook a finger at her sobbing brother. "I know you are disappointed about losing that tart, but you are better off, and if you will stop sniveling long enough to think about it, you will agree."

"I loved her, but she wanted a man with a title!"

"She wanted a man who spent more money on her than you were, wisely, willing to pay."

"I loved her," he moaned.

Aurelia threw up her hands. "We have discussed this over and over. I know of no way to make him see."

Handkerchief still to her nose, Joy studied the miserable little man, trying to envision how Mama or Papa might handle this situation. She decided to go with the most horrid fate she could imagine. "There is nothing to be done but send him to Bedlam, Jansen. I will not have him around our children." She prayed Jansen and Aurelia would understand that she in no way meant that and was merely attempting to shock Ambrose into pulling himself out of his malaise.

"Bedlam?" Jansen repeated, peering at her with an intensity that made her want to squirm.

"Yes. Bedlam. He has obviously gone insane. They can handle him there." Pressing her handkerchief to her temple, she hid a wink that she hoped Jansen would take to heart.

He did. "Very well then, I shall have him committed immediately. Aurelia, inform Severns that Ambrose is to be ready to leave within the hour."

Thankfully, Aurelia had seen the wink as well. "As you wish, brother." She paused and gave Ambrose a sad look. "I shall miss you, Ambrose."

"No!" Ambrose jumped to his feet and stood there slightly weaving. "You will not be rid of me that easily." He pointed a trembling finger at Joy. "Just because that woman says—"

"Careful, brother," Jansen warned.

Joy kept her victory hidden behind the filter of her handkerchief.

"I am not a danger to children," Ambrose sputtered, then wiped his mouth on his grimy sleeve.

"Well, you are certainly not an example to be upheld," Joy retorted. "Not only that, but your stench is crawling out into the hallway.

You will be pleased to know that you even smell worse than the Marquess of Debt—Lord Smellington. You, Mr. Ambrose, have surpassed a member of the nobility."

Jansen exploded with a barking laugh. "I believe she means Lord Pellington."

"Either way," Joy said, "he wanted to outdo someone with a title—well, he did."

"I have no debts either," Ambrose said with a growl, but Joy detected the barest hint of a little pride. They needed to tend to that little bit of pride and make it grow.

"Well, there you are," she said. "Why don't you go out to the country, enjoy your status as a gentleman of the gentry, and win some adorable young miss's heart with your charm and wisdom? Aurelia assures me you possess both in massive quantities when you choose to allow others to see them."

"Yes," Jansen said, "preferably a young miss who won't infect you with any diseases."

"That is no way to speak in front of ladies, brother," Ambrose scolded. He raked both hands through his hair, slicking the greasy mess back from his face. "Would you truly send me to Bedlam? You know what they say about that horrid place."

"Without hesitation," Jansen said. "In your current state, I want you nowhere near my children either."

"And if I improve upon my current state?"

"You may stay here for one month while your home in the country is opened, aired, and furnished. I am happy to share whatever resources might be of help to get you started as the master of your manor." He wrapped an arm around Joy, warming her heart—she had apparently handled the situation properly. One never quite knew for certain when it came to such matters. "After all, my angel and I will soon marry and set to the task of growing our family," he said. "We will need the extra space here in Town."

"But I will still be welcome to visit here and at Winterswick?"

Ambrose asked Joy. "I swear I am not a danger to children. I *swear*."

"You will be welcome as long as you take pride in yourself and see yourself for the fortunate man that you are," Joy said. "Our family would not be the same without you in it."

"You are not even in our family yet," Ambrose said quietly.

"No. I am not. But I intend to be. And when an Abarough woman makes up her mind, the devil himself shakes with fear."

A knock on the door interrupted them.

"Yes?" Ambrose said, running his hands through his unkempt hair yet again.

Severns entered, then came to a hard stop, blinking as though the stench burned his eyes. "Mr. Rathbun is here to see you, Sir Jansen."

"Good. Severns, please round up every male servant we have and help my brother get cleaned up."

Nose wrinkled against the filth, Severns nodded. "Gladly, sir."

Joy offered Ambrose her best curtsy. "I look forward to meeting the brother Aurelia has told me so much about."

Ambrose gave an uncertain nod. "Thank you, my lady."

❦

WHILE JANSEN PREFERRED to speak to the Bow Street Runner without Joy and Aurelia present, now that they knew the man awaited them in the library, there was no keeping them out. He escorted the ladies downstairs with the cloying feeling that his brother's stench still clung to him. He kept snorting to clear his senses of the disgusting odor.

"You sound like a raging bull about to charge," Aurelia told him.

Joy laughed. "I was thinking the very same thing."

He snorted again, this time with a laugh. "And when have either of you ladies encountered a raging bull?"

"Fine," Joy said, "then you sound like a horse about to snot on someone."

"That analogy, I will accept." He held the library door for them. "Mr. Rathbun, allow me to present my sister, Aurelia Winterstone, and my intended, Lady Joy Abarough. Ladies, this is Mr. John Rathbun of the esteemed Bow Street Runners."

Mr. Rathbun removed his hat and bowed. "Pleasure to meet you both."

The ladies nodded, then seated themselves together on the settee so the men wouldn't feel the need to stand.

"What news have you, Rathbun?" Jansen motioned to the chair in front of his desk as he seated himself behind it.

The detective glanced toward the ladies with a pained frown, then seated himself. "It would seem the letters were posted from the same place, at the same cost, with a private service."

Jansen's hopes rose. "Good news, then. Was the service able to tell you where the letters originated?"

Mr. Rathbun worked the brim of his hat through his fingers. "They were able to narrow it down to two possible points of origin."

"That is excellent news," Joy said as she excitedly caught hold of Aurelia's hand.

"Perhaps." Mr. Rathbun gave Jansen a pointed look that he didn't understand.

"Well, out with it, man," Jansen said. "Where are the two possible points of origin?"

"That would be this residence and Broadmere House."

"What?"

Mr. Rathbun gave an apologetic shake of his head. "We are quite certain, Sir Jansen. Those letters came from either this residence or Broadmere House. There is no doubt."

"That is impossible." Joy jumped up from the settee and rushed forward. "Surely you must be confusing the points of delivery with the points of origin."

Hat in hand, Mr. Rathbun rose to his feet and backed up a step. "I am afraid not, my lady. My men double-checked the facts, and then I checked them again myself. I personally spoke with the private service as well."

"So, someone in *this* house," Jansen said, "or Broadmere House, is our blackmailer."

"It would seem so, sir." Mr. Rathbun tipped his head to one side. "Of course, to continue the investigation, we will need to speak with members of both households, servants and residents alike."

"But then Chance will find out." Joy's voice trembled.

Mr. Rathbun nodded. "It would be extremely difficult to keep it from His Grace." He turned to Jansen. "What do you wish done, sir?"

Jansen eyed Joy, knowing she both wished to discover the blackmailer and keep her brother unaware of the true nature of the Reader's Dare Club. But they needed to catch the miscreant. They simply had to before the demon stirred more unrest. "Start with this household. With any luck, you will find the blackguard here within these walls."

"A sound plan, Sir Jansen. With your permission, we shall start right away."

Jansen blew out a heavy sigh, feeling as though the weight of the world teetered on his shoulders. "Do so, Rathbun. And keep me informed every step of the way."

"We will, sir. We will."

Chapter Twelve

"I AM THANKFUL your sister allowed you a private carriage ride to Wolfebourne Lodge, since we promised to make the journey in a day. After all, one can get quite *close* during a long carriage ride."

"Yes, but do not forget that my maid is in the next coach, riding with the abundance of gifts for Gracie, little Remy, and Gwynnie." Joy glanced out the back window and waved at Flora. The maid had chosen to ride atop with the driver in order to be somewhat of a chaperone, even though Joy and Jansen were in the carriage in front of them. Thank goodness Flora and Jasper had such a good rapport. So good, in fact, that Joy often wondered if the friendship between the maid and the Broadmere coachman was more than the simple friendship of working in the same household. "At least we may speak uninhibited."

"Which raises the question: What wedding date are you going to choose, my angel?"

"I am not certain." The horde of creatures in her stomach furiously batted their wings, making her swallow hard. "What date would you pick, sir?"

"Yesterday."

She laughed and arched a brow. "I fear that is not an option. Unless you have a direct line to the Almighty so He might turn back the clock for you."

Jansen took both her hands in his. "I am ready to be your husband as soon as possible. Today is not soon enough, my love." But his troubled expression gave her pause.

"What is it?"

"What is your true reason for delaying in choosing a date?" He slowly shook his head. "We both know that meeting your sisters was not the real reason you refused to have the banns read."

"Capturing the blackmailer." That wasn't the truth of it either, but he was not to know that.

"Joy."

"I hate it when you say my name like that."

"Then tell me the truth, so we might work through this. I do not wish for more delays once we have met with your last sister."

She stared down at their clasped hands, scrambling for a witty retort. Problem was, she had none. "I fear becoming an adult," she whispered, closing her eyes like a child afraid to look.

"What?" He shifted closer, making her open her eyes. "Did you say you fear becoming an adult?"

She barely nodded, chewing on her bottom lip until it almost hurt.

"But you *are* an adult."

"Not really." She eased her hands out of his and turned to stare out the carriage window. "I do not manage a household, servants, or any schedule other than my own. I don't host parties, mother children, or consult a husband whenever I wish to do something." She twitched a shrug. "I answer to and take care of no one but myself."

"You answer to your brother."

"Only after he has bellowed my name several times over."

"But you *are* going to marry me?"

She bit her lip harder and nodded. "Yes. Because my love for you is stronger than my fear of change. I am simply struggling to listen to the love part rather than the fear."

"Let me help you listen to the love." Jansen leaned forward for a kiss but was interrupted by a very loud "*Oy!*" from the carriage behind them.

Joy laughed and scooted farther away from him into the corner on her side of the carriage. "It appears that Jasper is helping Flora in her chaperone duties."

"It would seem so." Jansen shot a glaring scowl out the back window.

The carriage rolled to a stop, making Joy peer outside. "This should be the last stop before we reach Wolfebourne. It's not all that much farther. Good. I could use a bit of a walk around and a cool drink."

As they descended from the carriage, she frowned up at the ever-darkening sky. "It appears we had better enjoy our walk while we can do it in the dry. Look at those clouds."

"Aye, milady. Storm's a-comin'," shouted a lad as he ran to help Copper water the horses. He stuck his stub of a nose in the air. "Smell that rain? Me mam says a fierce one's coming today. Feels it in her bones, she says."

They hurried inside the small home that served as a way station for those passing through the area. The boy and his mother had discovered a fine way other than farming as a means of survival.

"Mam just laid a table full of meats and cheeses," the boy said as he showed them to the benches beside a long trestle table. "Fresh-baked bread there, and today's butter too. If'n you are hungry, that is. The cost ain't too dear."

"A glass of cider wouldn't go amiss with our feast," Jansen told the boy. "Or beer. Have you either?"

"Gots'm both, milord. Just tell Mam what you want."

"Sounds lovely." Joy seated herself at the table in the center of the large room that made up most of the house. Jansen joined her, as did Flora, Jasper, and Copper.

A cheerful lady with rosy cheeks and wild hair stuffed under a white ruffled cap hurried to serve them. She kept their glasses and their platters full. Thunder rumbled in the distance, but the rain held off, giving Joy the hope that perhaps it would blow through without storming after all. She truly wanted to get to Wolfebourne Lodge sooner rather than later, and a storm would slow them.

Her sister Grace would understand her dilemma about setting a wedding date. She had always been the independent sort who everyone thought would fight against marrying. But once Grace met Wolfe, she hadn't hesitated to love him and embraced a short courtship. Grace was so brave. Joy wished she possessed such courage.

"We best get going, sir," Copper told Jansen after a second glance out the window. "It's holding off for now. Mayhap we can make Wolfebourne afore the skies open up and pour."

Jansen dropped a generous number of coins onto the table and nodded his thanks before they all hurried out and climbed into the carriages.

They'd not traveled far at all when the angry gray skies split open wide. The storm broke, lashing the carriages with sheets of rain driven by high winds that made the vehicles rattle and sway. Lightning lit up the woods, and deafening thunder shook them.

Joy dove into Jansen's arms, cowering against him with her hands over her ears. She had never liked storms. Especially ones so fierce. But Jansen surrounded her with a solid, safe strength, enabling her to swallow hard and fight to slow her pounding heart. The blackness of the tempest blotted out what was left of the late afternoon sun, only enabling them to see whenever the lightning flashed. The carriage slowed to a crawl. Joy could only imagine the poor, terrified horses laboring to pull the conveyance through the mud that was surely axle deep by now.

Thunder boomed like cannon fire, and one of the horses screamed.

"Bloody hell!" Jansen clutched her even tighter. He curled himself around her and tucked his cheek against hers. Something about the bristly scrape of his jaw against hers helped her remain calm. Jansen was real, and he would keep her safe.

Then the coach stopped, and Copper yanked open the door. "Another way station up ahead," he shouted through the din of the raging fury. "Small, but it'll be shelter. Can't make it no farther, sir. Just can't do it."

Jansen squinted against another blast of lightning and thunder, then nodded.

"Must we walk to the inn?" Joy shouted to the driver.

"'Fraid so, my lady. I'll be unhitching the team and walking them. Too much rain, mud, and fear for them. Poor beasts just can't pull through it."

"Would you rather stay here and try to ride it out?" Jansen asked her, his eyes dark and wild with something she didn't quite understand until she realized it had to be the same terror that was in hers.

"No. I want shelter. Good shelter," she shouted. "I can make it." And she would make it—even if she had to crawl. With Copper and Jansen's help, she climbed down from the carriage and sank up to her knees. The road had become a river of mud.

Without asking, Jansen picked her up.

"You cannot make it carrying me," she shouted, thumping her fist against his chest. "Put me down. I can make it."

Jaw hard and expression grim, he shook his head and kept plowing through the deluge.

She shouldn't fight him. It would only make his journey even more difficult. Instead, she tucked tighter against him and held on, praying he wouldn't injure himself in the slow, laborious journey to the small way station.

A dim light up ahead, barely flickering in the deafening rain and darkness, gave her hope. It had to be their safe haven.

When they reached the door, he eased her down onto her feet and smiled. "We made it, my angel," he said, breathing hard from his labors.

"*You* made it, my knight in drenched armor." She hugged him closer, trying to steady him as much as she could. "Come. Let's get inside and wait for everyone else."

They sloughed off as much mud as they could, then went inside, blinking in relief at the warm, dry cheeriness of a hearth fire and candles.

"Bless my soul, come close to the fire," said an older gentleman with wild white hair. "Not a fit night out for a man and his wife. Daren't be worrying about the mud. My missus will have the lad sweep it out in the mornin' once it be dry. I be Mr. Mosely."

"Thank you, Mr. Mosely," Jansen said. "Our driver had to unhook the team and walk them here. They should be along shortly."

Joy noticed that Jansen didn't correct the man about their status as husband and wife, but she didn't say a word. Something about his demeanor advised her not to. "My maid and the driver of our second coach should be along soon as well. Have you room for us all?"

"Boy!" the old man shouted at a lad sitting in the corner. "Outside with you. Find that man and help him get his team to the shelter, and then help find the other one, too. Make haste now. These good people have had a hard journey."

"We've naught but the one room to let, my lady," said a woman who was just as ancient as the gentleman. "You and your husband can have it. Your servants can sleep here by the fire with our lad." She offered an apologetic shake of her head. "Me and my man here be too old to sleep on the floor. Wouldn't be able to fetch you a decent breakfast in the morning, if'n we did. Hope you understand how we can't be givin' up our bed."

"The one room will be fine, my good woman," Jansen said. "Thank you. Might you show us to it and send up some hot water and food when you get the chance?"

"Right away, my lord," she said, and Jansen didn't correct her.

Joy's cheeks burned with a fire like they had never known before. One room? One bed? With Jansen? All night?

"Oh dear, my lady," the elderly matron said, pausing as she walked past her. "I hope you do not mind my saying that you look as if you might be coming down with a fever. Them cheeks of yours are mighty red. Shall I send up a tonic as well? I have a grand one, if I do say so myself."

Joy swallowed hard, then nodded, not fully trusting her voice. "That would be lovely," she finally forced out.

The way station's keeper picked up a candlestick and waved for them to follow him up a rickety set of stairs. When they reached the top, he pushed open a door and stepped back. "It ain't much, but Mrs. Mosely keeps it good and clean, and it be dry and warm. The hearth's already laid for a fire. All you need do is light it."

Jansen took the key from him. "It is more than ample, good sir. Thank you. And please let the others in our party know we made it here."

"Happy to, my lord. Good evening to you. The water and food will be up shortly."

"Thank you again, sir."

Once inside, Joy had no idea what to say. This was sin itself. She was in a room with a bed. With a man. And it was nearly nightfall.

She went to the small window centered in the gable of the roof's sloped ceiling. "I should not be here," she whispered, staring out into the inky darkness. "Flora should be with me."

"They think we are married," Jansen gently reminded her. "And should we ever come this way again, we will be."

"But what will Flora think when she arrives?"

"Flora will be thankful to be in the warm and the dry, and that her mistress is safe." The floorboards creaked as he moved closer, making her jump. He halted. "I will neither harm you nor force myself on you, my love. I simply wanted us to be together—safe and dry on this terrible night."

Heart beating so wildly she almost couldn't speak, she bit her bottom lip again as she turned and eyed him. How could a man as wet as a drowned rat still be so devilishly tempting and handsome? A shudder rippled through her.

Jansen jerked as if suddenly awakening from a dream. "You must be cold. Let me get the fire started to warm you."

She was by no means freezing with the cold, but his lighting the fire at least gave them both something to focus on other than the bed tucked up against the wall beneath the eave. There was a low dressing cabinet beside it, bearing a pitcher and bowl. Two straight-backed chairs sat against the wall with a small, round table between them. She caught a glimpse of the chamber pot under the bed. *Oh, dear heavens.* How on earth would she ever manage whenever she needed to relieve herself, and why the devil had she drunk so much of that infernal cider at the last stop?

"There now." Jansen rose, staring down at the crackling fire with pride. "Thank goodness the proprietors saw fit to keep the wood dry and at the ready."

"Yes. It is very nice." She drew closer, unable to resist the warmth of the golden flames. "Thank you."

"I will always take care of you, my angel. Always."

She pulled in a deep, shuddering breath before risking a glance his way. "I know you will," she whispered.

A knock at the door made them both jump.

"Sir Jansen?"

Jansen strode to the door. "Copper. Thank goodness you made it all right. How did the team fare?"

"All tucked away for the night, sir." But the coachman shuffled from side to side, obviously worried.

"What is it, man?"

Copper glanced Joy's way and slowly shook his head. "No sign of Miss Flora or your Jasper, my lady. Me and the lad backtracked quite a ways after we got the horses settled, and we didn't find them any-where."

"They couldn't have just sunk into the mud and disappeared," Joy said, panic rising.

"No, my lady. Certainly not. They must have had to stop a lot earlier than we did. Mayhap the road got blocked. Trees down or some such thing. Leastwise there is no bridge or sides of a river to collapse. I feel sure they be fine. We just won't see them till the storm stops, and all is calm." He looked at Jansen, then back at her. "Probably won't see them until tomorrow sometime."

"Tomorrow?"

"Yes, my lady. I am afraid so."

Joy pulled in another shuddering breath and held it, determined to remain strong. There really wasn't anything all that wrong with this. After all, she and Jansen were engaged. Why, if they had gotten a special license, they could have even been married by now.

"Thank you, Copper," she said softly, praying the man wouldn't think her a lowly lightskirt.

"Thank you, Copper," Jansen repeated. "Go get yourself some food, man, and try to dry out."

"Yes, sir. Thank you."

Joy stared down at the fire as the door closed with a soft thump.

"Once our hot water and food arrive, we shall get out of these wet clothes," Jansen said.

"What?" She cringed at the squeak in her voice, swallowed hard, and tried again. "Beg pardon, I mean?"

"If we remove our clothes, they will dry quicker by the fire. We can wrap ourselves in the blankets. There appear to be several on the bed."

"I see." Dare she admit that his reasoning disappointed her? She almost gasped aloud. Perhaps she was an immoral lightskirt at heart.

⊱✦⊰

GO SLOWLY. JANSEN struggled to heed the sage warning. If he frightened her, he would be sleeping on the floor, and he wanted to share that bed with her, his precious Joy, his angel. Yes, he knew it was wrong, but he didn't care. He'd ached for her forever, and fate had seen fit to drop this opportunity into his lap. He'd be damned if he let it go to waste. And maybe then she would set a much closer date for their wedding out of fear she might be with child.

He smiled to himself. With any luck, and even more providence, she *would* be with child by the time this night was over.

Gads, he wanted her more than he had ever wanted a woman in his life. But it was more than a matter of wanting her body. He wanted *her*—all of her. To be joined forevermore, body and soul.

He added more wood to the fire, then pulled the straight-backed chairs in front of it and gently helped her sit. "The water should be here soon," he told her again. The way she stared into the flames worried him. It was almost as if she wasn't really there. "Joy?"

"Yes?" She turned, met his gaze, and smiled. "I heard you. It...it is just that I am getting warmer, and I find the blaze mesmerizing. Silly, I know."

"Nothing about you is silly, my love."

Her smile faded but didn't disappear completely as she returned her focus to the fire. "I hope Flora and Jasper are all right."

"They are more than likely taking shelter in the coach. I am sure they will be fine." He wasn't sure of that at all. So many things could happen, but he wasn't about to fuel her worries with stories of horrible carriage accidents during weather like this.

After another knock on the door that made them both jump, two steaming kettles of hot water sat on the dresser, along with a bucket on the floor for the discarded water. The tiny table in the corner groaned beneath the weight of cold meats, cheeses, and crusty bread. Two bottles of wine sat on the floor against the wall, since there was no room on the table, and a tray with a small, cracked teacup and an ominous-smelling pot of something awaited Joy on the floor at the foot of the bed.

Jansen sniffed at it again and barely held back a gag. "I do not recommend drinking that unless you fear yourself at death's door. Who knows what old family recipe the matron used to make that noxious substance? It is black as ink, too."

"Is it really?" Joy was rooted to the same spot beside the fire, making Jansen wonder what it would take to get her to relax.

Wine. Wine might help her relax. He hurried to pour them both a glass.

"Oh my goodness," she said after her first sip. "Elderberry. My favorite."

Jansen took that as another good omen.

Lightning flashed again, and thunder rattled the window, as if reminding him that fate was in charge here.

"Shall I help you with your dress?" he asked quietly. "Rivers are still running off your skirts. I am surprised if you can feel any heat at all." He felt heat, but it had nothing to do with the fire. "And you are still wearing your bonnet."

She removed the bedraggled thing and hung it on a nail in the wall. "Poor bonnet. I hope Flora can save it." She winced, then looked up at him with heart-wrenching worry. "She has to be all right, Jansen. She is not just a maid. She is my friend."

"Jasper will keep her safe. You know that." He went to her and nodded at the buttons on the front of her high-waisted traveling dress, the outermost layer of her ensemble. "If you will remove that, I shall try to find another nail on which to hang it."

"Thank you," she whispered, then bent her head to stare at the tiny buttons on the bodice. Her fingers trembled as she attempted to undo them.

He itched to help her, but didn't dare. Not yet. He had to be patient.

She handed it over and kept her head bowed.

Searching the walls, he spotted several hooks on the same side of the room as the hearth. They had to have been placed there for just that purpose. At least the garments would be close to the fire and hopefully almost dry by morning. He hung it in place, then turned back to Joy and nearly choked at the sight of his beloved angel. She had undone her glorious hair, releasing her shimmering locks, which had been turned an even darker, richer gold by the rain.

"Forgive me," she said as he stood there, staring. "When it is wet, it grows so heavy that the pins pinch and pull."

He fetched a blanket from the bed and handed it to her. "Your beauty stuns me, my lady. There is nothing to forgive. Allow me to help you with the rest of your wet things."

"Thank you," she said so quietly that he almost didn't hear her. She turned and pulled her hair aside, revealing the buttons on the back of her inner dress.

His own hands now trembling, he undid the buttons and couldn't resist kissing her bare shoulder as he peeled the wet material away.

She caught her breath, thrilling him even more.

After he had hung that garment on a hook, she stood in nothing but her chemise, stays, and stockings. As he reached for the laces, she said, "Jansen?"

Frozen in place, he wet his lips but didn't touch her. "Yes, my love?"

"Can you stop going so slowly? It is like removing a bandage stuck to a wound. If you pull it away slowly, the pain lasts longer than if you simply rip it off in one fast yank."

He bit the inside of his cheek to keep from laughing. "Gladly, my love." He made short work of the corset, silently cursing the wet laces that kept trying to knot. As it fell to the floor, she turned and handed him the blanket.

"Hold this out and close your eyes while I remove the rest. All right?"

Aching but dutiful, he did as he was told. "Ready, my lady."

Wet plops on the floor almost made him groan because he knew they were her stockings and chemise. She was naked. His angel was naked, and here he stood with his eyes shut. Gads alive, how he wished to open them.

"No peeking."

"No, my lady. Of course not."

She took the blanket out of his hands and after another moment said, "All right. I am ready."

He was ready as well, but he doubted she meant the same thing.

She had wrapped herself in the blanket, leaving nothing but her bare shoulders showing as she sipped her wine. He had never seen a lovelier sight.

She nodded at him. "Your turn."

"Allow me to hang your things first, my lady." He nearly groaned as he finished hanging the rest of her garments on the hooks and nails. The damp clothing smelled of her, of roses and warm, enticing woman.

"You know," he said as he removed his muddy boots and set them by the door, "if we were in Scotland, we would already be considered man and wife because I failed to correct the innkeeper when he called us that."

"We are not in Scotland, sir. We are just outside the Lake District."

"Yet and still."

"Yes," she said as she nibbled on a crust of bread, reminding him of a mouse stealing a treat. "Yet and still."

He stripped off his coat and jacket and undid the buttons of his waistcoat. "I fear all the hooks and nails are filled, my lady. Whatever shall I do with my clothes?"

She rolled her eyes and placed one of the chairs in front of the fire. "There you are, sir." She went to the pitcher and bowl on the dresser, poured some of the hot water from the kettle into the bowl, and started scrubbing her face and arms. "I suppose it was very rude of me to eat a bit before I washed."

"Nothing about you is rude, my lady," he said as he stripped off his shirt.

She turned and stared at him, motionless and open mouthed.

It was then that he remembered the scar on his shoulder. "From the war. The surgeon swears the bullet passed through, but I am not so sure. Sometimes, I still feel it." He moved closer, took her hand, and trailed her fingers across it. "It only hurts when it rains."

"It is bloody well pouring, Jansen." But she didn't take her hand away.

He laughed and pressed her palm tighter against his flesh. "Then it must be you, my angel. Healing my scars. Taking away all my pain."

She stared up at him and wet her lips. "So, in Scotland, we would be considered married?"

"We would, my love. And here in England, we will be married as soon as I can get a special license. Who needs banns?"

"Yes," she whispered, moving closer still and placing her other hand on his bare chest as well. "Who needs banns?"

He slid his hands along her bare shoulders, up her graceful neck, and cradled her face between them. "I adore you, my angel. Adore you more than you will ever know."

She wet her lips again. "Show me," she said in a breathy whisper.

"Gladly, my love. Gladly." He took her mouth, kissing her with everything he had ever felt for her. Elderberry wine and excitement flavored her lips, her tongue. "You taste divine."

She smiled and pulled him down for more. "So do you."

He nibbled and kissed along her jaw, down her neck, and along her shoulder. With an impatient yank, he pulled the blanket away and let it drop to the floor, revealing her beauty, of which he had only dreamed. Skin like silk, sweet as warmed honey, the taste of her made him even more ravenous. He worked his way downward, sampling each of her perfect breasts, nibbling and sucking on her pert rosettes as she arched her back and moaned.

And then he kissed his way lower as he knelt, cupping her perfect hips and breathing her in with every nibble.

"Oh my," she gasped, burying her fingers in his hair.

"I adore you," he said, pressing his mouth where he knew no man had ever touched her before, making her make the sounds that would only get better as the evening wore on. He smiled and dipped his tongue deeper. The storm wasn't the only thing raging this night.

She pulled his hair and cried out, shuddering so hard that she nearly stumbled.

It was time to go to bed.

He eased her back and laid her across it, kneeling and placing her legs over his shoulders. He would take her to the pinnacle and beyond before he joined her in bed.

"Oh, Jansen...never have I... Oh my."

He ran his tongue deeper while teasing the nubbin of her sex with his thumb. "Enjoy, my love. This is just the beginning."

"But—Oh, Jansen." She shuddered again and clenched her thighs tightly against either side of his head. And then she cried out and shook with wave after wave of pleasure.

He kissed his way back up her body, worshipping the honey of her skin, licking and nibbling her sweetness, of which he had only dreamed.

"No wonder we need chaperones," she said, still breathless. "That was absolutely..."

"And we are only just beginning, my love." He paused long enough to divest himself of his trousers and stretched across her, only to discover that crossways on the bed was not good at all. He lifted her and set things to rights, stretching across her. "I love you, Joy. Always will...I swear it."

Staring up into his eyes, she cupped his face between her hands. "I never knew what it was to love someone the way I love you. I didn't know such feelings were possible."

He kissed her deeply as she wrapped her legs around him, hugged him with her thighs, and arched to encourage him to complete the union that begged—no, that demanded—to be completed. He thrust himself inside her hot wetness, not going slow because his lady love had told him slow was bad. She winced for the briefest moment, then smiled and matched his pace with her own. The ancient dance began, and it was perfect. The bed creaked and groaned. The storm raged. But they didn't hear anything other than themselves.

Determined to bring her to ecstasy before he reached his, he struggled to maintain control. "Gads alive," he groaned. "Gads alive."

"Gads alive, yes!" she shouted, surpassing the thundering tempest outside with one of her own.

And that undid him. He pounded into her, harder, faster, then exploded with a ferocity that made him shout.

Breathless and spent, he collapsed, locking his arms in time to keep from crushing her.

She hugged him tighter, kissing his cheek. "No wonder we need chaperones," she repeated in a breathless whisper. "To think we could do this all the time."

He chuckled and kissed her again. "The night is young, my lady—and there is no chaperone in sight."

"Indeed, sir. Yes, indeed."

Chapter Thirteen

JOY KNEW SHE should be ashamed of herself, but she wasn't. Snuggled with Jansen in the small bed, her head nestled in the curve of his shoulder, she smiled as she listened to the steady rain pattering against the window. The tempest had blown itself out—much like she and Jansen had loved each other into a delightful, boneless weariness.

It had to be close to dawn, and she knew she should sleep, but she didn't want to miss a moment of this languid deliciousness. No wonder mothers watched their daughters so closely. They knew they had to keep them from this unbelievably wondrous pleasure until after they had said, "I do."

She eased in a deep breath, mesmerized by the shadows dancing along the walls, the room only lit by the fire in the hearth. The candle had burned out long ago, but it didn't matter. No amount of darkness or shadow could ever keep them from finding one another after this.

Jansen twitched, making her wonder what he was dreaming. His soft snores of earlier had stopped, replaced by erratic breathing and soft groans. Maybe he was dreaming about what they had just done? But then he shifted with more urgency, as if something pained him. Was she hurting him? She hadn't realized she was on his scarred shoulder.

She tried to move, but his arm tightened around her. "Jansen? Are you all right?"

He didn't answer. His breathing became pained gasps. He

wheezed as if stricken with consumption. A faint sheen of sweat peppered across his brow. "No!" He lashed out with a rumbling growl. "You will not!"

A bad dream. It had to be a bad dream. "Jansen!" She tried to shake him, but he shoved her away so hard it shocked her. "Jansen! You must wake up!" she shouted, cowering back against the wall.

He went still. She couldn't tell if his eyes were open or not.

Then he rolled out of the bed and went to the fireplace, leaning against it with both hands splayed on the stone chimney, breathing hard as if he had just run a race. "Did I hurt you?" he rasped without turning.

"No," she said, then decided to be truthful. "You merely frightened me when you shoved me away. I was afraid I wouldn't be able to wake you."

He whirled about and dropped to his knees beside the bed. "Forgive me, my angel. I beg you, forgive me."

"You did not hurt me. I was afraid *for* you. Are you all right? Was it a bad dream? Are you unwell?"

He rolled from his knees to his arse and sat on the floor, dropping his head into his hands. "Demons of war. They come for me every night and try to kill me on that damn battlefield."

"Every night?"

"Every night." He raked his hands through his hair. "That is why after we marry, you will have your own room, and I will have mine. I never want to hurt you, my love, and I fear I very well might."

While she didn't much like the sound of that, she wouldn't argue the point now. She was more concerned about his welfare. "How do you live with no sleep?" He hadn't been asleep that long, no more than an hour or so. If he went through this every night, how in the world did he survive? "Are you not exhausted all the time?"

"I have adapted, I suppose. What else could I do?"

"And nothing helps you? Laudanum? Whisky?" There had to be a way for him to block the demons out.

"Laudanum makes them worse, and it takes more whisky to numb them than I care to drink. I refuse to be a stinking sot."

She patted the spot beside her. "Come back to bed. I am not afraid now that I know what troubles you. I simply wish I could somehow help."

"Not yet. Not for a while. It would be best if I stayed right here on the floor." He sat there with his head in his hands. "Do you hate me?" he finally asked after what felt like forever.

"Hate you? For something over which you have no control? Absolutely not." She yanked the blanket free, wrapped it around herself, and got onto the floor beside him. "That would be like you hating me for having blue eyes."

He stared at her for a long moment, then whispered, "I do not deserve you."

"Teetering pedestals, sir. Remember how I feel about teetering pedestals."

"I do not deserve you," he repeated, even more slowly.

"I love you, Jansen. Nothing can change that. I swear it."

"Get back in bed, my love. I am not the only one who needs sleep this night."

"But Jansen—"

"Get back in bed, Joy. Please. Leave me with my demons."

She did as he asked but didn't like it. There had to be a way to help him, and by heavens, she would find it.

✬

JOY HELD THE front of her corset in place while Jansen tugged on the laces. "Tighter. If you do not pull them tightly enough, the stays do no good. They must support me."

"How the bloody hell do you breathe?"

"I have often wondered if women absorb the air with their faces or something, because we are unable to take deep breaths due to our corsets." Something was wrong with him. Something had changed between them, and not in a good way. But she would change it back. She refused to have unhappiness squatting between them like an ugly toad, especially after the perfection of last night.

He yanked on the laces harder. "You would bloody well need to absorb the air through somewhere other than your lungs when wearing this ungodly contraption."

"Jansen, what is wrong?" She turned and caught hold of his hands, trying to force him to look her in the eyes.

He turned away. "What makes you think anything is wrong?"

"You have said *bloody* twice and *ungodly* once. It is unlike you to speak in such a manner in front of me." She tapped a toe on the ray of sunshine stretching across the floor. "The rain is gone. The sun is shining, and we had an exemplary night. Now tell me, what is wrong? Have I done something to make you unhappy?"

"No!" He jerked back around and took her hands again. Staring down at the floor, he deflated with a heavy sigh. "I am ashamed."

"Of what?"

"Last night."

"Forgive me, Jansen. I know I am inexperienced, but in my opinion, you did *nothing* to be ashamed of." She cleared her throat and swallowed hard, every part of her becoming very warm and achy with renewed yearning at the memory. "As I said, I consider last night exemplary."

"My night terrors."

"Oh."

"Yes...*oh*, my lady. Now, do you remember how my demons shoved you away?"

"So, you are angry with me because my eyes are blue, then?"

"Do not be ridiculous."

"I am never ridiculous. You are the one being ridiculous. You should not be ashamed of something over which you have no control." It was time to change the subject. She refused to argue with him after last night. She tried to fluff out her bonnet, then finally gave up and tossed it onto the bed. "That is well and truly ruined. And how did it get so muddy? I do not recall standing on my head."

"Mud was everywhere, my lady." Jansen went to the window, squinting against the brightness of the day pouring through it. "While you slept, I went downstairs. Copper and the lad are taking a team of oxen to pull the carriage free and bring it here."

"What about Jasper and Flora?" His silence and expression did nothing to reassure her. "Jansen? What of Jasper and Flora?"

"After I deposit you safely at Wolfebourne, I shall ride out and search for them."

"I do not like leaving them that long."

"I know, my darling, but there may be no alternative. The Moselys have nothing but oxen and mules."

"I see." She still didn't like it, but she couldn't very well expect Jansen to ride out on an ox or a mule, and their team of horses for the carriage were not meant for riding, and also had none of the saddles or tack required that would protect them or him from injury. "I am sorry. I'm worried about them. As I said last night, they are not just servants. They are friends."

"I know." He scrubbed his eyes.

"You kept yourself awake all night while I slept, didn't you?" She hated this wall he had built between them all because of something he couldn't control. "Jansen?"

"I shall be fine, my angel. Please...let me handle this the way I need it handled."

Joy made a mental note to speak with Aurelia and see if she knew of her brother's problem. Perhaps, between the two of them, they could discover a way to help him. "Jansen?"

He straightened from pulling on his boots. "Yes?"

"I still want to marry you."

He rewarded her with a weary smile. "And for that, I am grateful." He offered her his arm. "Let us get you some breakfast and see what the morning has laid at our feet."

"Probably a great deal more mud. It was still raining when I drifted off." She took his arm and allowed him to escort her downstairs.

"Good morning, my lady," Mrs. Mosely called out. "Sit yourself down, and I shall be getting you a fine pot of tea."

"Thank you, Mrs. Mosely. That will be wonderful."

After a rousing breakfast of breads, beans, mushrooms, and kippers and a visit to the outside privy and the well to wash her hands, Joy felt well and truly refreshed and ready to embrace the day. She just wished Jansen felt the same. She'd never seen him like this. Unsmiling. Speaking little. Avoiding eye contact. The man was drowning in shame, and she knew no way of fixing it.

Copper and Tom, the Mosely lad, had recovered the coach, and thanks to Copper's quick thinking and abandonment of the vehicle, it was a little muddy, but other than that, quite whole and undamaged. He soon had the team back in place and they were on the road to Wolfebourne Lodge once again.

Joy and Jansen rode along in silence until she could stand it no longer. "When exactly did you intend to tell me we would sleep apart due to your night demons?"

"I had hoped to never tell you. Is it not customary for lords and ladies to sleep in their own rooms?"

"Firstly, we are not lords and ladies. Secondly, my parents shared a bedroom until Mama's consumption separated them. My siblings and I often wondered if it was the separation from Papa that hastened Mama's death, rather than the illness itself."

With a heavy sigh, Jansen bowed his head. "I am sorry, my love, but we cannot share a room. If I ever hurt you while fighting my demons on that battlefield, I would never forgive myself."

"I understand that, but what I cannot understand is your feeling such shame. The war did this to you, Jansen. It scarred your mind just as surely as it scarred your shoulder. You said yourself that your shoulder sometimes pains you. Well, it appears your memories do the same. I can accept separate rooms if that is what we must do. What I cannot accept is your berating yourself and thinking yourself less, because I now know why."

He pulled her into his arms and kissed her with a desperation that almost made her weep. She clung to him, pouring reassurance and love into him as fully as she could. When he lifted his head and stared down at her, his eyes were wet, but since no manly man ever shed tears, she pretended not to notice.

"We are getting a special license," he said with such vehemence it made her smile.

"Yes, my love. As soon as you can. And then we will marry."

"Yes, and then we will marry."

∞

EACH TIME JANSEN so much as twitched, the four foxhounds and one ungainly, short-legged dog of questionable ancestry showed their teeth and growled.

"Oh dear," Joy said. "Have you never gotten on well with dogs?"

"I like all animals, and they usually like me."

"Well, these don't appear to like you. Not even Gastric." Joy clicked her fingers. "Gastric. It is I. What on earth has come over you?"

The long-eared, overly fed Gastric wrinkled his muzzle, bared his teeth even more, and growled again, only a bit softer this time, as though apologizing for his behavior.

"Gastric!" Joy huffed. "Shame on you. You used to sleep in my bed whenever Gracie wasn't home."

"It is the twins," a lovely blonde woman said as she swept into the parlor. "All of them have been that way since little Remy and Gwynnie came along."

"Gracie!" Joy rose from the settee, but sat back down because the line of furry protectors advanced on her. "Will you call off your army, please? They appear to have forgotten me."

Grace split the air with a sharp whistle, then pointed at the dogs. "Enough. You know Joy and will soon know this gentleman who is with her. These are friends and are to be treated as such. Stand down, my babies. Remus Jamison and Gwyneth Jennette are safe thanks to you all."

The dogs wagged their tails so vigorously that their behinds wiggled back and forth.

Grace snapped her fingers and pointed at the hallway. "Off with you now. Hie to the kitchens before Nanny needs you upstairs for the babies."

The herd of canines galloped out of the room.

"Now then." Grace crossed the parlor and curtsied to Jansen. "I am the keeper of this madness. The Duchess of Wolfebourne, but of course, you may call me Grace—not *Her* Grace. Just Grace, because that happens to be my name, as I am sure Joy already told you."

"Sir Jansen Winterstone, your future brother-in-law, as soon as I can get a special license." Jansen liked Grace. She was down to earth, like the rest of the Abaroughs. All the sisters approved of him, which negated the fact that the brother did not. A sense of completeness filled him.

Laughing, Grace and Joy embraced. "Congratulations, sister! A real love match, yes?"

"Most definitely." Joy returned to Jansen's side and squeezed his arm. The way she looked at him made him swallow hard. He was the luckiest man alive.

"I am so glad you came," Grace said, but then she frowned. "But where is your maid? Flora. Your chaperone? I do not recall Mrs. Perridone mentioning their arrival and the need for accommodations."

"With your permission, I need to borrow a horse to go in search of Flora and Jasper. The other coach bearing gifts and some trunks you requested did not make it through the storm to the way station where we spent last night." Jansen braced himself for the duchess's outrage about Joy's compromising situation. If only she knew just how perfectly compromising that situation had been. At least until his demons had appeared.

He realized Joy held her breath, waiting for her sister's reaction as well.

Grace arched her brows, looking entirely too thoughtful. "I see."

And she did. Jansen could see it in her eyes.

"Well then," she said, "a special license is most definitely in order." She cleared her throat. "And of course you may borrow a mount. I shall ring for Mathias to take you to the stable to see Mr. George about choosing a horse. If you wish, you may ride mine. Pegasus is very fleet of foot. In this mud, he would be an asset, and he adapts to new riders quite readily."

"Thank you, Your Grace." He chose to use her title because her demeanor had turned stilted since her learning of last night's compromising situation. Until it changed back to her earlier relaxed friendliness, he would rely on good manners to keep her at bay. He noticed she didn't correct him as she went to the bellpull and gave it a hard yank.

When a small, wiry, older man arrived, Jansen kissed Joy's hand, patted it, and rose to his feet, expecting that to be Mathias, the footman.

"Feebson, please have Mathias escort Sir Jansen to the stable and request Pegasus be saddled for a ride."

Feebson bowed. "Yes, Your Grace." He turned to Jansen and waited.

"I shall return as soon as possible," Jansen told Joy.

She squeezed his hand. "Be careful."

"Yes. Do," Grace said in a sharp tone that clearly implied she was worried more about what would happen to her sister if anything happened to him.

"I will return. Never fear."

⚮

"JOY, PLEASE TELL me I did not hear your intended correctly. *Please*. All night at a way station? Without benefit of a chaperone? Please tell me it was the larger one that has two rooms. Pray, do not tell me it was the Moselys'."

Joy didn't answer. There was no need. She felt sure Grace could see the change in her.

Her sister groaned. "Oh, Joy."

"Do you mean to tell me that you and Wolfe never—"

"Not before we married!" Grace slowly shook her head. "We wanted to, but...did not. Are you saying that you and Jansen *did*?"

Again, Joy remained silent.

"He must ride for that special license straight away," Grace said. "As soon as he returns with Jasper and Flora, he must ride for it."

"It was just the one night. Surely I cannot be with child already." Joy covered her stomach with both hands, more excited than not about the possibility of a little Winterstone already safely planted within her.

"As fruitful as the rest of us have been, I would think you would have more concern." Grace pointed toward the hallway. "Remy and Gwynnie were born within ten months of my wedding, remember? Rorie came along in Blessing's first year, and Quill was born before Fortuity and Matthew's first anniversary. Abarough women waste no time when it comes to childbearing. Just look at Mama!"

"Well, scolding me about it will not undo anything either. We have been engaged. I simply refused to set a date until he met all of you."

"I had better be the last so you can marry immediately."

Joy almost smiled. At least she had found a way for Grace to be glad rather than upset that she was the last. "As soon as he returns with Jasper and Flora, we shall send him on his way for the special license. As persistent as he has been, I am sure he'll be happy to do as you ask."

"Good." Grace pulled in a deep breath and let it out. "He does seem amiable enough. As long as you are happy and remain that way, I shall not have to set the dogs on him. By the way, they did not really take to him, you know. I read that as a poor sign."

"He has a cat. No dogs." Joy couldn't imagine any other reason. "A black cat named Nimbus who steals anything he can carry."

"That is probably the reason. Also, I am sure they sensed his unease about this trip's *circumstances*." Grace yanked on the bellpull again. "I believe brandy to be in order."

"Excellent idea." Joy reseated herself, then noticed Grace's deeper scowl. "What now?"

"Seri wrote to me about your blackmailer. Any word on that front?"

Joy allowed herself a heavy sigh. "The Bow Street Runner on the case says the letters came from one of two places. He feels sure of it."

"And?"

"The blackmailer resides either at Broadmere House or Winterstone Townhouse." Joy swallowed hard. The smoked kippers she'd had for breakfast had suddenly decided to flutter their tails and try to swim back out. They too found that news reprehensible.

Grace stared at her, blinking slowly in disbelief. "Either our house or Sir Jansen's. Our house is impossible. Did you tell him that?"

Joy nodded. "Jansen told him either house was impossible, but the man insisted. Mr. Rathbun is interviewing everyone at Winterstone Townhouse as we speak. Every servant. *Everyone.* That is why Jansen's sister, Aurelia, didn't accompany us here."

"And if no satisfaction is found there?"

"He will interview everyone at Broadmere—including Chance. Oh, Gracie…what am I to do?"

Grace slowly shook her head. "You know what you are going to have to do."

"I know." Another heavy sigh left Joy. "I know I have to be the one to tell him. Heaven only knows what would happen if the Bow Street Runner enlightened him about the Reader's Dare Club. My only saving grace is that by then, I shall be married, and Chance will be too enthralled about an increase in his monthly allowance to really give a care."

"Chance cares about rumors and perceptions as much or more than he cares about money. You know that."

"I know. I fear I am in for the tongue lashing of the century."

Feebson appeared at the parlor door. "Your Grace?"

"Brandy, Feebson. And then a full tea, please," Grace said.

"Right away, Your Grace."

As the butler disappeared, Joy decided to change the subject. At present, she simply couldn't deal with the matter of the blackmailer. "Where is Wolfe? And Connor and Sissy?"

"London. Seeing the modiste, the tailor, and interviewing a possible new tutor. Connor cannot seem to help himself when it comes to tormenting his teachers, no matter the subject. I honestly believe it's because he is jealous of Sissy's brilliance. The child reads something once, and remembers it word for word." Grace smiled proudly. "She is amazing."

"I hate that we missed them."

"They will hate it too." Grace pulled a face. "If Connor would attend to his studies as avidly as he does the card games you taught him, he would be as brilliant as his sister." She rolled her shoulders. "I owe the little fiend a crown."

"Well done, Connor!"

"Yes, well…he is banned from gaming until he improves his mathematics and Latin."

"His mathematics should be good if his gaming is successful."

"Oh, he can add and subtract money with no problem when he is figuring his winnings or losses," Grace said. "Numerical columns are what impede him."

Feebson returned with the brandy, served them, and bowed his way back out without a word.

"I cannot believe Wolfe left you alone with the babies." Joy sipped the brandy and smiled. Elderberry again. A prosperous sign indeed.

"He didn't wish to, but he needed some time with his brother and sister. I urged him to go because I think the poor dears are feeling a bit overshadowed by the babies. Connor adores them, and so does Sissy, but I've caught a few longing glances at Wolfe when they didn't think anyone was looking. They needed some quality time with their older brother." Grace sipped her brandy, then set it aside. "By the way, there will be no more patty fingers until you and your knight are married. Understood? I'll not have Mama looking down from heaven and shaking her finger at me. While you are here, you will have a chaperone. Please?"

"That seems rather like closing the barn door after the horse has already escaped. Does it not?"

"Joy." Grace glared at her, reminding her of their mother.

"Fine." Joy finished her brandy and poured another. "Once he gets the special license, shall we marry here so you can lord it over the others?"

"Absolutely," Grace said. "I would have it no other way."

Chapter Fourteen

J OY TURNED AT the knock on the dressing room door. Grace had offered her a bath, and she was looking forward to it. "Come in."

Flora entered wearing a big smile and carrying a steaming kettle in each hand. "Sir Jansen got me back just in time to help you with your bath. Exactly as is proper."

Three other maids followed her, each of them bearing more water meant for the grand copper tub waiting in the center of the elaborate dressing room. They emptied their kettles into the bath and filed back out without a word.

"Oh, Flora! Thank heavens you are all right. I was so worried about you and Jasper." Joy couldn't resist hugging the maid who had taken such wonderful care of her for the past few years.

"It did get quite scary there for a while, my lady. I shan't deny it." The young woman blushed as she set the kettles beside the tub. "But Mr. Jasper assured me we would be safe, and we were."

Joy couldn't resist pointing out the obvious. "It would seem neither of us had an appropriate chaperone last night, then, did we?"

Flora ducked her head as she emptied one of the kettles into the tub. "No, my lady."

"Sir Jansen is leaving today to fetch a special license. Should Jasper go with him to fetch one too?" Joy didn't wish to pry, but she couldn't resist. After all, Flora was...well, Flora. Not just a maid but a confidante and trusted friend.

But the girl sighed and shook her head. "No, my lady. Mr. Jasper and I had quite the discussion about that, and I'd prefer if we talked about something else, if you do not mind."

"Do I need to speak to Jasper? Does Sir Jansen need to speak with him?"

Flora's eyes flared wide as she added another kettle of hot water to the tub. "No, my lady. Mr. Jasper and I are quite clear on what each of us wants. Now, shall we get you into this bath for a nice, long soak?"

"You know I will defend you, if need be." Joy wanted to make certain they were clear on that.

"Yes, my lady, and I thank you for that." Flora made a spinning motion with her hand. "Turn, please, so I can get you undone for your bath."

Joy did as requested, hoping she hadn't pried too much. Flora had her pride, and Joy would do nothing to take that from her.

"Good heavens, my lady, who tied the laces on your stays? They are knotted something fierce."

Joy cleared her throat. "I shall give you three guesses."

"The way station keeper's wife?"

"No."

"Did the way station keeper have a daughter or a beer wench?"

"No."

Flora tugged harder than usual and muttered something under her breath. "I shall not use my third guess, my lady. I believe I know the answer."

"Do not be judgmental, Flora. After all, I am marrying the man within days."

"It is not my place to judge anyone, my lady." But the maid's tone said otherwise. "I may have to cut these knots and replace the laces."

"Do what you must." Joy refused to feel guilty about last night. After all, as Jansen had said, had the way station been in Scotland, they would have been considered married as soon as Jansen allowed everyone to think she was his wife. "By the way, which gowns did we bring? I would like the blue muslin when I say my vows. Did we happen to bring it?"

"We did, my lady. Along with the matching spencer, bonnet, and ribbons, but if you marry here, you'll not have your mama's jewels like your sisters did."

Joy's heart fell. She had forgotten about Mama's jewels, which each of the Abarough girls had been promised for their wedding day. "Surely Mama would understand. I can always wear them once I get home—when I attend my first ball as Mrs. Winterstone."

"I am sure that will be fine, my lady. Into the tub with you now. I have added your favorite oils. Her Grace provided them, and they are of the highest quality."

Joy slid into the wonderfully hot water, leaned back against the linen-covered slope, and closed her eyes, breathing in the rose-scented steam. "Oh my. This is heaven. Why do you not get yourself a cup of tea? I intend to soak until I fully shrivel."

Flora laughed. "I have unpacking to do, my lady, since we now have everything safely arrived."

"Tea first," Joy said as she closed her eyes, knowing Flora had to be exhausted from last night's ordeal. "Then unpacking. Please? You deserve it, and I know you want to catch up with your auntie, Mrs. Perridone. I am sure she was worried sick about you."

"Yes, my lady, and thank you."

It was the least Joy could do. Gracie had told her how worried the housekeeper, Mrs. Perridone, had been about Flora when she hadn't arrived with them because of the storm.

She treated herself to another deep inhale of the rose oil and slid even deeper, tempted to douse herself completely, but really not in the mood to wash her hair. She vaguely thought she heard the door click again, but ignored it. After all, Flora had barely had time to get downstairs, much less enjoy a cup of tea. And then another familiar scent washed across her: sandalwood and citrus.

She opened her eyes to Jansen's devilish smile. "You shouldn't be in here," she whispered sharply.

"I was offered a bath, my lady. Far be it from me to decline such hospitality."

"Not in *this* dressing room. I am sure Gracie meant the one across the hall, in *your* dressing room!"

He ambled closer, slowly untying his neckerchief as he moved. "I prefer this one. Most definitely. We can be of great help to one another and our servants. If we wash each other, they'll not have to do anything but dress us when we are finished."

"Gracie said no patty fingers until we're married!"

"And do you always listen to your sister?"

"Rarely, actually." Joy sank deeper until her chin touched the water and everything else was properly submerged in the liquid made milky white by the scented oils. "But in this case, in her house, I would prefer to keep her happy—just this once, anyway. After all, she and Felicity are closest to me in age." She didn't add that she would need the support of all her sisters if Chance heard about the Reader's Dare Club. He would be most disagreeable and unpleasant.

Jansen crouched beside the tub and trailed a finger along the surface of the water. "You really wish for me to leave?"

"I *wish* for you to be in here with me, but I am trying to be responsible and lay our foundation appropriately with my sister." She blew a floating rose petal away from her chin before it stuck to her face. "I do not wish you to start out on the wrong foot with any of my sisters, because if you are on the outs with one, chances are good you will be on the outs with all."

"You truly do not wish to share your bath?"

"What did I just say?"

"When we are married, I shall commission a special tub for us. A tub for two. Agreed?"

The wicked glint in his eye sent a rush of heat through her. If he kept speaking in such a manner, she would soon have the water boiling. "Agreed. A tub for two, my knight. A tub for two. Now, out!" She shooed him away with a flick of her hand, splashing him with water. "Out, now, I say! Behave yourself."

"Only if you grant me a kiss, my angel."

"A kiss only. Nothing more. Understood?"

"Of course."

She braced herself as she lifted her face to his, knowing the temptation would be almost impossible to bear.

And then he kissed her, transporting her back to last night and all the pleasure she had known in his arms. Oh, how she yearned to return to that ecstasy and languish in that bliss. But she had to remain strong. She simply had to. With a gentle shove, she pushed him away, breaking the exquisite connection. "Out. Now."

"Well, damn and blast," he said with a grin. "Next time, I shall work harder."

"And I shall hold you to that, my knight in sinful armor." She pointed at the door. "Now, out!"

UNABLE TO SLEEP, Joy stood on the balcony overlooking the peacefulness spread out before her. Moonlight bathed the grassy meadow, casting everything in an eerie yet soothing blue-white light. The cool evening breeze tickled across the tops of the tall grasses, making them sway and ripple like waves in the ocean. A heavy sigh left her. This visit had not started out well at all. What had been planned as a pleasant introduction and attending Grace's churching had turned into a rather strained situation in what could only be described as Abarough sisterly hell.

Grace's churching had been Sunday past, so they had missed that.

The storm had soaked through the trunks and ruined the gifts for the twins. The dogs still didn't fully trust Jansen, therefore Grace didn't trust him either. And for some inexplicable reason, Grace had become more prudish about *things* than any mother launching a daughter into Society. It was a wonder she hadn't placed a guard at the bedroom doors.

But worst of all, Joy wanted Jansen with such a fury it frightened her. He had postponed leaving to get the special license until morning because heading out in the afternoon would have forced him to travel at night, and the roads were still too hazardous to traverse in the dark.

Besides, Grace had decided—and Joy grudgingly agreed—that they should wait to wed until the family joined them in the country. The wedding would still be at Wolfebourne Lodge to appease Grace for being introduced last, but all the family would be present. Even Wolfe and his siblings would return by then. Joy knew in her heart that was as it should be, but since she had tasted a particular benefit of wedded bliss, she wanted more of that wondrous intimacy sooner rather than later.

"Thinking of me, I hope," Jansen said from behind her.

She whirled about. "How did you get in here?" Even in the shadows, she caught the mischief in his eyes.

"I used the door, my lady."

"You know what I mean."

"Stealth is another thing I retained from the war." He opened his arms wide. "Pray, tell me I didn't waste it."

She didn't hesitate, flying into his waiting embrace with a happy, albeit quiet, laugh. "You did not waste it, my beloved knight. I am oh so glad you are here. I fear you have turned me into an unrepentant wanton."

"Good." He lowered his head and kissed her breathless, then swept her up into his arms and carried her to the bed. "I could not sleep for thinking of you. Lying here in your thin night rail." He trailed kisses along her jawline and down her throat, tickling ever lower with his exquisite mouth. Cupping her breasts, he groaned as he nibbled each of them, then untied her chemise and slid it off her shoulders. "I am a greedy man, my love. I fear I shall never get my fill of you."

"Good." She rucked up his shirt and pulled it off over his head. Who had time for ridiculous buttons? She arched into him, molding herself to his body. "Velvet-smooth skin covering rock-hard muscle. I cannot get my fill of you either."

"And remember Scotland," he said in a raspy whisper, hoarse with need. "There, we would be man and wife already."

"I love Scotland." She bit back a moan as he kissed his way lower, pushed apart her legs, and set about tasting her. "We must be quiet," she whispered as he pulled her legs up over his shoulders. "You must not make me shout. There is no storm to drown my cries tonight."

"I love your cries and don't give a damn if the entire world hears your pleasure."

She clenched her teeth and fisted her hands in the sheets as he ran his tongue deeper. How in heaven's name would she ever keep from shrieking? She bucked as a warning wave of bliss washed across her. She was so close. Turning her head into the pillow, she grabbed it and jammed it against her face, biting into it as he pushed her into ecstasy. Wave after wave crashed through her, making her need to scream oh so badly. But she bit the pillow harder and restrained herself to a faint moan.

Jansen pulled the pillow away as he settled inside her and began the wonderful dance their bodies knew and loved. "You are going to smother yourself, my angel. We cannot have that."

She tangled her fingers in his hair and pulled him down for a long, deep kiss. As he drove in harder, she moaned into his mouth. She couldn't help it. They fit together so nicely. In fact, nicely didn't begin to describe the way he made her feel when they were one.

Her moans made him pound harder, deeper, if that were possible.

This time her bliss returned with a vengeance, sending her into the highest heights of pleasure. She bucked and almost screamed. He covered her mouth with his, swallowing the sound to keep their clandestine love hidden. Then he rumbled with a barely contained growl, shuddering as he drove in deep and stayed. As he collapsed on top of her, both of them breathing hard, he rained kisses along her neck and shoulder.

"Gads alive, woman," he said in gasping whisper. "Quiet is difficult with you."

She started giggling and struggled to stop. "Quiet is most difficult, my sinful knight, but it is also most exciting. Do you not think so?"

"It is most *something*, my love. That is for certain." He rolled to the side and pulled her into the curve of his arm. "Might I be allowed to stay for a little while?"

"You may stay for as long as you like." She rose and smiled down at him. "I love you, Jansen. You have made me love you more than you will ever know."

He tenderly touched her cheek. "And I love you, my angel, with a ferocity that frightens the bloody hell out of me."

"Good." She stretched forward and brushed a kiss to his shoulder. "Mama always said a little fear was good for the soul."

Jansen laughed. "Then I am most definitely heaven bound."

❧

JANSEN HAD FULLY expected the Bow Street Runner's report to name Ambrose as the blackmailer, even though he wasn't quite certain how his brother might have come about information on the Reader's Dare Club. Of course, Ambrose and Aurelia were quite close. Perhaps she had told him, and Ambrose possessed such a hatred for those of the *ton*, he had chosen to profit from it. But according to the paper in front of Jansen, everyone at Winterstone Townhouse had been cleared. Even Ambrose.

Mr. Rathbun was now requesting permission to interrogate the Broadmere household. Problem was, no one would be there other than a few servants to maintain the residence, since everyone was coming to the country for the wedding. Mr. Rathbun and the mystery of the blackmailer would have to wait. At least they hadn't heard from the blackguard again—much to everyone's relief. And there was also the matter of Broadmere himself being told about the club and the blackmail. Joy was not looking forward to that conversation and refused to allow Jansen to handle it for her.

The distinct feeling of being watched made the hairs on the back of his neck stand on end. He looked down to his left and discovered Gastric studying him. "What say you, old boy? Ready to be friends?"

The dog cocked his head but didn't wag his tail. At least he didn't growl either. That was an improvement. The foxhounds no longer growled, but they gave him a wide berth. Never had Jansen ever had so much trouble with animals liking him. He didn't understand it. It was as if he had smeared some sort of dog repellent on himself.

"Feebson said you received a letter," Joy said as she entered the vast Wolfebourne library.

"The butler is reporting on me?" Jansen found that somewhat insulting.

"Don't take offense. Feebson is as protective as the dogs. You will eventually win him over as you are winning over the four-legged challenges. I noticed you have a friend here with you. Good afternoon, Gastric." Joy held out her hand.

The rotund dog ambled over, wagging his tail in a large circle.

"I have yet to get a greeting like that or the slightest friendly woof, but at least there are no more growls."

"Progress, then." She bent and rubbed the canine's long, floppy ears and scratched him under the chin.

"Yes, progress." Jansen offered her the letter. "Mr. Rathbun's report."

Joy chewed on her bottom lip as she read, cringing more the longer she stared at the page. Pitiful in her despondency, she handed the letter back to him. "How can it possibly be anyone at Broadmere House? How?"

"If you were to guess, who would you suspect the most?"

With a slow shake of her head, she threw up her hands. "No one. It cannot be anyone at Broadmere House. Mr. Rathbun has to have gotten this wrong. It simply does not add up. Seri, Felicity, or Merry would never. Chance knows nothing about the truth of the club, and most of the servants don't know either."

"Servants know everything, my angel. You know that." He refolded the letter and tucked it back inside the inner pocket of his jacket. "Try to view it impartially. Look at Broadmere House as if you were an outsider looking in."

"I cannot think of a single servant who might bear a grudge against us. We treat all our people fairly." She wrung her hands together as she paced in a slow circle. "And as I said before, my sisters would never do this."

"And your brother?"

"How could Chance be the blackmailer? He thinks the Reader's Dare Club is a Tuesday meeting to discuss books."

"Are you certain?"

She snorted like an angry bull. "I am not certain of anything at this point other than I am ready for it to be finished and done with. I wish I had never started that ladies' club." She nodded at Jansen's pocket. "Are you so certain that Mr. Rathbun isn't mistaken? I know he is a Bow Street Runner, but everyone makes mistakes."

"I agree, but perhaps we shall learn more once we speak to your brother."

"We?"

"Yes—I intend to be a part of that conversation." Jansen resettled his stance, knowing a battle was about to break out, but on this one, he would not relent. "You are not facing him alone."

"He is my brother. It is not as if he is going to hurt me. He'll simply gift me with one of his infamous tirades."

"Be that as it may, I am going to be a part of that conversation. End of discussion."

Both her fair brows rose higher, a sure sign he had hit a nerve. "End of discussion?" she repeated. "You are not my husband yet and have no right to use such language with me. In fact, even *after* you are my husband, I would strongly recommend you avoid it then as well."

"Married or not, it is my duty to protect you. Physically, emotionally, however is needed. I am your safe haven, my love. Whenever you are threatened, you should be able to run into my arms and feel protected."

"I do not need to be protected from my brother. Trust me. He is not fond of eels in his bed and has learned to tread lightly with me."

"Fine. But I will be there when you speak with him. It is only right."

"You are impossible."

"And you are exquisite."

"That is not how insults work." She glared at him, but her determined resolve was softening. He could see it in her eyes.

"I would never insult you, my love." He patted his other pocket. "Especially not when our special license merely awaits the arrival of your family."

"So, what do we tell Mr. Rathbun?" she asked, and her tone suggested this was a test to see if Jansen answered correctly.

"We tell him to double-check his facts beyond a shadow of a doubt regarding Broadmere House, and he will not speak to anyone in the household until we return." Jansen couldn't resist a grin. "Correct?"

Her smile turned wry. "Correct."

"I BROUGHT THE dark-blue sapphires that Mama always said would be yours someday." Serendipity fastened the precious necklace around Joy's throat, smiling at her in the dressing table mirror.

Joy swallowed hard to keep from weeping as she touched the deep-blue pendant surrounded by diamonds. "I wish Mama could be here."

"We all do," Serendipity said, then turned away and cleared her throat. "You are certain about this?"

"I never believed I could feel this way about anyone." Joy pulled in a shaky breath and eased it back out. "I know it will take years to obtain what Mama and Papa had, but I feel as if I have a good start. The foundation is there to build upon."

Serendipity hugged her, pressing her cheek to hers. "I am glad, sister. I am truly glad." She squeezed her again. "And you look so beautiful in the blue."

"He said blue was the color I wore the first time he saw me, Season before last. I thought it appropriate."

"I agree."

Felicity burst through the door with Grace and Blessing hot on her heels, all of them chattering at once and sounding rather heated. "Joy," Felicity said, her eyes snapping, "will you please inform *your* sisters that you approved meat to be served at your wedding breakfast?"

"Last I checked, they were your sisters, too."

"Joy! Please!" Felicity appeared to be on the verge of tears.

Joy rose and pointed first at Grace, then at Blessing. "Leave her alone. I gave her my approval to prepare whatever she wished, and she has done so. I am sure it will be wonderful. If you see something you do not like, don't eat it. Understand? Why must you two always push her to tears?"

"She uses tears to get her way," Blessing said.

"That's right," Grace agreed.

"Just listen to yourselves. Are you two not married with children of your own?" Joy couldn't believe their behavior. "Mama would be ashamed of you both, picking on Felicity the way you do."

"I sided with Felicity," Merry said as she entered the dressing room. "You should see the banquet she has overseen. It looks absolutely scrumptious."

"I am sure it does." Joy hugged Felicity and gave her a reassuring smile. "Stay the course, Feli. Be *you*, not someone's idea of you...all right?"

"What will I ever do without you, Joy?" Felicity gave her a sad pout.

"I am marrying—not setting off for the Continent or the colonies. I'll either be in London or Winterswick, here in the country. Always within visiting distance, and you are always welcome—understood?"

"And me too?" Merry asked.

"Everyone is always welcome," Joy said, feeling generous. "This is my wedding day. Peace should reign. Please?"

Grace and Blessing had the good manners to look abashed. Fortuity and Serendipity assumed a superior demeanor for not chiming in on the battle, and Felicity and Merry seemed victorious. All was once again as it should be.

Joy nervously smoothed her hands along the silk folds of her gown. "I suppose I am ready." The tea she'd had earlier churned even harder at the announcement. "Good heavens, I hope I don't cast up my accounts all over his shoes."

Fortuity handed her a knotted handkerchief. "Fresh mint leaves in the sachet. Breathe it in. It will help settle your stomach. As it starts to fade, crush it more to make it stronger."

After a deep inhale of the cleansing scent, Joy did feel as though her tea would stay put. "Thank you, Fortuity. I feel much better."

"Shall we go downstairs, then?" Serendipity asked.

"Yes." Joy breathed in the mint again, then kept tight hold of it as they filed out and joined the rest of the family outside in the garden. It was a glorious day for a wedding, sunny, bright, and breezy, as if the Almighty Himself had already blessed the union.

Jansen looked magnificent, smiling and proud as though he had just battled the greatest of enemies and won.

Joy's heart fluttered into her throat as she strolled toward him. Who would have thought she could ever feel this way? As if she had finally found that part of her life she'd been missing so long.

"You are stunning as always," Jansen whispered as she took her place at his side.

"As are you, my wonderful knight."

The vicar—a Mr. Peabody she had never met—cleared his throat. His unsmiling countenance made it clear he did not approve of pre-vow whispers.

Joy squared her shoulders and lifted her chin higher. "Press on, Mr. Peabody. We have a wedding breakfast to get to."

The man's bushy black brows knotted over his eyes, reminding her of the woolly worms she often saw in the garden. "Yes. Well, then. I have been informed you do not wish the service read from the *Book of Common Prayer*, as is usual? I do not approve, but I will allow it."

"Very good of you," Jansen said.

Joy held her breath to keep from laughing.

Mr. Peabody glared at Jansen, then nodded as he unfolded a piece of paper and began reading, "Do you, Sir Jansen Winterstone, take Lady Joy Elizabeth Marigold Abarough to be your lawful wedded wife? Vow to keep her in sickness and health, protect her while in the light and in the darkness, and cherish her for all the remaining years of your life?"

Jansen took hold of Joy's hand and pressed a kiss to it. "I do so swear upon my body and soul to be the husband this woman deserves."

"Yes. Well." The vicar cleared his throat again and turned to Joy. "Do you, Lady Joy Elizabeth Marigold Abarough, take Sir Jansen

Winterstone to be your lawful wedded husband? Vow to cherish him in sickness and health, support him in the light and the darkness, and cling to him in love and joy for all the remaining years of your life?"

"I do swear upon my body and soul to be the wife this man deserves." Joy swallowed hard, then took a deep inhale of mint to keep from vomiting up her tea.

"Then by the power vested in me by the Almighty and the Church of England, I do hereby pronounce you husband and wife. Let no man put asunder that which God Himself hath joined. Amen."

Amen echoed through the garden, then everyone cheered and clapped. The Abarough family was anything but quiet.

"Here you are, vicar," Chance said as he handed the man a bulging leather wallet. "Thank you for the preferred ceremony, and do feel free to join us at the breakfast."

Mr. Peabody bowed. "Thank you, Your Grace. I would be most honored to have a nibble or two."

"I do not like that man," Joy whispered to Jansen as they turned to go. "I cannot believe we had to make such a sizable donation to get the brief ceremony we wanted." She felt sure the Almighty would share the same dim view of the avaricious vicar.

Jansen patted her hand as he settled it more snugly into the crook of his arm. "We are married. That is all that matters, my love."

"Yes." She took another long sniff of her mint sachet and silently thanked Fortuity for her wisdom. "We are man and wife at long last." At present, she had no desire to eat, but wasn't about to disappoint Felicity. What weighed heavily on her mind now was capturing their blackmailer so she could avoid a confrontation with Chance. "If only we could discover our blackmailer. Wouldn't that be a lovely wedding present?"

"It would indeed, my darling. It would indeed." Jansen turned her toward the library rather than the dining room. "After we sign the registry, perhaps we can observe everyone while they relax with cakes and chocolates. With any luck, someone will slip."

"Fine. I wish Aurelia were here to help us. She is such a keen observer."

"Yes, but she wanted to ensure Ambrose was out by the time we returned. She knew he couldn't be trusted to leave without someone there nipping at his heels. And we certainly didn't want him here."

"To be honest," Joy said, "I suspected him." She halted, afraid she'd offended her new husband. "I am sorry."

"Do not be sorry, my darling. I suspected him as well."

"But according to Mr. Rathbun—"

"Mr. Rathbun is double-checking, per my instructions."

A sense of relief filled her. "What a lovely wedding present," she said. "Now I do not have to speak with my brother. At least—not yet."

"No, my angel." Jansen smiled down at her. "Not until you are ready."

Chapter Fifteen

JOY FOLLOWED MRS. Copper through the sprawling townhouse, trying to commit all the servants' names and the route through her new home to memory. Good heavens. Winterstone Townhouse was as magnificent as Broadmere House. She hadn't realized that when she'd visited previously. Of course, then she had not received the grand tour. Owning this place was quite the feat for a member of the landed gentry.

She silently scolded herself for the unintended hint of prejudice in that thought. How dare she? She rolled her shoulders, shaking off the stink of such a *ton* way of thinking.

Nimbus trotted along beside them as if proud to show her his home. Mrs. Copper chattered nonstop, only pausing long enough to draw in a quick breath, then chattering on some more. Joy struggled to keep up with the conversation because the woman tended to switch topics as quickly as she blinked her eyes.

"And be sure to let me know your favorite foods and those you detest," the housekeeper said. "I shall ensure Cook knows, so you've no trouble with anything." The kindly woman went quiet and peered at her, reminding Joy of an owl about to swoop down on a mouse—and Joy was the mouse.

"Uhm…thank you, Mrs. Copper. I am none too fond of kidneys, liver, or beetroot. Other than that, I enjoy almost everything. Mama and Papa frowned on choosy eaters, always reminding us that those less fortunate often went without and would gladly accept that which caused us to turn up our noses."

Mrs. Copper smiled, making her bright eyes crinkle into cheery slits. "I always heard wonderful things about your mama and papa. Now I know they were true."

Joy swallowed hard, suddenly stricken with the need to weep uncontrollably. "Yes," she said, struggling for control. "I miss them terribly." She batted her eyes, willing herself not to cry. What in the devil was wrong with her? Mama and Papa had been gone for four years now, yet the sense of their loss kept hitting her as strongly as it had the day they had passed. She pulled her handkerchief from her sleeve and pressed it to the corners of her eyes.

"Oh, dear. I am that sorry, my lady," Mrs. Copper said. "Do forgive me for upsetting you. One never quite gets over the loss of one's parents. I know that was the way with Miss Aurelia, Mr. Ambrose, and Sir Jansen with their mother's loss. They were quite young when she passed, but their father's accident was only a few years ago."

Joy sniffed and shook her head. "No, forgive me. I am not usually so prone to tears. It must be all the change that has my emotions in a stir."

Mrs. Copper gave her a knowing smile. "Indeed, my lady. Change can do that to a body."

Joy decided to be completely honest with the housekeeper. "Mrs. Copper, I know absolutely nothing about running a household. I am depending on you to guide me—especially when it comes to entertaining. Can I count on you and Severns for that?"

"Of course, my lady. We have been with the Winterstone household for many years and are proud to help you any way we can."

"By the way, in what condition did Ambrose leave his rooms?" Joy shuddered. "As I remember, they were very *ripe* the last time I visited."

Mrs. Copper wrinkled her nose in agreement. "The paint is peeling off the walls, my lady, and the furniture still reeks even though we have aired it well and scrubbed it several times. We already had to discard the rugs. I strongly recommend redecorating completely."

"Yes. I had feared as much." Joy would speak to Jansen about it, even though she felt sure he would not have an issue with doing so.

Severns came around the corner and bowed. "My lady, the Bow Street Runner is in the library with Sir Jansen. He sent me to fetch you, knowing you would wish to be a part of that conversation."

Joy perked with interest. "Most definitely, Severns. Thank you." She turned to Mrs. Copper. "Please excuse me."

"Of course, my lady. Summon me if you need me."

"I will. Thank you." Joy hurried to follow Severns to the library. As soon as she walked in, an air of displeasure, perhaps even anger, hit her like an insurmountable wall. She offered the Bow Street Runner a curtsy. "Mr. Rathbun."

The man offered a polite nod while nervously running the brim of his hat through his fingers. "My lady."

Jansen stood behind his desk, glowering down at several pouches strewn across it. Joy recognized some of them as the coin bags left in the hollow oak tree in the mews.

"You discovered the blackmailer and recovered all the money?" she asked.

Jansen didn't lift his gaze to hers. "Yes. Mr. Rathbun gave me some irrefutable proof. I spoke to the guilty party, and after absolutely no cajoling, they surrendered the money and apologized for a misguided plot gone so terribly wrong." He looked at Mr. Rathbun. "Good day to you, sir, and thank you."

"Good day, Sir Jansen. Lady Joy."

Joy clenched her teeth, holding her questions until the door clicked shut behind the Bow Street Runner. "It was Ambrose, wasn't it?"

Jansen slowly shook his head. "No, my love. It pains me to tell you that it was Aurelia."

Staring at him, Joy realized her mouth gaped open and snapped it shut. No. That couldn't possibly be true. Not Aurelia. Not her best friend. "That cannot be."

He nodded at the money on the desk. "Every last penny is accounted for, my angel. Turned in by Aurelia before she went to her room to pack."

"To pack?"

"I asked her to leave—after she returns the money to whom it belongs and apologizes to them, of course."

"But she is your sister—"

"And yet she did this to us. To you."

"She had to have good reason." Joy shook her head, still unable to believe it. "She had to have done it to get back at Lady Prudence and Lady Constance. That was her reason, wasn't it?"

"She did it to distract you so you would not send me away. She felt it would draw the two of us together if we had a common enemy." He sucked in a deep breath and released it with a low, rumbling growl. "Or at least, that is what she claimed when I confronted her with Mr. Rathbun's witness's statement."

Joy slowly dropped into the chair in front of the desk, staring at the pile of money. "What did she intend to do with that?"

"Donate it to London's Children's Home as soon as the topic cooled enough for it to be safe for her to do so."

Tears overflowed even though she fought to hold them back. Her dearest friend had betrayed her—well meaningly so, but betrayed her nonetheless. "She truly thought that blackmail would ensure you and I would not part before we married?"

"That was her excuse. I found it somewhat weak as well." He scrubbed his eyes while slowly shaking his head. "She claims it was because she knew us so well that she thought that. How you always relish a challenge perceived as dangerous and daring, and how I would protect you at all costs."

Joy snorted a wry laugh. She couldn't help it. "She does know us well." Throat aching with more tears, she covered her face with her hands, trying not to wail aloud. Good heavens, what on earth was wrong with her? It wasn't as if Aurelia had done it to separate them. She had done it to keep them together, to bind them over a common enemy. "Where are you sending her?"

"To a distant cousin. I am too angry presently to allow her to stay here."

"She is your only sister, Jansen."

"She is our mutual betrayer, my angel. Think of the pain she caused you."

"At least I haven't spoken to Chance yet." There was that. If she had endured Chance's fury, perhaps she would feel differently about Aurelia. But thankfully, they'd had Mr. Rathbun check Winterstone Townhouse's residents once more. "Who was the witness?"

"Mrs. Copper. She knew of Aurelia's game but had always indulged her. If not for her years of loyalty, she would be gone too. She thought it a harmless prank and begged me to allow her to stay."

"I suppose it was harmless—in most ways." But the betrayal. Playing the part of a victim herself. Joy closed her eyes and swallowed hard, suddenly nauseated by the whole ordeal and very, very tired.

"I am sending her away, Joy. She has to learn that all actions, all decisions, have consequences."

She pushed up from the chair and turned to the door. "I must lie down for a little while. Do not make her leave until I have spoken with her. Please?"

"I will have her come see you before she leaves."

"Thank you." She hurried up to her room. Her room, where she slept alone because of her husband's nightmares. More tears sprang forth. She so wished she and Jansen could wake in the mornings in each other's arms, but it was not to be. Sometimes during the night, she heard his shouts through the door that connected their rooms. She had come to hate the darkness and knew he did too. But nothing she had found, no books she'd read, told her how to help him. All she could do was pray, and that she did every night. She fell asleep begging the Almighty to heal Jansen or show her a way to help him. But so far, her prayers had gone unanswered.

"My lady?" Flora called as she tapped on the bedroom door. "Mrs. Copper saw you rushing upstairs. Can I be helping you?

"Come in, Flora." Joy sat on the window seat, staring out at the garden below. Maybe some tea or some of Flora's herbals would help her manage this infernal weepiness, so she could sort through this Aurelia mess and Jansen's nightmares.

Flora entered carrying a tray with a cup and a small teapot, as if reading her mind. "I know it is time for your courses. So I took the liberty of preparing your herbals. All your pads are laundered and ready. I unpacked them yesterday and placed them in the small dresser behind the privy screen."

"My courses haven't come yet, Flora, but they must be on the way because I am crying about everything." Joy patted the cushioned seat beside her. "Just set the tray here. I can pour."

Flora eyed her. "Your courses still haven't started?"

"No. All this *change* must have them off kilter. Like my tears and my stomach upset."

"They should have started days ago, my lady. Regular as you are, a farmer could plan his crops by your cycles."

Joy closed her eyes and sipped the noxious tea that always made her feel better. It cured headaches, calmed belly pain, and made her less likely to cast up her accounts. "It is all the changes. The wedding. The blackmailer. Learning to run a household when I have no idea how to run one. I just want to go to sleep, then wake up and find all my worries resolved. Wouldn't that be wonderful?"

Flora took the cup out of her hands and set the teapot out of reach. "I believe you might need a different tea, my lady. Let me fetch it for you. All right?"

"This one always works. Why is it suddenly the wrong one?"

"Because your courses have not come yet. You need a different tea to settle your nerves."

"Fine." Joy felt sure her courses would start anytime. As Flora said, she was more regular than the phases of the moon—unless undue excitement or unrest happened. When Mama and Papa had died, her courses had fallen off by several weeks. But once she had calmed down, they had returned. Of course, she didn't have a husband then. A husband who came to her bed every evening.

She looked up to find Flora staring at her with her brows slightly raised, waiting for her to realize the possibilities. "So soon? I cannot be."

"It only takes one good seed sowing for a flower to take hold and bloom," Flora said with a nod at Joy's middle. "Begging your pardon, but have you not experienced several *sowings*, my lady?"

"That is a very bold question."

"But a good question, nonetheless. As your maid, I need to help you prepare."

"Prepare for what?" Joy pressed her hands to her middle. "There is too much going on right now. A child would be one more weight on my already out-of-balance scale."

"Let me get you that tea." Flora gathered up the teapot and cup, placed them on the tray, and hurried from the room.

Joy didn't know whether to sob uncontrollably out of happiness or misery. There was already so much to deal with right now—Jansen's nightmares, Aurelia's betrayal, redecorating Ambrose's rooms, learning the household, and now she had to contemplate setting up a nursery? "Oh, bloody hell. Not right now. Please."

A soft pecking on the door drew her attention. It couldn't be Flora already. It had to be either Aurelia or Jansen. "Who is it?" She wasn't in the mood for surprises.

"Aurelia."

"Bloody hell," Joy muttered again. "Come in."

The door creaked open, snagging Joy's already raw nerves like a jagged fingernail across fine silk.

"Jansen said you wished to see me before I left."

"Why, Aurelia? Of all the things you could have done—why?" Tears welled and rolled down Joy's cheeks. She didn't even try to stop them.

Bleary eyed and her nose red from weeping, Aurelia started crying again too. "I was afraid the two of you wouldn't end up together if I didn't do something. You didn't wish to marry, and even though Jansen loved you so very much, he was taking his sweet time about getting around to courting you. He is nine and thirty, for heaven's sake. Far too old to be dragging his feet about taking a wife."

"But blackmail? Seriously? What if I had told Chance about the club? Do you have any idea of the fury I would have had to listen to for the rest of my days?"

"But it worked out. I was going to confess before you spoke to Chance. I would never force you to go through that. And now you are married. And happy. You are happy. Yes?"

"That is not the point! You do not manipulate friends."

"But it not only brought you and Jansen closer, it paid back Connie and Prudie for being such a pair of cows."

"And what of poor Frederica? She won't even speak to me anymore out of fear that she will be targeted again."

"That is regrettable," Aurelia said. "I always liked Frederica. But she is marrying and will soon be off to the Continent. Her intended is Prussian royalty. She is quite fortunate, and we will rarely see her again—if ever."

"Aurelia." Joy had no words. She was simply too weary and disappointed to argue.

"I know." Aurelia swiped away her tears, sniffing as she searched for her handkerchief. "I am sorry. It seemed like a fine idea at the time."

"And now you are leaving me. Being sent away until Jansen's temper cools. And aren't you the one who told me he never forgets a slight? How many years will he keep you there?" Joy waved her away. "Just go. I cannot deal with another thing right now, and the loss of a trusted friend is a very big thing to deal with."

"I am so sorry," Aurelia whispered as she backed toward the door. "I truly am."

"I am too," Joy said with an exhausted sigh. "I am too."

⟨⟩

JANSEN HANDED THE Earl of Denby, his old war friend, a drink. "It is not working, I tell you."

"It takes longer than a mere few days." Denby accepted the glass, lifted it for a quick toast, then sipped the whisky both men preferred. "It took me almost a year before the demons stopped completely. You have to envision a different outcome to the nightmare. See yourself conquering the bloody bastards *every night* before you fall asleep. Since you have a new, quite lovely wife, I'll wager you're too exhausted to envision anything before you drop off."

"All I see here of late is the sadness in her eyes whenever I leave her bed." Jansen couldn't express how frustrated he was with himself. "Her parents enjoyed a phenomenal love match and always shared a bedroom. Joy is doing her best to be understanding, but I see the disappointment in her eyes. The loneliness. And I feel it too. What I wouldn't give to wake each morning with her in my arms."

"Envisioning myself fighting back, winning, going home victorious, worked for me," Denby said. "Keep at it, man. You are the most disciplined person I have ever known. You can correct this and vanquish that scar from your mind."

"Some scars are forever."

"If you think like that," Denby said, "you are defeated before you ever start. Believe in yourself." He snorted. "Never in all my wild and woolly years did I ever think to tell *you* to believe in yourself."

Jansen sipped his whisky, letting the liquid slowly burn its way down his gullet. "I do not handle failure well and have never been known for my patience."

"Well, in this, you must learn some patience. The mind is a stubborn thing. Once it learns something, once it is scarred, it takes a great deal to convince it otherwise." Denby stretched more comfortably in the leather chair and crossed his legs at the ankles. "Do you die in your dreams?"

"No. I awaken just as they start stabbing me with their bayonets."

"See yourself snapping off those bloody blades and gutting them with their own weapons. Conquer them. Stop letting them conquer you."

"I am trying."

"Try harder."

LEANING CLOSE TO Joy's bedroom door to better hear the slightest noise within, Jansen knocked. No answer came. She hadn't emerged from her rooms all day, not even for tea with Nimbus, a daily ritual she had come to adore. He was worried. Had she already tired of him? Had the ordeal with Aurelia changed her heart? "It is Jansen, my angel. May I come in?"

"No. Go away."

"I am not going away. I am worried about you. Shall I send for the physician?"

"No. I am just not feeling well, and I look like something Nimbus mauled in the garden. Leave me alone. Please."

Jansen stared at the door. At least she had softened the dismissal with a *please*. "Let me come in for just a moment and see with my own eyes that you are living and breathing."

"If I were not living and breathing, I would hardly be speaking to you, now would I? Go away."

Then the unmistakable sound of retching came through the door. Jansen winced and backed up a step. His poor beloved sounded quite ill. "Shall I have Mrs. Copper send up one of her remedies? She is quite good with ailments of the stomach."

Silence.

He tapped on the door again. "Joy—you are frightening the bloody hell out of me. Please let me in."

"It is not locked, you unrelenting arse."

Restraining the urge to throw the thing wide open, Jansen eased into the stuffy, shadowy room. "Shall I open a window for you? Some sunshine and a cool breeze might help."

"Flora will just shut it again."

"Why?"

"Because she is a relentless arse too."

"If you want it open, it shall be open. I will not have you suffocating in here." He strode across the room, yanked open the curtains, and threw open the doors to the balcony. "There. Much better." He turned and came up short at the small mound under the covers in the middle of the bed. "Joy?"

"Go away," came her muffled reply.

He drew closer and eased down onto the edge of the bed, taking care not to jostle it or bump the chamber pot on the floor. "I shall have the surgeon come immediately."

"There is no need. I know what is wrong with me."

"What?" He braced himself, dreading what malady she might name.

"We are going to have a child, you oaf."

He stared at the mound beneath the bedclothes as it gently rose, then fell with her every breath. "What did you say?"

"A child," she sobbed. "We are going to have a child, and I am not ready."

His heart shattered into a thousand pieces and plummeted to his feet. "You do not want our child?" He was barely able to utter the words.

She whipped back the covers and glared at him with red-rimmed eyes. "Are you that great of a fool?" She shook a finger at him. "I want this baby more than anything. But I have so much to do already. So much to learn. Redecorating Ambrose's rooms. Learning how to run the household. Missing my best friend, who betrayed me. Being a wife who cannot sleep with her husband because of that bloody war that scarred him. Entertaining and settling in as a married woman of the *ton*, and straightening out the donation dilemma to my charities. And now, setting up a nursery. I cannot stomach any additional obstacles to conquer! I simply cannot!"

His shattered heart immediately healed and leapt with happiness. He caught hold of her hands and pulled her into his arms. "I will help you, my love. I will help you with everything."

"Let me go. I smell worse than one of Gracie's dogs after it's rolled in something nasty. I've not washed since yesterday morning and perspired buckets because of Flora and her superstition about those infernal windows and fresh air." She pushed away and backed up against the headboard. "I do not know any more about being a mother than I know about running a household. This poor child is being saddled with a complete fool."

"Now that is just ridiculous. You are wonderful with children. Your sister's newborn twins adored you. You were the only one who could appease them when they cried. We will have nannies and nurses to help. I am sure your sisters will help, and I will help too."

"What do you know about caring for babies?"

"I will learn." At least he would try. He hoped he sounded braver than he felt. "And I can help with all those other matters you are worried about—at least, most of them I can help with. Ambrose's rooms will not be an issue. I shall turn that over to a decorator. The same with the nursery and the nanny's rooms. Of course, everything must be approved by you. I cannot help you with Aurelia, but I am not opposed to your writing to her if you wish. See if she has learned her lesson yet. And we will figure out your charities." He made a show of squinting and tapping his chin. "And what else worried you? Ah, yes...not being able to sleep with your husband."

"I know there is nothing you can do about that. I am sorry I said it." She held her head and slightly weaved back and forth as if about to retch again. "I should not have mentioned it. That was rude of me."

"Denby is helping me try something that he swears will help. Just give me a little more time, my love. Soon, very soon, we shall unite our bedrooms into one."

She peered at him through her fingers, her expression dubious. "Suddenly, you are cured from a condition you have endured since the war?"

"No, not yet, but I am working on it."

"I see." She shuddered with a heavy sigh, her head still in her hands. "I wonder if Mama felt this way when she realized that Chance had taken root?" Shoulders quivering, she unleashed a keening wail. "I need my mother. Why did she have to die? And why am I constantly on the verge of tears about it even though it was over four years ago?"

Carefully nudging the chamber pot out of the way with his toe, Jansen scooted closer. "Life can be unfair, my love. If crying helps, then sob to your heart's content." *Gads alive.* What else could he say? He had never seen a woman so inconsolable. "Shall I send for Lady Blessing or Lady Fortuity? Might they help you with any questions?"

She snatched up her pillow, curled herself around it, and lay on her side. "I do not know. All I know for certain is I am currently very miserable."

He rose. "I shall send for them both."

"No! Do not leave me."

He seated himself once more, thankful that she had changed her mind about banishing him from her life. "I am right here, my love. Nothing could pry me away from you."

"Then how are you going to send for my sisters?"

"I shall ring for Flora and have her tell Mrs. Copper. She will take care of it." He stretched and yanked on the rope beside the bed. Twice. Hard.

"Are you going to retch?" Joy asked as she wiped her nose with a handkerchief.

"No. I do not have any ailment. Why would I retch?"

"Because my aroma rivals that of Lord Smellington."

"Never, my love. Trust me. If you were that bad, my eyes would be watering."

"Tell Flora to let me have a bath."

"I shall tell Flora several things as soon as she decides to grace us with her presence. What the devil is taking her so long?" He yanked on the bellpull twice more.

"She is fetching more tea and some biscuits. If I do not have anything to cast up, the retching is worse."

"Oh, my darling, I am so very sorry."

"You should be. You did this to me."

His heart fell again, but then it rose as she gifted him with a smile.

"But I am glad you did this to me," she said with a softness that touched his very soul. "Our first child. Already."

Flora burst into the room with a tray balanced on her hip. She came up short and appeared to panic when she saw Jansen, then noticed the open doors allowing a refreshing breeze and warm rays of sunshine stream into the room.

"'Tis bad luck for the babe. We must keep everything dark and warm."

"I actually feel better with the fresh air," Joy said. "Please leave it open."

"But my lady—"

"Your mistress wishes it open. It stays open," Jansen said. "And she wants a bath. Prepare one for her immediately. It stands to reason that if the mother feels better, the babe feels better as well. Is that clear?"

Flora bowed her head. "Yes, sir."

"Now, tell Mrs. Copper to send word to Lady Fortuity and Lady Blessing that Lady Joy needs to see them right away. I shall take care of pouring her tea. You may tend to her bath upon your return."

The maid stared at him as if she hadn't quite understood all that he had said.

"Flora—did you understand my requests?"

"Yes, sir."

"Then do it," he urged with quiet steeliness.

Flora twitched as if waking from a dream, curtsied, and hurried out.

"How do you like your tea, my love?" he asked Joy.

"A great deal more honey than is wise and lots of lemon as well. No milk." She nibbled on the edge of a biscuit, wrinkling her nose at the taste. She returned it to the plate.

"Shall I fetch you a toasted crust of bread?" He handed her the teacup, then poured and prepared just as she had requested.

With a thoughtfulness that gave him hope she was calming, she sipped her tea. "A toasted crust of bread?"

"Aurelia always nibbled on a toasted crust of bread with no butter or jam after having stomach ailments. She said it seemed to calm the upset. I tried it one morning after drinking myself legless the night before, and it helped immensely."

"I should like to try that, but wait till Flora returns. If you ring for her again, she will think something is sure to be wrong."

"I can fetch it for you."

"No." She took another sip of her tea. "I want to hear how Denby thinks to cure you of your night demons."

"He has instructed me to relive my nightmare but change the outcome."

She leaned forward the slightest bit. "He said to do what?"

"Before I go to sleep at night, I am to run the nightmare through my mind but change the outcome to where I am the victor and overcome the demons." When she didn't comment, he continued, "After I have done that over and over, the nightmares should either change or go away completely."

"I see." But her tone said she thought it a load of rubbish.

"He swears it worked for him."

"He had night demons, the same as yours?" She finished her tea and held out the cup. "More, please."

As he prepared it the way he had done before, he nodded. "Yes. Denby was on that battlefield with me. He lived through those horrors just as I did."

"But it has yet to work for you?"

"I just started trying it. He said it could take some time."

"I am sure it could." She accepted the cup, then eyed him while slowly stirring, ever so gently clicking the spoon against the porcelain sides of the vessel. "I suppose you could say that your believing it would matter as much as anything. Papa always said if we truly believe in something, it will come to be."

"Denby did stress that believing is most important." Her willingness to entertain the idea also helped. "If you believe, it will help me; that will help too."

"Then I most certainly believe," she said. "Soon, maybe even before the baby comes, we shall share a bedroom, permanently."

"That is my goal, my love. To fall asleep each night and wake each morning with you in my arms."

"That would be lovely." Her look changed to one of shock, and she shoved her tea into his hands. "Chamber pot! And get out!"

He hurried to hand her the spare chamber pot he'd spotted under the bed, then vaulted across the room to the door. "I love you, my angel!"

"Get out!"

Once in the hallway, he leaned back against the door and closed his eyes. A child. Already on the way. The Almighty had truly blessed him beyond belief.

A sense of elation rushed him down the hall. There was much to be done.

Chapter Sixteen

"**I**F YOU CLOSE those doors and windows again, I shall have you shot," Joy said to Flora, then immediately felt guilty about threatening the poor maid. Of course, she would never have her shot and therefore should never say so. It wasn't Flora's fault that Joy felt like something Nimbus had dragged in from the gutter.

"Never you fret, my lady." Thankfully, the maid ignored Joy's fractiousness and moved a small table against the door on the right. "I am merely propping it open. This one keeps trying to swing shut. Shall I tell Severns so he can have a man check the hinges?"

"Not until my constitution calms enough for me to leave this room." Joy resettled herself yet again in the mound of pillows the maid had propped around her. "And I am sorry for being such an ill-tempered cow."

"She has never handled illness well," Blessing assured the maid as she wrung out a cloth, then offered it to Joy. "Press this on the back of your neck. That always helped me in the early days of my Rorie. Thankfully, the little one I'm growing now seems quite agreeable. Must be a milder-tempered girl."

"Or perhaps an easygoing boy? Here is another mint sachet," Fortuity said to Joy. "Quill made me feel wretched for the first month or so. Never you worry. You shall feel right as rain soon enough."

"A month?" Joy shoved the bundle of mint against the end of her nose and inhaled, wishing it worked on her nerves as well as it worked on her stomach. "I cannot be like this for an entire month. I have a life. Things that demand my attention."

"Take heart, dearest, and make the best of it. Some women suffer even longer," Blessing said. "I had bad days off and on throughout the entire time. You remember how I was."

"I remember you ate everything that didn't bite you first," Joy said, then found herself awash with guilt all over again. "Sorry." She swallowed hard, trying to keep the burning bile from rising in her throat. The mere mention of food almost made her retch.

Blessing perched on the edge of the bed and gave her a sympathetic smile. "You will be impossible until you hold the babe in your arms. That is part of it—and you are allowed to be so."

Fortuity sat on the other side of the bed. "What early name shall we call the new Winterstone?"

"Early name?" Joy said.

"Rorie was Starpeeper," Fortuity said. "Quill was Quill Seshat. What early name shall your baby have before it is born?"

Joy pressed the cool cloth to her eyes, trying to alleviate the pounding in her head. "I have no idea. *Menace* comes to mind because the little rogue is making me so miserable."

"No," Blessing said. "It cannot be something bad or the little one will think itself unwanted. Think of something, Fortuity. You are a novelist."

"Wager." Fortuity grinned. "Joy loves gaming. This is the most precious wager she will ever make in this game of life."

Blessing bounced on the bed and clapped her hands. "Perfect! Little Wager."

"Chamber pot!" Joy shouted. "And stop shaking the bed."

Blessing fetched it for her, cringing as Joy hung over it and started heaving.

"I am so sorry," Blessing said. "Quite thoughtless of me."

Joy gagged and strained, feeling as though she were turning herself inside out. "Does this hurt the child?" Her voice echoed in the empty porcelain chamber pot. She needed to drink something to have something to vomit back up.

"No." Blessing pressed a fresh, cool cloth to the back of Joy's neck and another to her temples. "Your baby is safe. Rest easy on that count, dearest sister. We Abaroughs were made to be mothers." She wiped Joy's face and gave her a sip of water.

Joy concentrated on taking slow, deep breaths to keep the water down. Aurelia's toasted crusts of bread had worked wonders this morning. Perhaps an afternoon serving would work again, too. "I wish Aurelia were here."

"Where is she, by the way?" Fortuity asked.

"She was the blackmailer, and Jansen sent her to live with a distant cousin."

"Aurelia? The blackmailer?" Blessing dropped the cloth she had just wrung out back into the bowl. "But why?"

"She thought it a guarantee to keep Jansen and me together. Common enemy and all that."

"Well," Fortuity said, "I suppose it worked."

"And now she is gone." Tears welled and overflowed. Again. Joy pointed at the top drawer of the nightstand. "Handkerchief, please."

"The incessant need to weep will ease off too, dearest." Fortuity pressed a fresh handkerchief into Joy's hand. "You are having to adjust to the new little resident in your middle. Your insides are somewhat in a state of disrepair. Redecorating, so to speak."

Joy dabbed at her eyes, swollen and gritty from so much crying. "I do not recall you two being this ridiculous."

"Oh, we were," Blessing said. "We simply hid it as you are doing. You won't be this way when you finally feel sturdy enough to emerge from your rooms."

"I never thought a Wager would make me feel so terrible." Joy smiled at the name Fortuity had chosen. "Wager. If it is a boy, perhaps we should work that into his name."

"Wager Winterstone?" Blessing cringed. "That would be too cruel for a real name. We shall help you write down several choices for boys or girls. You will be amply prepared before little Wager comes into the world."

"Amply prepared," Joy repeated as she sagged back into the pillows and handed off the chamber pot to Blessing. "I look forward to being amply prepared rather than floundering. I wish Mama were here. I need her wisdom, too."

Blessing smoothed Joy's hair back from her face. "Mama is here, and she is overjoyed that there is going to be another grandchild for her to watch over. Close your eyes and listen closely. You shall hear her voice when you need it most."

"Thank you, Blessing." Joy smiled at her sister, and then at Fortuity too. "And you as well. Thank you both for being here."

"We would never think of being anywhere else," Fortuity said. "Now, sleep. Maybe you will dream of Mama."

⊸⧓⊶

SIX NIGHTS IN a row, Jansen had conquered his night demons and slept through till morning. He felt so rested it was ridiculous. He couldn't remember the last time he had slept so soundly and so well. Now, as soon as his angel felt better, and he had at least another fortnight of calm nights, he would tell her they could attempt an entire night together.

She had started emerging from her rooms for a few hours each day, every day, a little longer than the one before, but she still wasn't well. Her pallor concerned him. Bearing children was a dangerous business indeed. He knew many a man with a second or third wife because childbirth had stolen the others. What gave him hope, what kept him from tumbling off the ledge of worry into the abyss of sheer panic, was that she had three sisters who had successfully brought forth healthy children and survived it quite well. Blessing was even with child again and not suffering nearly as much as she had the first time. Or so Joy had told him. He prayed this was true and not just a tale to give her hope. Blessing had seemed hearty enough when she had visited to lift Joy's spirits.

"Jansen?"

He turned from perusing the garden through the library window. "My angel, I do believe your color is better. Dare I hope you are having a good day?"

"I *am* having a good day. Just avoid any mention of *f-o-o-d*."

"Absolutely, dearest." Although he didn't understand why spelling the word didn't make her sick as well. But whatever it took was fine by him.

"I thought to stroll in the garden. Would you like to join me, or are you busy?"

"I am never too busy for a stroll in the garden with you." He hurried to her side and offered his arm, thrilled at the rosiness of her cheeks and the sparkle in her eyes. As he led her out to the garden via the library's terrace, he patted her hand. "Soon enough, you will be doing so well that we can ride in the park."

"I hope so. I tire of *riding* that bed." As they stepped onto the path that meandered through the roses, she paused and sniffed a crimson bloom. "Exquisite…and speaking of being tired of my bed, how is your project coming along? Any hope of my moving into your rooms?"

"I have had six good nights in a row, but I still feel we should wait. At least another fortnight."

"Why?"

"Because I do not wish to harm you or little Wager."

"I do not think you would ever harm us. I think you would stop yourself."

He halted and forced her to look him in the eye. "I shoved you on

225

our first night together. Never will I ever forgive myself for that."

Her gaze hardened with stubbornness. "You pushed me away. You did not attack me, nor did you come after me. When I left you alone, you continued fighting yourself. If you should revert and start losing to your demons, which I do not think you will, I will take cover and wait for you to awaken."

"You will not, because I am not ready to try it just yet."

"I am not afraid of you, Jansen. You would never hurt me. I know it in my heart."

"No, Joy. Now leave it." He immediately regretted the sharpness of his tone. "Please, my love. Were anything to happen to you because of me…never could I bear it."

"Fine."

"Joy." He knew what she meant when she said that word that way. "Please?"

"I said *fine!*"

Instinct told him he best be on his guard. Her *fine* meant she was plotting.

STANDING ON HER balcony, the cool night breeze wafting through her hair, Joy smiled up at the sliver of moon rising in the night sky. No one ever told Joy Abarough Winterstone to leave something alone and lived to tell about it. Whenever they did, she considered it a challenge. Tonight, she would slip into Jansen's bed, then when he awakened in the morning and found her there, he would realize she was right and, more importantly, that he was wrong.

Ever since sharing her news of the baby with him, he had ceased coming to her bed. Granted, she had been too ill to share it with him up until the last day or so, but now…now she was ready. And Blessing and Fortuity had both assured her it was quite safe to resume her wifely duties. No harm would come to her or the child.

Her bed was a cold, uncomfortable, sick bed. His bed was a warm bed of love. A surge of heat rushed through her. She stretched out her arms and let the wind kiss her heated flesh through her thin chemise. Thankfully, her balcony faced the gardens and was shielded from the other residents of Mayfair by the tall, solid wall that separated their property from the mews.

She decided to wait a little longer, gauging the time by the moon's position. It had to be well past midnight by now, perhaps even closer to dawn than she had hoped. Jansen was known for keeping late hours, so she had to be patient. She meandered back inside, wrinkling her nose at the sight of her waiting bed. Not tonight. Tonight, she would sleep with her husband.

Unable to wait any longer, she silently moved to the connecting door and ever so quietly tried to open it. "Locked?" she muttered. "How dare he!" It was then she noticed that her key to that particular lock was missing. She glared at the door as if doing so would will it to give way and cower itself open. It remained shut. "Fine. I shall simply enter through the main door in the hall."

Fetching the candlestick from her bedside table, she swept out into the hallway and went to his door, only to discover it locked as well. A low growl escaped her. She couldn't help it. Did he truly think something as insignificant as a locked door would stop her?

She hurried back to her room, went to the dressing table, and rooted around in the drawer until she found the perfect tool to solve the current dilemma: a hairpin. Little did her beloved husband know she was quite adept at picking locks. After all, she had grown up in a household of girls who always tried to hide things from each other, including locking things away. Of the seven sisters, she was the best at coaxing open any lock, and took great pride in that accomplishment.

Returning to the door that connected their rooms, she inserted the hairpin into the keyhole and listened for the lock to speak to her. And speak to her it did. It said, *Welcome—I am now open.*

She allowed herself a victorious smile, snuffed out the candle, and eased into Jansen's room. After waiting a moment for her eyes to adjust to the shadows and listening for any sign of wakefulness, she silently moved closer to the bed, taking care to remain out of the circle of light shining from the night candle on his bedside table.

He looked so peaceful. It took her breath away, and she almost sobbed, overcome with love. She pressed the back of her hand to her mouth and stood there, forcing herself to remain calm and silent. She must not wake him, for she had no doubt that he would carry her back to her room and block the door with furniture too heavy for her to break back inside.

The slightest movement on the pillow behind his head caught her eye. Nimbus stared back at her, lazily blinking his huge golden eyes that reflected an ancient wisdom known only to felines.

She pressed a finger to her lips, silently begging the cat not to give her away or awaken Jansen.

Nimbus yawned, repositioned himself, then settled back down and closed his eyes.

Thank heavens. She eased out the breath she'd held. Silently, she crept to the side of the bed and slipped under the covers, lying back without touching Jansen or moving the bed in the slightest way. Turning her head on the pillow, she watched him, smiling as she breathed in his warm, familiar scent. The scent that made her ache to touch him, but she didn't dare. He must not discover her in his bed until morning.

She closed her eyes, satisfying herself with reveling in his fragrance and listening to his steady breathing.

✦

JANSEN SMILED WITHOUT opening his eyes. The dream of his angel had been so real, it had left her delicious scent of roses and irresistible woman behind. He had dreamed of loving her—ever so gently, since they had a child on the way. The dream had left him rock hard and aching, but it had been so worth it.

He rolled over onto his side and became aware of a warm, familiar softness that did not belong in his bed—at least, not yet. His eyes sprang open, along with his mouth, in shock. How had his wily minx of a wife gotten past two locked doors and climbed into his bed? When had she done so?

Sunlight flooded the room, attesting to the lateness of the morning hour. She lay curled on her side, facing him, reminding him of a delicate flower in sweet repose. Gads alive, he loved her to distraction—even when she defied him to prove her point. His smile returned. Prove it she had. Never again would she sleep in the room next door. Unless she wished it, of course.

He reached out and trailed a fingertip along the soft curve of her cheek and was rewarded with a sleepy smile.

She opened her fabulous blue eyes and wrinkled her nose. "I told you so."

"How did you get in here, my love?" He ran his thumb down along the graceful curve of her neck and teased open the neckline of her chemise.

"I picked the lock," she said with no small amount of pride. "You underestimated me, my love."

"Indeed, I did." He slid her chemise off her shoulder and cupped her breast. "I will not make that mistake in future."

She touched his face and whispered, "I missed you."

He closed the distance between them. "I missed you too," he rasped, then united them with a searing kiss. The dream he'd had the night before could never compare with this.

Chapter Seventeen

Some months later…
Late March 1824

"I HAVE BECOME larger than your horse." Joy waddled around the library, glumly rubbing her back as she scanned the many shelves of books.

"You are beautiful, my angel." She *had* become astonishingly large, especially in the belly, but he wasn't fool enough to admit that to her. He wondered if there was but one in there. Perhaps they should have added a second cradle to the plans just to be sure. Regardless, she was still the most breathtaking woman he had ever beheld. "Come sit with me. You seem more restless than usual."

"I cannot sit, stand, or walk with any comfort. Existing is an achingly troublesome effort." She snorted much like his horse and ambled around yet another circuit. "Perhaps I should go to the garden. It is warmer today, and the sun is actually shining. Am I bothering you?"

He went to her and offered his arm. "You never bother me. Come…we shall stroll through the garden together. This early, though, I fear only the snowdrops and daffodils will be blooming."

"I don't care what's blooming." She took his arm, then paused, bending forward slightly.

"Joy?"

"I am certain it is belly gas. If we send for the accoucheur one more time just because I have a case of the winds, he is likely to refuse us when it really counts."

"If he does, I shall see the man ruined." Jansen eyed her, concerned about the high color to her cheeks and the puffiness around her eyes. "We are sending for him. You look decidedly unwell."

"What a horrible thing to say!"

"Do not be hurt by what I say." He touched her forehead. "You are blazing hot, even perspiring, and it is not at all warm in here. Something is not right."

"Perhaps we should send for him, then." She leaned against him. "I do not feel well at all, but I did not wish to cause you concern."

"I am carrying you to the bed." He swept her up into his arms, kicked open the library door, and shouted, "Send for the accoucheur. Lady Joy is not well."

"Do not cause panic," she said, sounding so breathless it concerned him.

"Are you having trouble drawing breath?"

"It is because I am so huge. Once the baby comes, I am quite sure I will be fine."

"Get that accoucheur here now!" he bellowed.

"Jansen." She patted his chest, wanly smiling up at him. "I am fine. Maybe the baby has finally decided to join us."

"I hope so." He prayed that was all it was. She did not seem *fine* at all.

"You must not worry," she whispered, staring up at him with those deep-blue eyes that pulled him in and made him hear the ocean. "Wager and I will be fine."

"Of course, my love. But I want the accoucheur here…now. The monthly nurse should be back from her errands at any moment. I cannot believe she left you in this state."

"I insisted that she do so, my dearest, most impatient knight."

"Damn well right I am impatient. When it comes to those I love, I have no patience for anyone else."

By the time he reached her bedroom, the room she insisted be used as the birthing room, she had curled against him in pain. He took that as a positive sign that the baby was coming. As soon as he laid her on the bed, she rolled off to her feet and resumed her pacing.

"I cannot lie," she said. "I simply cannot." She caught hold of the bedpost and clutched her enormous belly while trying to draw breath. "Oh my goodness, this is not at all like Blessing and Fortuity described. Do you think something is wrong?"

He did, but was not about to tell her. "I am sure every birth is different. Even your sisters said so, did they not?"

That seemed to ease her. "Yes...yes, they did say that."

Where the bloody hell was that accoucheur? Jansen stayed close to her side, supporting her whenever she needed to lean against him. "Richard Wager if we have a boy, and Charlotte Wager if we have a girl, yes? Is that what we decided?"

"Yes," Joy said with a breathlessness that concerned him.

He caught her as she stumbled. "You must get into the bed, my love. Now. Please."

"All right," she gasped. "But only for a little while."

"Yes, just for a little while to please your worried husband." Terror struck Jansen hard and deep. She must be feeling weak for her to agree so readily.

The bedroom door burst open. The accoucheur entered, followed by two attendants, the monthly nurse, and the wet nurse. The man glanced at Joy, then caught Jansen by the arm and yanked him to one side. "You may be required to make a choice, Sir Jansen. What shall it be?"

"What?"

"Save the child or the mother?"

"You will save the child," Joy sang out loud and strong. "Don't you dare try to harm my baby to save me. I will never allow it!"

The accoucheur never twitched, keeping his glare locked with Jansen's. "Sir Jansen?"

"Do what my wife says. It is not my choice but hers." Gads alive, it killed him to say that when everything within him begged that his Joy be saved. He didn't know this baby, this child...at least, not yet. He knew and loved his wife with a fury greater than all creation. But he would not go against her on this. It was not his choice to make. No matter what the accoucheur said.

The man acquiesced with a single nod, then nodded again at the door. "I recommend you leave."

"I am not leaving her."

"Fetch Essie and Tutie," Joy said before gasping for another breath. "Please fetch them for me. I need them."

Jansen went to her. "I do not want to leave you, my love. I am afraid."

"Get Essie and Tutie. Please?" She touched his cheek so tenderly, so bravely, that he almost sobbed. "I shall be fine," she promised, sounding as though even she doubted that lie. "I promise."

"Swear it."

She smiled. "I swear it on every eel I ever placed in Chance's bed."

"I hope you placed a lot of them there."

"I did, my love. Now, please...fetch my sisters."

He bolted from the room, bellowing, "My carriage! Now!"

Servants scattered like marbles tossed across the floor. Severns chased him down the hallway. "Your hat, sir. Your gloves."

"I don't give a bloody damn about any of that. Where is Copper and my carriage? My wife needs her sisters. Now!"

Noise out front assured him that the carriage had finally arrived. He charged out of the house, leapt into it, and shouted, "Lady Knightwood's first. Then Lady Ravenglass's, and for heaven's sake, make haste!"

Surprisingly, or perhaps not, both sisters were expecting him. It was almost as if the wind had carried the news of Joy's travails. Thankfully, Lady Blessing had just been churched after being safely delivered of a son in January, but Jansen had no doubt that nothing would keep her from her sister's side.

Once they were all in the carriage, he shared his greatest fears. "She is not well. Swollen. Pale. Cannot catch her breath. Feverish, even." When the sisters shared a shocked glance, his terror stabbed deeper. "She cannot die. She cannot leave me."

Blessing reached across the carriage and thumped him on the knee. "Pray. Hard and meaningful. Pray as you have never prayed before."

Instead, he dropped his head into his hands and wept.

❧

"LORD DENBY TO see you, sir," Severns said from the hallway adjacent to the private sitting room.

Jansen kept his gaze locked on the door to the attached bedroom, the entrance to Joy's bedroom. Even though her earlier cries had struck fear into his heart, the silence behind that door now horrified him. It had been too quiet for far too long. He would not look away from it.

"I came to offer my support," the earl said as he fell in step beside Jansen while he paced. "My beloved Henrietta has been through this three times. It never gets any easier for us, old man. Or them."

Jansen snorted. "We think them delicate flowers. They are steel, Denby. Steel forged by the hottest fires imaginable."

"I agree." Denby clapped a hand on Jansen's shoulder. "Take heart. The Abarough sisters are even stronger than most. My wife says so, and she would know. Women talk among themselves about these things. They are far wiser than we are about life's beginnings."

"It isn't the beginning that worries me. It is the ending."

"Best not to think like that. Remember our theory? What you believe becomes so. Believe she and the babe will be well."

Before Jansen could comment, the bedroom door opened and

Fortuity stepped into the sitting room, carrying the tiniest bundle—an entirely too-still bundle, in Jansen's opinion. And she had been crying. Red eyes. Red nose, but now Fortuity bore the expression of an almost forced calm. He had not heard any cries. Had his and Joy's child died?

"You have a son, Sir Jansen," she said, her voice quivering. "He is very small and very weak, but he lives…for now."

Jansen hurried to her and stared down at the precious infant. As he carefully pulled back the blanket, he noticed a purplish-red mark near the child's jawline. "His neck. That mark?"

"The cord, dearest brother. It nearly strangled him. Thankfully, the accoucheur was able to save him in time. He revived him when the rest of us feared all was lost."

"And my beloved Joy?" Jansen cupped the baby's warm, velvety-soft head in the palm of his hand. When Fortuity didn't answer, he let it drop. "Tell me she is not gone. Do not tell me otherwise, sister."

"She lives…for now." Fortuity cuddled the infant closer, sniffing and blinking against another onslaught of tears. "She has gone to sleep, dear sir, and we cannot seem to awaken her."

"Give me my son." Ever so carefully, Jansen cradled the softly squeaking mite to his chest. "Come along, Richard Lionheart Wager Winterstone. Let us speak to Mama. We must tell her it is very rude to frighten us this way."

He shouldered his way past Fortuity and marched into the room. The first thing he noticed was the bloody rags piled in the buckets and bowls. So very much blood. He felt as though he had stepped back onto the battlefield. Ignoring the accoucheur and his aides, he went to the head of the bed and pushed his way in to see his precious angel. "Joy Elizabeth Marigold, Richard and I need you to awaken. You are frightening us, my angel. Awaken and share in the happiness of this fine son. Awaken, Joy."

Her long lashes were almost lost against the dark purple circles under her eyes. She was so pale. So still. So damned lifeless.

"Joy," he whispered. "I beg you. Please open your eyes and live."

"Sir Jansen." The accoucheur appeared at his shoulder. "The wet nurse needs to work with the babe. See if she can get him to eat. It will not be as good as his mother's first milk, but it will be something to give him strength. I must warn you, he is very weak, and I am not certain he will live longer than a few hours."

"My son will live long enough to cast a tall shadow across my grave," Jansen said, "and I will not hear otherwise." He kissed the baby's forehead. "I love you, my boy. Eat hearty and be strong so you can meet your mama when she awakens." Reluctantly, he handed off the babe to the awaiting nurse, then turned back to the accoucheur. "My wife?"

The man released a heavy sigh and slowly shook his head. "It is in the hands of the Almighty. I have done all I can. This birth was most difficult."

"She just needs some rest," Blessing said from the other side of the bed. She placed a cloth across Joy's forehead, then bent and kissed her sister's cheek. "Joy is the most stubborn of us all. She will not leave us without holding her son." Tears streamed down Blessing's cheeks as she hiccupped and sniffed. "She would never leave us without saying goodbye. It just is not done, and she knows it."

Jansen glared across the room at the wet nurse. "Feed my child, then bring him back to me. Richard wishes to wait with me for his mother to awaken. We will not leave her side."

The accoucheur cleared his throat. "I do not recommend—"

"I do not give a damn what you recommend. I will do as I see fit to care for my wife and son." Just as the nurse went to leave with the child, he spoke louder. "Woman. Are my instructions clear to you?"

She nodded so hard that the ruffles on her bonnet quivered. "Yes, Sir Jansen. Once your son eats his fill, I shall bring him back to you. I swear it."

"Very good." Jansen settled into the chair beside the bed and took hold of Joy's limp hand. "I know you are weary, my darling, but if you could give us a sign, it would be most appreciated." He squeezed her hand, then held his breath, waiting for her to squeeze his in return. Nothing happened. His precious Joy had gone to a place where he could not follow.

The accoucheur approached him. After a long moment, he bowed. "Summon me if needed, Sir Jansen. The monthly nurse will assist in keeping your wife comfortable."

Without taking his eyes off his angel, Jansen nodded. "Thank you for saving my son. I will send for you if my wife has further need of your services. Or perhaps I shall have the surgeon come by and see to her."

"That might be wise," the accoucheur said. "Good day to you, Sir Jansen."

"Good day."

✖

JANSEN DIDN'T CARE that Blessing had told him that most newborns had eyes of blue; Richard's eyes were the deep yet startling blue of his mother's, and they would never change. The Abarough blood in this boy was strong, and for that, Jansen was exceedingly glad. The tiny mite would need every ounce of Abarough stubbornness to survive. The babe could barely cry. He squeaked more than cried, and Jansen worried that the cord that had nearly taken the child's life had damaged the baby's voice. But he didn't care. As long as his son lived, and as long as Joy awakened someday to behold him. They would worry about the boy's ability to speak at a later date. For now, the tiny but mighty one lived, and that was enough.

"I can sit with her a while so you may rest," Fortuity said as she entered the room. "If we let you fall ill, Joy will never forgive us."

"I do not need rest. I need her."

Fortuity took the baby from him and settled the infant in the cradle beside his chair. "Richard's color is better, and the nurse said his appetite is hearty."

"Praise God for that, but I am a greedy man, Fortuity. I want my wife healed as well."

"Do not be greedy, sir. Be thankful."

"I will—when she is healed."

Blessing came into the room, bearing a tray with tea and a bottle of brandy. "I thought you might prefer brandy over milk in your tea."

"Your mother named you wisely, Blessing." Jansen rose to help her set the tray on the table at the end of the bed. "I wish Joy would awaken. I know she would enjoy some too."

Fortuity looked up from where she was pressing a wet cloth against Joy's mouth. "She is swallowing. I take that as a good sign."

"A good sign, indeed." Jansen accepted the cup of tea Blessing offered him and returned to his chair beside the bed. "She doesn't know I added *Lionheart* to Richard's name. Do you think she will mind?"

"I think she will love it," Fortuity said.

"Yes," Blessing agreed. "She always enjoyed the ballads of Robin Hood and good King Richard the Lionheart. I feel certain she will heartily approve."

As Jansen sipped his tea, he studied his slumbering wife, willing her to open her beautiful eyes and join them in celebrating sweet Richard. But she remained still and deathly pale. "When will she awaken?" he muttered more to himself and God than Fortuity or Blessing.

"When she is ready," Blessing said without hesitation. "Wherever she is, she is healing and will not return until she is strong enough to hold her own."

"Didn't Mama frighten Papa this way when Felicity came?" Fortuity asked. "Didn't he tell us that?"

"I do not remember," Blessing said. "He may have. Papa shared so many things after Mama passed."

"Did she stir at all when the nurses changed her bedding?" Fortuity asked Jansen. "Even the slightest bit?"

He slowly shook his head, loath to admit the truth of it. "Not so much as a twinge." He shuddered with a jaw-cracking yawn while settling more comfortably in the chair.

"Go rest," Fortuity pleaded.

"No. Leave me here with her. I rest better when I can listen to every breath she takes."

"Fine." Blessing gathered up the tray from the teatime before last and headed for the door. "Ring for us when she awakens. Come, sister."

"But I do not want to," Fortuity said.

Blessing waited at the door with one brow arched higher than the other.

"Fine." Fortuity hurried after her, fussing as she shut the door behind them.

Jansen huffed a sad laugh. "Your sisters remind me of you, my angel. Fussing all the time but ready to do battle for those they love." He leaned over and brushed her hair back from her face, relieved at the coolness of her skin. No fever. A blessing in and of itself. "Richard is a true gem. You did well with our son, but he needs you to awaken and hold him close. Every son needs a mother's love, and Richard is no different."

Her breathing remained steady, and her eyelids never so much as twitched. Jansen blew out a heavy sigh. "I need you, my angel. Without you, I have lost the will to breathe. I only continue doing so for the sake of the babe. I know you would want that."

He scooted the chair closer and laid his head beside her. Closing his eyes, he prayed, "Please, God. Thank you for granting life to our son, but I need her too. Please do not take her. Not yet."

"Not yet."

The words were faint and breathless, but he heard them just the same. At least, he prayed he did. Ever so cautiously, he lifted his head, but then his heart fell. She hadn't moved or opened her eyes.

"Joy—I beg you. Speak to me again. Give me hope."

"So tired," she said with as little movement as possible. "Must rest."

"Praise God!" Jansen kissed her forehead. "Yes. Rest, my darling. Rest." He ran to the door and bellowed, "She spoke!" Then he leapt back to the bedside and squeezed her hand.

She moved the fingers of her right hand with the barest twitch. "Baby," she whispered without opening her eyes.

"We have a fine son. Richard Lionheart Wager Winterstone. As soon as you are stronger, I shall place him in your arms."

The right corner of her mouth quivered a bit higher in a valiant effort to give a lopsided smile. "Lionheart?"

"Yes. I took that liberty. Do you mind?"

"Love it."

"I am glad. No. I am not merely glad. I am giddy." Jansen kissed her hand again as Fortuity and Blessing exploded into the room. "She is extraordinarily weak and seeks rest. We must not tire her."

They flitted and fluttered around her, cooing and murmuring like nesting doves. After a few moments, Jansen shooed them away. "Fetch the surgeon. He will know how we can best help her."

They each kissed Joy, then scurried back out of the room.

"Jansen?" Joy kept her eyes closed, but her forehead puckered with the slightest frown.

"I am right here, my love."

"Cannot move left," she said, her speech slightly slurred.

"Cannot move what?"

"Left. Fingers. Hand. Arm. Left cannot move."

"Rest easy, my darling. You are simply weary. The surgeon is on the way. I am certain he will tell us how to help you."

"Sleep."

"Yes, my dearest angel," Jansen said. "Sleep and grow stronger." But in his heart, a sickly sense, a gnawing dread, seeded itself and sprouted. The weakness she complained of, the refusal of her left side to obey her, the way she spoke, smacked of apoplexy. Heaven help them all if that dreaded attack had happened during the birth and left her permanently damaged. His precious Joy would not only be furious, she would be despondent. "Rest now, my love. When you awaken, I shall hold Richard close so you might see him."

The right corner of her mouth twitched higher. "Yes. Richard."

"Yes, my love. Richard the Lionheart."

She barely squeezed his hand. "Little lion."

"Yes, dearest. He is a little lion and his mother a true lioness."

Chapter Eighteen

"**I** DO NOT like having him on my left side," Joy said. "I am still too weak."

"Pillows support you both, and I am right here." Jansen adjusted the cushion under her arm. What better way to strengthen her left side than with the baby? "We shall not let him fall. Besides, you said your right breast is getting sore." He was probably the only man in the entire *ton* to know so much about putting a baby to the breast. He didn't care. It was his wife and son, and they were alive and getting stronger every day.

"I hope I have enough milk for him, but Mrs. Kalifenny is still here—yes?"

"Yes, love. She tops him off, so to speak. Just to be certain."

"Is he not perfect?" Joy gave her softly grunting son a lopsided smile.

"He is perfection itself. Just like his mother."

The surgeon had said it could take days, months, or maybe never for Joy to recover completely and be rid of the paralysis. She had yet to walk, but at least she was alive, able to speak, and getting stronger.

"Lion," she said in a singsong voice as she tickled the baby's cheek. "My little lion."

"He has the appetite of a lion." Jansen had never known such pride and contentment. The Almighty had indeed blessed them beyond belief. "Remember what the surgeon said about eating more to build your strength. Mrs. Copper was not pleased with what you left on your tray at luncheon."

"She knows I despise liver and beetroot." Joy made a face. "Disgusting. I shall revert to toasted crusts if she keeps sending that up."

"She said it is good for Lion."

"When Lion gets teeth, he may eat it. Until then, he shall forgo liver and beetroots via my milk."

Happiness swelled within Jansen. There was the Abarough fight and wit that would get her through this struggle. He would not have her feeling sorry for herself. They had too much for which to be thankful.

"Our son has gone to sleep, my love. Shall I take him to Mrs. Kalifenny just to be certain?"

"Yes. He is so tiny. I do not want to risk shorting him in any way. He sleeps because he is close and comfortable."

"Come to me, young man. You must eat a bit more to grow as tall as your papa." Jansen scooped the child into his arms and took him into the adjoining room, where Mrs. Kalifenny awaited.

"How did her ladyship do?" the kindly woman whispered.

"Stronger every day."

"Well done." She held out her hands and took the mite from him. "Come along, Master Lion. Time for dessert."

Jansen struggled not to laugh as he returned to the bedroom. "Mrs. Kalifenny informed Master Lion that it was time for dessert," he explained to Joy after he'd shut the door behind him.

She laughed. "She is such a nice lady. I must thank Fortuity for recommending her."

"Indeed." Then he noticed she went quiet. "Tell me, my love. Do not sit and stew."

"What if I am bound to a bath chair the remainder of my life?"

"Then we will make the accommodations needed and be thankful you lived through the tumultuous ordeal that nearly stole you away from me."

She fixed him with a grim stare. "But I do not want that for you."

"I do not want it for you, but I will gladly make whatever concessions we must to have you still here—alive and well. You frightened the living hell out of me, my angel. I thought you lost and about to get your wings."

"What if we cannot have any more children?"

"I am thankful for Lion and none too sure I wish you to endure that again anyway."

"You have an answer for everything."

"Well, of course I do. You have a very wise husband. Were you unaware of that?"

"I am aware he is a horse's arse."

Jansen threw back his head and laughed. "That I am, my love. That I am."

"But I love you anyway."

He laughed again, thrilled with the sparkle in her eyes. "I love you anyway too, my angel. More than you will ever know."

Epilogue

WITH HER BEJEWELED cane tapping the marble floor, Joy limped through the largest of the two parlors, overseeing the Christmas decorations. "The bough on the right still needs to go a bit higher, Severns. It has gone all lopsided again. Why will it not stay?"

The butler exploded with a vicious sneeze. "The fir and pine both are very *sappy*, my lady. The infernal things should stick up there with no ribbons and nails, but for some reason, they refuse to do so. The ivy stayed with but a tiny strand of ribbon. I shall add more to the evergreen boughs. Never fear. I shall prevail."

"Take heart, Severns," Jansen said as he toted his very chunky son in the crook of his arm. "She shan't ask you to move them again. She will merely want you to add more."

Little Lion clapped his pudgy hands and added his opinion in the form of raspy babbling. He had become quite the vocal child of late, but always sounded a bit hoarse. Joy didn't care. In her opinion, her son sounded like an angel. She also didn't mind being forced to depend on the stabilization of a cane due to the continued weakness in her left leg. At least she could walk and be more or less independent. They had so very much for which to be thankful.

"I cannot wait to see how Lion feels about figgy pudding," she said. "I am sure he will love it."

"Nanny will have a fit." Jansen chucked his son's double chin. "She gets quite cross when we feed him something other than his coddled eggs and gruel."

"Lion has the appetite of a lion. She might as well get used to it or seek employment elsewhere." Joy still wasn't all that sure about the woman. Blessing, Fortuity, and Grace had recommended the agency that sent her, but that didn't mean she had to accept the first candidate they tried.

Jansen laughed. "Spoken like a true lioness."

"Yes, well...*rawr*. By the way, where is Nimbus? We are missing more ribbon."

"Last I saw him, he was...*courting* his lady love. Very loudly, as a matter of fact."

The true meaning of *courting* was not lost on Joy. Especially since they had enjoyed some courting of their own, just this morning. "Well done, Nimbus. But I wonder where the ribbon got to?"

"Leave poor Severns alone and let him deal with it."

"I suppose I should." She tickled little Lion until he had them all laughing with his adorable baby cackles. A contentment she had never known existed filled her and made her wish the same for her remaining sisters that were yet to marry. "Felicity is next on the chopping block, you know. We must help her find the happiness we have."

Jansen backed up a step and lifted his laughing son high into the air. "Lion and I decline that invitation, my angel. That is an Abarough task if ever I heard one."

"Perhaps," Joy said with a grin. "Would you care to make a wager on that?"

"With you, my love?" Jansen laughed. "I am always up for a wager."

THE END

About the Author

If you enjoyed JOY'S WILLFUL WAGER, please consider leaving a review on the site where you purchased your copy, or a reader site such as Goodreads, or BookBub.

If you'd like to receive my newsletter, here's the link to sign up:
maevegreyson.com/contact.html#newsletter

I love to hear from readers! Drop me a line at
maevegreyson@gmail.com

Or visit me on Facebook:
facebook.com/AuthorMaeveGreyson

Join my Facebook Group – Maeve's Corner:
facebook.com/groups/MaevesCorner

I'm also on Instagram:
maevegreyson

My website:
https://maevegreyson.com

Feel free to ask questions or leave some Reader Buzz on
bingebooks.com/author/maeve-greyson

Goodreads:
goodreads.com/maevegreyson

Follow me on these sites to get notifications about new releases, sales, and special deals:

Amazon:
amazon.com/Maeve-Greyson/e/B004PE9T9U

BookBub:
bookbub.com/authors/maeve-greyson

Many thanks and may your life always be filled with good books!
Maeve

Printed in Dunstable, United Kingdom